MW01136622

LOST HOURS

LOST LAKE LOCATORS BOOK ONE

SUSAN SLEEMAN

Published by Edge of Your Seat Books, Inc.

Contact the publisher at contact@edgeofyourseatbooks.com

Copyright © 2025 by Susan Sleeman

Cover design by Kelly A. Martin of KAM Design

This book is a work of fiction. Characters, names, places, and incidents in this novel are either products of the imagination or are used fictitiously. Any resemblance to real people, either living or dead, to events, businesses, or locales is entirely coincidental.

PROLOGUE

Death. The ultimate payback, and he was the one to inflict it.

A deep, satisfying burst of pleasure exploded in his gut. His whole body throbbed with satisfaction over the well-deserved revenge. He wanted to bask in it. Relish the feeling flowing through his limbs.

Revenge. So sweet.

He sighed but looked at the spilled blood. The corpse wrapped in a striped rug. He couldn't stand around. Couldn't get caught. He had plenty of time for basking later. Now was the time for cleanup. A dull, laborious chore.

"Just remember where you're taking him. The surprised look on the soon-to-be suspects' faces." *Oh yeah.* He grinned and dragged the lifeless body toward the door.

The guy's head bumped like a driven soccer ball over the raised threshold, a hollow thump the resulting sound.

Oh well. No skin off his nose. Well, except the cops would waste time trying to figure out what caused the bumps and bruises when they would have six ready suspects to try to pin this on. Maybe miss all the obvious leads he was providing.

He tugged again and moved a good three feet. Thankfully this man was fit, unlike many men his age, and his weight was manageable. As a bonus, he'd found the guy visiting his daughter who lived in a remote cottage by the ocean where no one would hear or see the shooting or the body being hauled out the door to the van.

The daughter's face flashed in his mind. No one would see him move the body, but she'd witnessed her father's death.

Simple. Take her out too.

Pop. Pop. Pop. Just like her old man.

He tried. Failed. He should never have looked into her eyes. Into the eyes of the younger woman. Pleading. Begging. He couldn't pull the trigger. But he also couldn't let her go. Not when she could identify him.

He had a problem now. A big one. He shouldn't have let her live.

What was he going to do with her? He couldn't keep her captive forever. He'd have to eventually summon up the guts to kill her.

No other option existed.

The second she'd dug out her phone and dialed 911, he'd grabbed her. Ditched the phone before they could possibly figure out who she was or where she was located, then hid her in a secluded place where no one would look for her.

The rug caught on the rough sidewalk, bringing him back to the task at hand.

"Focus, man."

Tugging harder, he backed to the van and shoved the package inside, then took a long breath of the salty ocean air. A glorious March day. Actually even bordering on the side of hot with the sun's brilliant rays glaring down on them. At this time of year fog and rain ruined most every day, sunup to sundown.

He'd even had to turn on the portable AC unit in the place to keep from dropping sweat on the shiny tile floors. Wouldn't do to leave his DNA.

He stretched and took another long breath. He couldn't stand here all day. He would have plenty of days in the future to enjoy the view and weather. But the body? No. Not the poor deceased mayor. He wouldn't wait. He had to be moved into position now.

Then let the game of cat and mouse begin while he hid in the shadows to watch it all unfold, and that loser Lost Lake Locators team take the fall.

1

A killer of an evening.

Or so the anonymous invitation claimed. But did the claim hold up?

Nolan Orr was about to find out.

He grabbed the embossed invite for the black-tie event from the dashboard of his SUV and slid out. Why he let this expensive piece of paper entice him to show up at the Tidewater Mansion, he didn't know. One thing was sure. He hadn't come for the reason the sender hoped.

No. He didn't want a killer of anything in his life.

Zip. Zilch. Zero.

Even less, if possible. He'd lived enough of those threats as a secret service agent on the presidential detail. And, yet...here he was just to find out who organized the night.

The sun set over his shoulders and a soft breeze drifted across the lush landscape as he approached the wide steps leading up to the 1800s Victorian.

Looked calm. Serene. Peaceful even. But was it?

His steps hitched. Was he a sucker for coming here? Maybe. Possibly even. But not like he had a choice. He'd had to show up. Curiosity and all that. Besides, the rest of his Lost Lake Locators team waited for him on the veranda. He wouldn't bail on them.

"Keep going." Shoving the invite into the breast pocket of his tuxedo, he moved ahead to the sweeping stairs of the renovated mansion. It was perched on a cliff overlooking Lost Lake Bay and was now used as a party venue. He bounded up as fast as his slick dress shoes allowed without faceplanting.

The five other members of his team turned to face him. He'd known everyone since college, and they were like a family, but he'd never seen them in formal wear. Striking really.

All three of the guys had dark hair and close-cut beards and wore tuxedos like Nolan. Not so the women. Abby Day and Reece Waters were nothing alike. Sure, they both wore formal black dresses, but Abby was petite, had short dark hair, and held herself like the former sheriff she'd served as. Reece was tall with long blond hair, and her college modeling showed in her stance. Most people would never guess she was once an ATF agent.

Gabe Irving, a former Oregon state trooper, looked up from his phone and gave Nolan a once over. "Boss man. You clean up well."

"It's been a minute, though." Nolan tugged on his bowtie and resisted pulling it completely free. "I'm not used to it."

"At least you own yours, and it's tailored to you." Hayden Kraus, a former US Customs and Border Protection agent, adjusted his jacket. "This thing is binding up in all the wrong places. Give me hiking or skiing gear over this any day."

Nolan wasn't into the same things as Hayden, but... "Tonight I'd rather be rappelling down a cliff with you than be here."

"You're joking, right?" Hayden creased his forehead. "You're the one who sent the invitations. Never thought you'd fork out this kind of cash for a little team building."

"From me?" Nolan looked around the group. "Is that what you guys think? No wonder no one mentioned it. I wouldn't plan a party when we have work the next day. I'm as surprised by it as you."

Hayden faced the team. "One of you set this up?"

"Not me," Abby said. "I'm with Nolan. Monday night isn't a party night."

"I didn't send it either." Gabe shoved his phone into his pocket.

"Not from me." Reece looked around the area. "No way I can afford a party in an upscale place like this. Not with all my money going to buy into the business."

"None of us can." A hint of frustration crept into Jude's tone. He'd had to work the hardest to come up with his buy-in to become an equal partner in Lost Lake Locators and almost didn't leave the FBI to join the team because of it. Sure, Nolan used an inheritance to purchase the inn where they worked and lived, but the others had to chip in for upfront costs and buying needed equipment.

"Then who in the world sent out these invitations?" Reece asked.

Abby cast a concerned look around the area. "I don't like this. Something's up."

"What, is the question." Gabe rested a hand on the sidearm tucked under his tuxedo jacket.

The front door groaned open. Nolan's heart gave a kick, and he felt for his concealed weapon as he spun to face the building.

A man he put in his fifties stepped out. Thick gel slicked back his inky hair, and he wore a formal tux and white cloth gloves. "Wonderful. You're all here. My name is Smythe, and I'll see to your needs this evening."

What in the world? Nolan blinked a few times. Was this man an actor hired to play a formal butler or a real butler? If an actor, Nolan was buying into his role.

"Follow me." He spun in a precise pivot and entered the house.

Gabe frowned, his gaze locked on Smythe. "This is getting weirder and weirder."

"Yeah, but if we want to find out what it's all about, then we do as he says and follow him. But take care." Nolan gave each team member a pointed look, then strode into the mansion.

The well-groomed man stood just inside the formal two-story foyer, his posture military perfect. Nolan forced himself to look away and take in the building as his teammates entered behind him. He stood on gleaming marble tile with a sweeping grand staircase climbing to the second floor that overlooked the entry, and an impressive chandelier sparkled from above.

The butler moved, and Nolan jerked his focus back to him.

He held out his gloved hand. "The dining room is straight ahead to your right, and dinner will be served in five minutes."

"So who paid for this night?" Abby asked, not surprising as she was usually the first one to jump in when something needed clarifying.

"That's information I'm not privy to. I've just been instructed to facilitate a special evening for you." Smythe smiled, but this one was definitely fake. He held out a Faraday bag. "Before you go in, I'll need you to drop your cell phones in here, and I'll take your invitations."

Say what? The bag stopped all signals coming into or

leaving a cell phone. This made no sense. Why did he need their phones to basically be inoperative?

"Nah, no way on the phone." Gabe shook his head and planted his feet. "That's a deal killer for me."

"Please do not worry. This is just so you all will enjoy every moment tonight." Smythe jiggled the bag. "I will put this in the dining room with you. You can see it at all times and know your phones are safe."

Nolan wouldn't let this condition stop him. Not when he'd be able to see the bag and retrieve his phone if needed. "That should be fine then."

He handed over his invitation and dropped his phone into the bag. He stood back so his teammates could follow suit.

"I don't like this," Gabe said as he let go of his phone.

Nolan gave a sympathetic nod, but he wouldn't back out now. Not a chance. His gut burned even more to find out what was going on. "You're sure you don't know who paid for this event?"

Smythe glanced around as if checking for a spy. "I'm not supposed to tell you, but the night is courtesy of a client who is thankful for your work."

So someone was grateful that they'd found a lost loved one and decided to give the team a night out. Despite the person's desire to remain anonymous, Nolan would find out the identity so he could show his appreciation. "Can you tell me which client?"

"I've already said too much." Smythe gave a conversation-ending smile. "Please join me in the dining room."

His chin raised, he marched off.

"He obviously knows who it is and isn't telling us." One of Hayden's piercing expressions took over, and he fisted his hands. "Maybe I should give him some up close persuasion."

Nolan held out a placating hand. "Not necessary. I'm uncomfortable not knowing which client arranged this, but no need to intimidate the butler. We have other ways to find out."

"No surprise the two of you are so uncomfortable." Abby looked between Nolan and Hayden. "You both need to control everything."

Gabe shifted his stance. "I don't like it either, and if it bothers me, there's got to be something to it."

"All I can say is, if I wake up dead in the morning because we're being poisoned at dinner, I'm gonna be mad." Jude grinned.

The others laughed, the tension broken as Jude often accomplished as the team joker.

Nolan appreciated the humor, but he wasn't at peace with everything. Still, he'd stay at least until he had a logical explanation for the night. Or learned enough to investigate and find out what was going on.

Smythe turned at the doorway and gestured for them to join him. "When you finish your meal, I'll invite you to the next room for a night of games prepared just for you."

A vision of the invitation flashed in Nolan's brain. "Is this where it turns into a killer of an evening?"

"Indeed it is, sir." Smythe smiled. "Prepare yourself to be delighted and shocked at the same time."

Hayden's face lit up, and he pulled on his bowtie. "Sounds like my kind of night, and maybe this monkey suit will be worth it."

Shock and delight. Nolan wasn't as quick to get on board as Hayden was. Nolan couldn't imagine shock and delight going hand-in-hand. But did it matter?

Either he walked out now, or he had to wait for the shock. All he knew at the moment was if whatever was planned was enough to stun this team of former law enforcement officers, it had to be big. Very big.

~

Sheriff Mina Park sat behind her desk, her ear tuned to her radio and her eyes drifting closed as she stared at her computer.

Please. Let something happen that needs a sheriff's intervention before both of my eyes close.

She shouldn't complain or wish to be needed. She'd wanted this job for as long as she could remember. Being sheriff of the county where she was raised and providing protection for the people she loved was everything to her. Everything.

She loved most every bit of it. Overseeing not only the county, but the town of Lost Lake too. Kept her busy. Especially in the summer months, but the off-season boredom? Nearly drove her nuts.

Like tonight. Her big highlight? Reviewing and signing off on the recent city council meeting minutes, attesting that she'd read them. Highlight. Hah! More like a lowlight.

She'd take any call to get out of the office. Anything. Even a drunk resident at one of the local bars. An event that could turn interesting, but not in a way to challenge her brain. But she couldn't expect much more in the off-season when all the tourists had gone home.

But then, she didn't want a major crime to occur either. With the annual Founder's Day celebration coming up that weekend, she would make her share of arrests. Surely she could hold on till then.

Besides, she especially wouldn't want the ultimate in crimes. A murder. No, that meant someone lost their life.

She'd seen all the reports where tourists died on their vacations in some exotic destination. Exotic, hah! Not her county, holding Lost Lake and Lost Island. Interesting for tourists who loved pristine Pacific beaches and the historic island, filled with century-old Victorian homes, but not exotic.

Problem was, over the years their tourist trade had fallen. A lot. Even the centuries-old Portside Inn and Lighthouse out on the point hadn't been able to survive and had to close. It sat vacant for three years until Nolan Orr swooped in and bought it before she even knew what was happening. Not that she could've stopped the purchase, but if she'd known about it, she sure would've tried.

How she would have tried. With every fiber in her being she would've tried to stop the man who unceremoniously dumped her from coming back to live full-time in her hometown. He probably bought the place in secret because he thought she would try to halt the sale.

Or not.

More likely, he hadn't thought about her from the day five years ago when he'd left at the end of their summer fling without saying goodbye.

An ache wrapped around her heart even after all these years, and she curled her arms around her stomach. She'd been so in love and thought this was the guy she would spend the rest of her life with. She'd met all of his friends, and they seemed to agree she was the right person for him.

Obviously not Nolan. No, not him. They were supposed to meet out at the lighthouse. He didn't show. She waited two hours before going to his hotel. He was gone. Checked out early in the morning and hadn't tried to contact her. End of story.

Her radio squabbled, and she came to attention in her chair.

"Drunk and disorderly at the Thirsty Crab," Deputy Banfield said. "Backup needed."

"Perfect," she whispered to herself. "Something to take my mind off the traitor Nolan Orr."

And something to stop her wondering if her life was as fulfilling as she believed it to be before that man had come back to town and filled her brain with a boatload of *what ifs*.

2

Nolan and the rest of the team trailed Smythe down the dark hallway to a locked door on the right. Smythe blocked the electronic lock with his body to secretly enter a code, and the deadbolt gave way.

Nolan didn't like this. Not that Smythe was acting odd, but why would anyone need a deadbolt on an interior door, much less on the door for a room used to play games? He supposed it could also serve as a storage space for event items, so he would reserve judgment for now.

Smythe pushed open the door, flipped on a light, then stood back. "Please enter, and I will give you instructions for your first game of the evening."

"Hold up." Nolan raised his hand. "Let me check this out before we all go piling in there."

"By all means." Smythe stood back.

Nolan stepped into a long, narrow room. One wall was covered with six gray metal lockers. Next to them stood a bookshelf, holding books and stacks of newspapers. Then came a closed, glass trophy case loaded with various shiny trophies next to a bulletin board with what looked like notices. The back half of the room was set up to resemble one side of a college dormitory room including a twin-sized bed with storage drawers underneath.

Across from the lockers, a punching bag hung from the ceiling, with three pairs of gloves dangling from the cord. A bright wooden box sat on a table below the movie posters plastered on the wall.

"I don't know if you're familiar with the term *escape room*," Smythe said from the doorway, "but we've planned an escape room for you based on your academy days."

Nolan moved back to the door as he ran through what he knew about escape rooms. He didn't like them much. Not when he had to give over control of his life for an hour or so. Sure, it was up to him and whoever joined him to decide the actions they took to solve the puzzle and escape the room, but still, he was a prisoner of the game's creator.

He looked at Smythe. "You're going to lock us in here while we solve puzzles or look for clues to figure out how to get the door to unlock."

"Exactly." Smythe ran his gaze over the group. "How many of you have ever participated in one?"

Nolan raised his hand along with Reece and Jude.

"Good. Then you can help lead the others. We have cameras in the room, and I will be watching while you try to locate the clues. If you require help, all you need to do is call me on the cell phone we left for you, and I will give you a clue. You have one hour to solve the mystery. Any questions?"

No one spoke up.

"Dear me." He palmed his forehead. "I forgot one of the most important things. I will not actually lock the door, so have no fear. If you need to exit to use the restroom or for any other reason, all I ask is that you let me know you're leaving."

Nolan had to admit that last bit gave him comfort in

playing this game. One thing was for sure. He would find out who planned this night. And then what? Tell them it wasn't fun for a group of former law enforcement officers to be put in a small room with the goal being to escape? At least not Nolan's idea of fun, but the others were smiling as they entered the room, so he went along with them and stepped inside.

Gabe pivoted beside Nolan. "A blast from the past."

Abby pointed at a handmade poster by the punching bag that said *The fight may be tough, but so are you*! "Sounds like someone's idea of a motivational pitch."

Hayden tapped the movie posters one at a time. "*Men in Black*, *The Avengers*, and *The Hunger Games*. We saw all of those right after we graduated from the police academy."

Jude cast a quizzical look at the wall, then turned to take in the rest of the room. "Is this a mashup of a dorm room, the fitness room, and student lounge at OSP Academy?"

They had all graduated from the Oregon State Police sixteen-week training academy for law enforcement recruits in Salem. Took some doing, but they'd timed job hires so they could attend together.

"You are very perceptive, sir." Smythe set the bag with their phones on a small table just inside the doorway and rested his hand on the doorknob. "Please call me if you have any questions."

He pulled the door closed, and Nolan listened for the deadbolt as it seemed the others were doing as well. No sound, but he couldn't leave it at that and be able to relax and enjoy this game. He crossed the room and grabbed the knob. The door opened.

Satisfied, he turned to his team. "I guess the first question is, do you really want to do this? We can leave now if you don't want to stay."

"You kidding?" Jude asked. "The gauntlet has been

thrown down. We're not the type of team to run away from a challenge, even a pointless challenge like this one."

"Anyway," Reece added, "it could be fun."

"I say we go for it. Minus the heels." Abby kicked off her shoes. "Everyone knows since we started the business we don't have much time for fun. Seems like we're always working to pay the bills."

"Okay, I'm in," Gabe said. "Not sure if I want to do it, but I'm up for a challenge. Besides, I'll show you all the way to the finish."

"Ooh." Reece rubbed her hands together. "Challenge accepted."

Nolan loved to do puzzles and ciphers. Always had. And his past escape-room experience had told him that they would have to be creative and able to solve puzzles to find their way out.

"You should know," he closed the door, "escape room creators rarely put anything in the room that doesn't have to do with the solution. Not that on the surface the item will be a direct clue, so when you find a lead, it won't necessarily make sense at the time. It's only when we put a bunch of the clues together that the solution comes to light."

"Sounds intriguing," Abby said.

"It can be a challenge," he said. "Let's split up and look for clues. Bring everything you find to the table with the box, and we'll try to figure out what it means."

They broke up as if they were exiting a team huddle and began searching.

Speakers mounted near the ceiling suddenly started blasting out, "Stronger," sung by Kelly Clarkson.

"I remember this song," Reece yelled above the music.

"How can you not?" Jude asked. "It was played on the radio nonstop."

Nolan liked the song, but at this volume? It wiped everything out of his brain, and he could barely think.

The melody played three or four times and stopped as suddenly as it started.

Jude stared up at the speakers. "What was that all about?"

"Could just be to get us in the mood for the game," Gabe said. "Or further emphasize the time frame like the posters and other memorabilia would indicate."

Jude shook his head. "I don't buy that. If so, why not keep playing it?"

"So, is it the words?" Nolan asked. "*What doesn't kill you makes you stronger*. What is it referring to? What might kill you or make you stronger?"

"The poster." Abby pointed across the room. "*The fight may be tough, but so are you!* Could it be the punching bag or even a sports game where you had to fight to get one of the trophies in the case?"

"Could be." Nolan turned his attention to the trophy case. "What about the trophies? They all signify someone doing something great."

Reece joined him at the case and tried to slide the glass open. A small metal lock kept it closed. "We need a key."

"Let's not waste time looking for one," Nolan said. "I'll grab the phone bag, and we can use our phones to enlarge the engraving on the trophies to see if it tells us anything."

Nolan retrieved the bag and returned. He reached inside. Felt around. "No. Oh no."

He pulled out a small cardboard box containing something heavy. He opened it. A lead weight taped inside. He dropped it then grabbed another and another. "Our phones are gone."

Gabe looked up at one of the cameras. "You lied, man. Come in here and explain it."

No response.

"My life is on my phone," Hayden said. "We need to get him on the phone he left us, or I'm tearing this place apart until I find him."

"We first have to find the phone," Nolan said.

He didn't have to tell his teammates twice. They dashed around, searching in and under things.

"Here it is." Jude snatched it off the bookcase from behind a plant and held it up. "An old Motorola RAZR."

"Make the call," Nolan said.

Jude flipped it open. "It's dead. Just for show." He slammed it down.

"What about the door?" Gabe asked. "He lie about that and lock it? If so I'll—"

"I checked it. Remember? I'll go find him." Before Gabe could go off half-cocked, Nolan bolted across the room and twisted the knob. Didn't budge. "Locked."

Abby planted her hands on her hips. "He must've come back to lock it. Probably blasted the music so we couldn't hear him."

"Then we're on our own," Jude said.

"At least we're safe." Reece patted her purse. "I don't suppose I'm the only one carrying."

"Do you even need to ask?" Jude grinned. "The only thing we can do at this point is figure out the mystery to unlock the door."

"Not the only thing." Gabe glared at the door as if it were a living being and could see his response. "We could just break the thing down."

Nolan stepped closer to his teammates. "Let's not over-react and try figuring out the puzzle first. If that doesn't work, then we do what Gabe says and bust out of here."

Jude nodded. "The lockers seem obvious to me. These

should have padlocks but don't, so it's like we're meant to open them."

They descended on the lockers, and each person pulled up on a hasp.

"Locked." Gabe looked at the others. "All of them."

Reece made her way down the row. "They're numbered. Wait! Seventeen. That was my academy locker number."

"Mine was one," Nolan said.

"You're on my left and four is on my right."

"That's me." Abby ran over there.

Jude, Gabe, and Hayden located their numbers too.

"Maybe we all have to be at the right locker and open them at the same time," Nolan said. "Let's try it on the count of three."

He counted. They pulled. Nothing budged.

Jude frowned. "So much for that idea."

"So back to the poster then." Abby looked around. "*The fight may be tough, but so are you*! Time to try the punching bag in the corner."

Nearest to the bag, Gabe grabbed a pair of gloves and handed them to her, then slipped his hand into one. "There's something in here." He pulled out small pieces of paper. He dropped the glove and jostled the papers. "Letters. Just a bunch of letters cut out of a newspaper or magazine."

Abby took her hand from her glove. "Mine are numbers."

"Check the other ones." Nolan turned his attention back to the trophies. "I wasn't a jock, but could they be from championships or records set by any of you in high school?"

"Not me." Gabe moved to the table holding the wooden box and laid the papers on the table. "I was too into motorcycles and chicks to be bothered with sports."

"I played basketball," Reece said.

"You gotta know I wasn't tall enough to do anything

except make posters for the pep squad." Laughing, Abby joined Gabe and let a handful of papers filter down onto the table. "These are the cutout numbers from my glove but the other ones were empty."

"I was a football fanatic." Hayden crossed over to the case.

"Me too," Jude said, coming up behind them. "Quarterback, in fact. I set several passing records." He leaned closer to the trophy case. "Nothing I recognize in there."

Nolan stepped back. "Hayden, check out the trophies to see if any of them are related to you."

"We won state one year and got a big trophy." Hayden took Nolan's place in front of the trophy case. "Nope. Not in there. These look like individual trophies and not all look sports-related."

What in the world is going on here?

"Maybe these letters and numbers will tell us something," Abby said.

"I suppose they could help find the key to the trophy case." Nolan stepped over to Abby and Gabe.

Abby tapped the wooden box on the table. "Could be in here, but it's locked too. Looks like some fancy smart combination lock."

Hayden joined her and lifted the lock to study it. "You're right. Our host can access it remotely and open it at any time."

Reece grinned at him over her shoulder. "Being our resident geek, you would know that."

Hayden rolled his eyes as he often did when being called a geek, but the shoe fit. He'd helped them all with computer issues in college and when they'd attended police academy together. Now, he'd taken that role in their team, and Nolan couldn't be more grateful to have someone with exceptional computer skills on his side.

Abby moved a few pieces of paper around. "I'm assuming this is going to spell out a message of some sort. Do you think it's related to the academy or boxing since we found it in the glove or something else?"

"Not sure." Gabe shoved around nearby letters, then looked up. "If you go by the ink colors and background, we can sort this into words. So far I've got *the, is,* and *to.*"

"The numbers could be a date." Nolan rearranged the scraps until he formed a date.

"That's our academy graduation day," Abby said, still moving letters around. "I've got *best.*"

"And *yet,*" Gabe said.

Nolan shifted the last four letters. "*Come.*"

"The best is yet to come," Abby cried out but didn't need to explain as they all used this saying to help get through tough days at the academy.

Nolan spun. "What else are we missing related to the academy? Maybe specific to graduation."

"The bookshelf," Reece called out. "Our class graduation picture."

Abby charged over to the bookshelf and grabbed the framed picture. She flipped it over and ran her fingers along the back. "There's something in here."

She freed the backing. "A key. It has a key taped to it. Small, like it would fit the trophy case lock."

Reece ripped the key from the cardboard and inserted it into the lock. "It's turning. We've got it! We can open the case."

She removed the lock and slid the door open.

Jude reached in, took out a nearby trophy, and gave it a good looking over. "This is for you, Nolan. It's for the Victor G. Atiyeh Award."

He felt his face flush. The award was given to each basic class and was named after the former Oregon governor who'd helped make the academy a reality. The recipient was selected by students and staff for criteria of excellence.

"There wasn't a trophy for this," Nolan said. "So someone had to have had this made just for tonight."

"Reece and Jude, you both got awards," Abby said. "See if your name is on any of those?"

Reece bumped Hayden out of the way with her hip. She removed a trophy and followed Jude's lead, checking it out thoroughly. "Has my name on it for the marksmanship award."

"Looks like mine is on the top shelf." Jude reached into the case. "What in the world? It won't budge. It's attached to the shelf somehow."

"Don't be a wuss," Gabe called out. "Pull harder."

"Yeah, your motto," Jude said, sarcasm liberally coating his words. "If it doesn't work at first, use brute force and shove harder."

"Is there any other way?" Gabe chuckled.

Jude put both hands on the top of the trophy and pulled it forward. The trophy remained attached, but pivoted on the shelf. "This is like you see for hidden passages on TV and in movies when they pull on something on a bookshelf and a hidden door opens."

"No door opening," Nolan said. "But the lock on the wooden box is whirring."

The padlock suddenly dropped open. Nolan opened the box to reveal a stack of jigsaw puzzle pieces. He dumped them out and set the box on a chair to free up the table.

"Are you kidding me?" Gabe asked. "Another puzzle to solve?"

"But we have a secret weapon here," Nolan said. "Hayden does puzzles all the time."

"Out of my way, peeps." Hayden strode toward them. "Let the master get to work."

Abby spread out the pieces. "Um, Hayden. These are like toddler-sized pieces. I think we can handle it."

"But not as fast as me. Still, I'll let you work with me. Separate out the edge pieces, and I'll start putting them together."

They set to work, Hayden's intensity as fierce as if this lead might help him find one of the lost people they were hired to search for.

He soon had the frame done and began filling in the pieces by color. "I see crime scene tape and someone squatted in a Tyvek suit."

"That's me!" Abby cried out. "Remember when you made fun of me because I was so excited about forensics and shining my blue light around? But what does it mean?"

"Maybe we're supposed to find a blue light," Nolan said, already moving toward the bookshelf.

Hayden beat him there, found a flashlight, and turned it on. "It's a black light. Kill the lights so we can see if it clarifies something."

Jude flipped the switch on the wall, plunging the windowless room into complete darkness except for the beam of blue light.

Hayden waved it around the room but stopped on one of the lockers. "Someone's written something here." He focused the beam on the upper part of the lockers.

"*The right order is the key to everything.*" Nolan read aloud. "It could mean we need to open the lockers in numerical order."

"Let's try it." Abby headed for her locker. "You're number one so you go first, then me with number four."

They scrambled to their respective lockers. After a few missteps, they lifted the latches in order. The first five didn't open.

"One more to go," Jude said, the last number belonging to him. He pulled up the latch, and his door swung open.

"Whoa." He lurched back.

"Dude," Gabe said. "He is *so* dead."

Nolan bolted down the line until he caught sight of their local mayor squeezed into the locker. His purple-colored skin told Nolan all he needed to know.

"We need to get out of here and call the sheriff," he said, but as soon as the words left his mouth he wished they could be calling anyone but Sheriff Mina Park.

She was the most amazing woman he'd ever met, but she didn't think he was quite so amazing. Their summer fling had ended badly, and he didn't have a clue how she would react to seeing him again, not to mention finding him with a dead body.

3

Mina planted her hands on her hips and surveyed the scene ahead of her. She'd gotten her wish. Sort of. She got the excitement she craved as multiple units sat outside the Tidewater Mansion, lightbars running, illuminating the night and declaring a murder had occurred. One discovered by Nolan Orr. By her summer fling. By the man she'd hoped never to see again. The man she couldn't forgive.

Yet, here she was. Set to interview him.

With gritted teeth, she pounded up the steps, past the deputy on duty, and through the spacious and opulent mansion. Her sergeant had shared the preliminary details, including the big life-altering fact that Nolan and his team had found the body.

Nolan. Here. Unbelievable.

She'd known she would eventually cross paths with him. Sure she would. Her office might be in Seaside Harbor, the county seat, but she lived in Lost Lake, and the place was too small to avoid him forever.

But why couldn't that day be in the distant future? Maybe in passing on the street in town. Not here. Not with him as a prime witness—maybe suspect—in a murder investigation where they'd be thrown together.

She paused outside the dining room. The LLL team, along with Harmony Vance, the mansion's caretaker and leasing agent who was always on duty when the building was leased, were waiting for her. She took a breath. Then another. And stepped forward.

Her body failed her, and her feet came to a dead stop. Nolan stood on the far side of the room facing his team who were seated around the table. A single look at his profile and everything turned to mush. Just as it had when she'd fallen in love with him.

Okay, fine. You might be over the heartbreak, but the mere sight of him can still make your knees weak. So buck up and be careful.

She took another one of those deep chest-heaving breaths and started into the room.

He turned. Locked gazes with her. Her footsteps faltered again. That compelling attraction he'd always had for her radiated across the room as if drawing her to him. She'd never been able to fight it in the past.

So what? She was a sheriff now, in charge of a murder investigation, and she would fight it today. It would take everything she was made of, but she would succeed.

Please help me not make a fool of myself with him and to see the way to successfully work with him.

She curled her fingers into fists and strode forward, passing Deputy Banfield, located right inside the door. The tall guy, built from hours at the gym, raised his shoulders in a kind of salute.

She gave him a nod of acknowledgment and a thankful smile. It wasn't easy babysitting witnesses to keep them from comparing stories, but he'd been first on scene and had followed protocol.

Secure the scene. Make sure no one was in danger. Separate the witnesses if possible. Not possible in this case so babysitting was his only option.

She stopped in front of Nolan, widening her stance as if somehow a strong position could make up for the fact that he was more than a foot taller, and she had to look up to him.

"Nolan." Was all she could say without her voice cracking.

"Mina," he replied, sounding equally uncomfortable.

She ignored Harmony for now and turned to the team. "It's good to see all of you. Not under the circumstances though."

Gabe snorted. "I never thought we'd lay eyes on you again. Not with the way you dumped Nolan."

She blinked at him. "What? I—"

"Now is not the time for that." Nolan eyed Gabe.

"It's your deal, man, so I'll shut up." Gabe shrugged and sat back.

Nolan spun to face Mina. "You'll want our statements. We're happy to cooperate in whatever you need."

Okay, back to the business at hand, and no explanation of Gabe's comment. Had Nolan told his team she dumped him? If so, why would he lie about that? If he wanted to save face, he would've done just the opposite and explained how he'd left her. For some reason, it seemed like he wanted them to think badly of her. But what Nolan and his team thought of her was of no importance.

Yeah, keep telling yourself that.

She planted her hands on her waist. "I'll first take a look at the scene."

"The room is just down the hall," Nolan said. "I can take you there and walk through the events if you would like."

Like? Like? No. Not like at all.

If this were a normal crime scene, if such a thing existed, and she didn't have a room full of former law enforcement officers, she would absolutely refuse the offer. But Nolan, or anyone in this room except Harmony, could be trusted not to contaminate the scene and respect any boundaries she set. But did it have to be Nolan?

"I'm sure the team needs you here." She looked at the others, running her gaze from person to person. "Is there anyone else who would want to show me through the scene?"

She got a few mumbled nos and head-shakes. They'd obviously talked about her arrival and had decided Nolan would be in charge. Had they talked about the big breakup too? Hashing over the embarrassing event when he walked out on her without a backward glance?

"Fine," she said to Nolan. "I'd appreciate you walking me through the evening. But only if you agree to follow any directions I provide."

"Of course." A forceful shove of his hands into his pockets contradicted his cheerful response. "I'm glad to do whatever you say to help find the mayor's killer."

She held out her hand. "Then lead the way, but stop at the door where my deputy will give you booties and gloves."

He strode out. She was right on his tail but turned to look at the group. "I don't have to tell you not to discuss what you witnessed, but I'm going to tell you anyway. And Deputy Banfield will remain here with you to be sure you don't talk about it."

She got some grumbling and a challenging look from Abby, who, as a former sheriff, was used to being in charge in such situations. She had to be jonesing to get involved, and only loyalty to Nolan could've gotten her to sit back and let him accompany Mina to the crime scene.

"I'll be back," she said to Banfield and slipped out of the room.

Nolan was already talking to Deputy Ewing and putting shoe coverings over his shiny dress shoes. She hadn't really noticed the details of his attire, but his traditional black tuxedo looked like it was custom-made. And it likely was, the cut highlighting his broad shoulders and trim waist. He probably owned it from his days on the president's security detail.

Man, if only she wasn't on the outs with him, she would love to sit down and talk about when he worked the detail. Not to get gossip about the family or the president, but just to find out what it was like to protect the most powerful man in the country. Some would say the most powerful man in the world.

She put on her own booties and a pair of gloves. "Wait here while I get the lay of the land."

She stepped inside the doorway. She ran a quick look over the room, but her gaze landed on the bald head gleaming in the overhead light and held. *The mayor.* She swallowed. Once. Twice. She'd expected to see him, but nothing really prepared you to see a body. Especially not of someone you knew and worked closely with.

She gritted her teeth and turned away to face Nolan. "Walk me through the night."

He took a few steps closer to her. "We had dinner in the dining room. It was served by a man named Smythe, but we don't know him or who sent us the invitations."

"Perhaps from the property owner, as this is quite an elaborate scheme for one night's rental."

"I don't suppose you know who owns this place."

"Cody Palmer. I've never met him, but he purchased the mansion as a business investment a year ago and lives out of town. The business is registered, and we have property

30

records, so we can easily get his information and contact him."

"We should make that a priority."

She ignored the *we* part of his statement and scribbled a reminder in her notebook. "Do you remember if the invitation envelope had a return address?"

"It didn't," he said. "I double-checked because I wanted to know who it was from."

"I'd like to see the invitations and envelopes they came in."

"No can do on the invitations. We had to surrender them to Smythe when we arrived, but maybe someone kept an envelope. I'll ask the team. We also had to surrender our phones."

"Seriously?" She blinked at him. "You willingly gave up your phones?"

"Only because we thought they were safe."

"How so?"

"We put them in a Faraday bag that Smythe placed on the buffet in the dining room, in our sight at all times. When we moved to this room, he brought the bag of phones with him and set them on the table by the door. Or at least we thought he did, but turns out he swapped the bag with one holding small boxes with weights in them to mimic phones."

Creative. "Any thoughts on who this Smythe guy is and where he went?"

Nolan shook his head. "He seemed like a butler, but he could've been a trained actor. After we reported the murder, we searched the house and grounds for him. Found no sign of him ever having been here."

"Nothing? Not even in the kitchen where the food must've come from?"

"It wasn't cooked down there, that was obvious. Or if he

had cooked it here, he completely cleaned up, which I don't think he had time to do. But my guess is he brought prepared meals in from a caterer and simply served them to us."

"Still, we'll want to process that space for forensics. The dining room too."

"Agreed, but you should know he wore cotton gloves the whole time he was with us. If he didn't take them off in the kitchen, there won't be any fingerprints. That doesn't mean he wouldn't have left DNA."

He could be right, but she would have to wait for the state for forensic processing when she could get started on the investigation right now. "Do you remember what he looks like well enough to sit with a forensic artist to create a sketch?"

He nodded. "I don't suppose you have someone on staff who can do that?"

"Actually, I do," she said. "Most sketches are done electronically these days, and I have a deputy trained to do it. I can get him into the office right after we finish up here. I can give you a ride." She could hardly believe she was offering to spend time with him. "But you'll have to wait in the car while I notify Becca of her father's death."

"I could just meet you at your office."

"Suit yourself." She shrugged but was disappointed. Perhaps she was hoping he would share the trauma of doing a death notification call. She couldn't bring him into the house with her, but he would be there when she got out. And things she knew for certain about him, he was understanding and super supportive. At least, he was until he wasn't.

He'd been carefully watching her and let out a breath. "On second thought, I will take you up on the ride."

She waited for an explanation but didn't get one. Okay,

fine. She would move on and hope her body language hadn't given her away. "Back to the phones. Did you find them?"

Nolan nodded. "When we left the room in search of a phone to report the murder, we found the original bag on the buffet in the dining room."

She looked around the space. "I was told this was an escape room, so I assume the door was locked. How did you get to a phone to call us?"

"We played the game. Solved the clues." He shrugged. "We could probably have broken down the door, but once we found the mayor, we didn't want to disturb any more evidence if possible. We'd solved most of the mystery by the time we found him, but then we still had to do a few more things to get the door unlocked."

He sounded so matter-of-fact in his telling of the night. She didn't know how he could be so calm, as he surely hadn't seen many dead bodies in the Secret Service. Likely hadn't seen any at all. And here he was with his team locked in the room with the deceased mayor shoved in the locker. It took a strong man to handle such a situation. But then she'd known he was strong. It was one of the qualities that had drawn her to him.

Didn't matter.

She couldn't let that affect anything that occurred tonight or in the investigation. She had to remain objective. This was her first murder investigation, and she had a lot to prove to the county residents who'd elected her. She would not fail simply because she was crushing on a man she would never get involved with again.

Nolan explained the puzzles and mysteries they'd solved to Mina, making sure he was all business. He had to ignore the way her blond hair softly curved over her shoulder and covered up the county sheriff's logo on her chest. The way her uniform fit her five-foot-nine body as if custom-made for her. Or the way her large brown eyes were fixed on him, her attention to his every word.

His attention faltered, and he had to stop talking before he sounded like a complete idiot. He'd already agreed to get in a car with her when he could've driven on his own. But he'd had visions of her going alone to do a death notification call, and she seemed as if she wanted company. If being closed in the car with her was the cost of providing some support, so be it.

All he had to do was keep his focus on the investigation. Dig deep. Remember his past as a Secret Service agent where he learned to put on a game face twenty-four hours a day, seven days a week if necessary, no matter the distractions presented to him.

Tonight it was necessary. Imperative. Assuming he didn't want to beg her to tell him why she didn't respond to his note explaining his sudden departure. Why she'd blown him off instead of calling him.

Mina pointed, redirecting his attention. "So the lockers opened, and you found the body. Did they all open at that time?"

Nolan shook his head. "Jude's was first, revealing the body. Then like I said, once we got over the shock of finding the mayor, we were still faced with trying to get out of the room."

She cocked her head. "It must've been rough being in such a small space with Mayor Sutton deceased in the locker."

"It wasn't the greatest of times, but we'd already spent

fifty minutes in the room and Smythe said it should take about an hour. We figured we only had about ten minutes left and were even more determined to finish the escape and find our way out."

"Which you did, but how?"

"We tried the other lockers again. This time they opened. They contained our framed academy graduation pictures. Each one had a letter written on the back in marker, but mine had the alphabet typed on white paper."

"Interesting"

"More than interesting. I thought it might be a rudimentary cipher, so I laid the letters on the table. Moved forward a letter on the alphabet. No luck. Moved forward two. Still no luck. But three was the trick. The letters spelled *board.*"

Her gaze whipped across the room. "The bulletin board."

"Exactly. We each took an item down to study it. The back of the daily schedule held numbers. We tried them on the door lock, and they didn't work so I figured it was another cipher, and I used the same basic one I did for the letters except for numbers. It gave me the code for the electronic door lock."

She tilted her head. "It's either a coincidence that you're good at ciphers, or the person who locked you in this room knew you were."

"I don't think it's a coincidence. Not with all the other items in the room being personal to us. Some of which I'm shocked are here. Like our graduation pictures. And why make trophies that never existed?"

"Something I'll need to investigate." She narrowed her eyes. "This person who created the escape room could be trying to set one of you up for the murder charge. And since the items are so personal to each of you, I have to entertain the idea it could be you or one of your team."

"No!" He shook his head hard. "I refuse to believe that. I didn't do it, and you know the others—spent time with them. You know they would never murder someone. Besides, what motive would any of us have for killing the mayor? He's been our ally and supportive of our team and mission since we arrived in town to set up business. He even got a special tax credit approved for our business. And if we wanted to kill him, why would we make everything in this room all about us and put his body in here?"

"Perhaps it's something you don't know about."

Nolan shook his head again. "No. Emphatically no. Don't waste your time going down that path or the real killer will go free."

"I have to go down any path the forensics and leads take me."

He let his gaze bore into her. "Is this about our past? Are you wanting one of us to be guilty because you feel bad for bailing on me? Bailing on them?"

Her mouth fell open. "Me bail on *you*? You're the one who left without a word. One minute we're supposed to meet for breakfast, and the next I find out you've left town with no explanation."

What? He'd explained this in his note, so why was she pretending she didn't know why he'd had to leave? "Didn't you get my note?"

"No note," her steely tone cut him to the core.

He took a breath to mitigate some of the emotions taking over. "I would never leave without explaining. I had to go. An enterovirus spread from agent to agent assigned to the president, and my supervisor canceled everyone's vacation."

Her chin went up higher as if she wasn't buying it. "Okay, so you had a good reason for leaving. Didn't mean you couldn't have told me."

"Like I said I left a note."

She crossed her arms. "What about just talking to me? Was that too much for me to expect?"

"I tried, but I had to leave immediately to catch the only flight available. I couldn't call you—you lost your phone the day before. Remember? We were joking around, and you dropped it over the cliff at the overlook and into the ocean."

Recognition dawned on her face. "Okay, but there must've been another way to contact me before just leaving me behind like a meaningless summer fling."

"How? The only way was to come to your house to talk to you, but you never gave me your address. Still, I didn't just leave. I'd seen you talking to the desk clerk a few times, and it seemed like you knew him, so I figured he might be able to tell me where you lived. But he said he didn't know, and I didn't have time to go looking for you. He suggested I write you a note, and he would ask around town for your address and make sure to get it to you. So I did."

She frowned. "If it's the desk clerk I think you're talking about, it was Tommy. He was one of my good friends and had been to my house plenty of times."

"Then I don't know why he would say he didn't know where it was." Nolan described the guy, making sure to emphasize his red hair and freckles. "Is that him?"

"Yeah, that's Tommy. He was the only guy with red hair at the hotel, so it had to be him." She stared at Nolan for a long moment. "I didn't get a note, and if you gave one to Tommy, he would've passed it on."

Nolan locked gazes with her. "Are you saying I'm lying?"

She planted her booted feet on the floor, her chin raising in that stubborn look he remembered from when she got mad. "I guess I am."

"One way to solve this," Nolan said, trying not to get angry himself. "We find this Tommy guy and ask him about the note, though he'll probably lie about it because he never gave it to you."

"Just one problem with that."

Bad news was coming. Nolan didn't want more bad news today, but he also wouldn't run from it. Meet it head-on and deal with it. That had always been his philosophy. "And what's that?"

"Tommy died from leukemia a few months ago."

Nolan's heart sank in his chest. Since Tommy hadn't delivered the note, he probably wouldn't have told the truth about it. But if he were alive, there would at least be hope.

Now that he knew Mina hadn't simply ignored his plea to call him, he would've liked to resolve once and for all something else that had weighed heavy on him for years.

But that, like who killed the mayor, remained a mystery.

4

As Mina made her way around the escape room, she could feel Nolan watching from the doorway. She should be concentrating on the murder, but she couldn't get over the fact that he'd supposedly left her a note. He seemed sincere, but he could just be trying to get on her good side so she wouldn't suspect him or one of his friends of this murder.

Sincere or not, how could he have left a note without her receiving it? Tommy was a loyal friend until the day he died. If he'd gotten a note from Nolan, he would've delivered it.

Wouldn't he?

His mother had always hinted that he had a crush on her, and they would make the perfect couple. He'd protested and said that's the last thing he wanted. That they were just good friends. But could he have been covering up for his true feelings and kept the note from her because he hoped they would get together?

No. No. She was certain of that. Even if he wanted to be with her, he wouldn't have decided her future for her. Not Tommy. He was as loyal and honest as they came.

So let it go. It's all in the past. Spilled milk and all that.

Don't cry over it. She'd done plenty of that when Nolan had disappeared from her life.

Chalk it up to a summer romance. That was all it was. This kind of romance happened around these parts with tourists and college kids coming to work in the shops and hotels during the peak season. Love 'em and leave 'em. It still happened today, leaving lots of broken hearts.

Not hers. Not again. Though it would be different now. Nolan seemed like he planned to stay this time. Set down roots and all.

Also didn't matter. She was *so* not going there, but seeing him made clear an issue that had nagged at her for years. She needed to find a way to forgive him. Not for him, but for her. The Bible clearly said if she didn't forgive him his sins, her Father wouldn't forgive hers.

And then what if she didn't? She couldn't even begin to comprehend the consequences because she couldn't find a way to let go of the hurt long enough to forgive him.

She had to address it and soon. Not now. Now she had to get to the bottom of this murder.

Gritting her teeth, she spun to look at him. She wanted to move on to the murder, but her emotions betrayed her. "Why here? Why set up your business at the inn?"

"Lost Lake got under my skin when I visited, so when I decided to leave my post with the Secret Service to come back to Oregon, I thought this was where I wanted to live. So did the others. I was already in escrow on the inn before I knew you were still here, much less the county sheriff. Your goal was always to experience big city policing, and I knew you'd moved to Portland."

She wouldn't ask him how he knew that, because she really didn't care. "I got my fill of city living and came back as a deputy. When the sheriff stepped down, I decided to run. Folks around here didn't much like that I'd left, so no one was more shocked than me when I won."

"They must've liked you better than your opponent."

"I guess so, though the deputy I ran against had been a deputy here longer than me."

"Is he or she still on the team?"

She nodded and left it at that. She didn't want to talk about the challenge of supervising Sergeant Abell, who'd vied with her for the sheriff's office. He often pushed her buttons simply to get a rise out of her, which she wouldn't fall prey to. "I've seen enough here. As much as I want to keep this investigation in-house, our county is too small for a full-time forensic staff. I'll need to call in the state team."

Nolan nodded, but his gaze flitted around the room.

"What are you not saying?" she asked.

He hesitated for a long moment. "Don't get me wrong. I'm sure the state team is quite capable."

Before she said something she would regret, she clamped her mouth closed, then took a breath. "But you've worked at the federal level, and you don't think the state staff possesses the necessary skills."

"I'm not saying that, but I was going to suggest we bring in the Veritas team from Portland."

She snorted. "No way we can afford a world-class team like theirs."

"I get that, but I have a buddy who owes me, and he has a connection to the team members. It's possible he could get them to process the scene pro bono."

Interesting but... "Say that's possible. They've got to be booked up. How long would it even take before they could work this scene?"

"If you'll authorize me to ask, I can find out the answer while also finding out if they'll do it pro bono." He leaned closer to her. "What do you have to lose by asking?"

"What? I'll tell you what. Number one, it keeps you involved in the investigation. Maybe they'll be obliged to give you results. That won't work. If I agree, and it's still a *big* if, I would insist on every bit of the forensic reports and updates coming directly to me. Not to you."

"No worries," he said as if it were no big deal when it was a huge deal to her. "They'll sign a contract with you stating who the results are to be delivered to. Trust me. They don't share information unless authorized to do so."

"Fine," she said, giving in to the lure of having a top-notch team at her disposal in this investigation. At the same time, she was certain she was making a mistake. "As you said, what do I have to lose by asking? So go ahead and ask." She feigned indifference, but her gut clamped down tight.

"Roger that." He wasted no time but stepped into the hallway.

She half expected him to gloat about her giving in to his wishes, but he didn't. He was simply straightforward and acting like he wanted to solve the murder. She could honestly use his help in the investigation. The help of his team too. Certainly one or more of them had participated in a murder investigation and had better skills than most of her deputies possessed.

Maybe even better than hers.

And Nolan had been on the president's team when there was an attempt on his life. She suspected he'd been involved in finding the shooter. She couldn't say that for certain, but he was on the detail the day of the shooting, and he wouldn't let something like that rest.

If she contrasted their skills to her deputies' skills, there was no question. The LLL team had more experience in large investigations. There hadn't been a murder in her county for twenty years, and the only murder-investigation skills her team possessed were what they'd learned at police academy. Same thing went for her too.

She was a newbie. A greenhorn. Had only been the sheriff for two years. But she'd been around long enough to know that when the news got out about the mayor, she was going to receive a parade of phone calls from the citizens demanding she find his murderer. He was beloved by all, and if she didn't solve his murder quickly, they would definitely call for her to resign or find a way to remove her from office.

So the question was, did she want to stay in office more than she wanted to avoid working with Nolan and his team? She loved her job and didn't want anything to take it away from her. She especially didn't want to be removed and disgraced for not handling a murder investigation as quickly as the citizens wanted her to.

But an even bigger question she needed answered before she could work with the team was, did they have airtight alibis for the time of the mayor's death or was one or more of them guilty of this murder?

Nolan dialed his friend Colin Graham. A former FBI agent, Colin was now a member of the Shadow Lake Survival team, a group who taught survival skills to people who wanted to change to off-grid living. His boss, Reid Maddox, knew the experts at the Veritas Center and could hopefully be Nolan's way in.

"Yo, Nolan," Colin said. "How's the new business going?"

"You know." Nolan tried not to let the murder color his tone. "The usual start-up issues, but otherwise it's good."

"Doesn't *sound* like things are good."

Nolan laughed. "You asked about the business, not if things are going good."

"Right. So what's up?"

"I need your help." He explained their situation.

"Whoa. That must've been a shocker."

"It was. Still is, really." He took a deep breath. "And that's why I called. I was hoping you would talk Reid into seeing if Veritas would get on board with doing the forensics. Not only handle them, but do it pro bono."

"You don't want much, do you?"

"I know it's a big ask."

"Not too big, man. We owe you and your team for helping out my brother when he needed it, so I'm glad to ask Reid. I'm sure he'll make the call, but I don't know if Veritas will go for it."

"All we can do at this point is ask, right?"

"Yeah, will do as soon as we hang up." Colin let a long breath of air through the phone. "Anything else I can do for you? Like maybe you need manpower?"

"We're good for now, but I'll let you know if something comes up. And thanks, man. I appreciate the help." Nolan ended the call and stowed his phone.

Mina exited the escape room, closed the door, and stopped by her deputy. "I don't want anyone else in here without my approval. You got that?"

Her deputy gave a sharp nod. "Roger that, boss."

She approached Nolan and looked up at him. "Any luck with that phone call?"

"I got a hold of my friend, and he'll get the ball rolling with Veritas. I'll let you know as soon as we hear anything from them."

"Sounds good." She started to walk away, then stopped. "I didn't ask you. Any ideas on who might want to kill Mayor Sutton?"

Nolan shook his head. "I didn't know him very well. We worked together on some of the issues regarding refurbishing the inn and applying for a tax break, but other than that, I didn't have any dealings with him. And we've all been far too busy getting the business up and going to socialize and catch any gossip about him."

She frowned. "Then why would someone want to try to connect this murder to you? And connected it is, considering the personal nature of the escape room. That's what I'm having the hardest time with."

"You're having a hard time! Think about our confusion when we don't have any connection. Maybe it's just someone who wanted to pin the murder on the new guys in town because no one knows much about us. Maybe making it easier to do."

She eyed him, fire burning in her gaze. "You mean because they don't think I have enough experience to handle investigating your backgrounds to find a connection?"

"Not you particularly, but yeah, something like that." He regretted upsetting her, but he had to tell the truth. "I know that's not true. I know that you're very skilled in law enforcement, and I have no doubt that you'll solve this murder with or without our help."

She studied him carefully, her gaze boring into him but suddenly softening. "I honestly don't believe anyone on your team is behind the murder. However, you know that whoever finds a body is an automatic suspect until proven otherwise. And in this situation, with everything in the murder scene related to you and your team, that further implicates you in this investigation."

"I understand, I do, and I think you're about to tell me that we can't work together on this investigation until our names are cleared."

"Yes." She planted her feet, a stubborn stance she'd always taken when she'd felt threatened. "I hope you understand this isn't anything personal."

"I do, and I hope you understand there's no way the team and I can leave this alone. We'll be investigating this murder one way or another. Either with you or alone."

She gritted her teeth. "I can't allow you to get in the way of my investigation."

"Then maybe you need to reconsider us working together. After all, if we did join forces, you would know everything we were involved in."

"Sure, during the time you're with me, but when we're apart, I would have no idea what you were up to."

"Then you'll just have to trust me."

"Hah!" She scoffed. "It's going to take far more than this conversation for me to trust you ever again."

He knew she was angry at him, but this obviously went deeper than that. She didn't trust him, and he had no idea if or how he could get past it.

"Well, then." He made eye contact with her. "The only other option is for you to spend all of your time with us."

She continued to meet his gaze but suddenly jerked it toward a gray-haired man walking down the hall. He was dressed in a white Tyvek suit and carrying a medical bag. Had to be the county medical examiner.

"Dr. Osborne." She held out her hand and smiled. "Thank you for coming so quickly."

"When you told me it was Mayor Sutton, I could do no less than get over here as fast as I could. My assistant is right behind me with our gurney." He shook hands, but he released hers before shoving it out to Nolan, giving him the once-over. "Lawrence Osborne. GP in Seaside Harbor and county medical examiner."

"Nolan Orr." Nolan shook the doctor's firm grasp.

"Nolan's the leader of the team who found Mayor Sutton's body," Mina said.

His eyes narrowed. "Must've been quite a shock to discover him in that locker."

"That's putting it mildly." Nolan released the man's grip. "So Osborne. Any relation to the former owners of the inn?"

"My family." He fished gloves out of his pocket. "Glad you bought the place. I hated to see it stand vacant so long and worried it would fall into disrepair."

"No disrespect," Nolan said, "but it was already in need of major repairs when I bought it."

"Yes, of course, and I'm glad to see you're restoring it to its former glory." Osborne smiled and put the gloves on.

"It's our pleasure. Once we've made more progress, I'll invite you over to see it."

"I'd like that very much. If it's not too much trouble, could my parents come along too? They'd be thrilled to see the restoration."

Nolan had only just met this guy and already liked him. In his experience, MEs and coroners could lack interpersonal skills, but he seemed compassionate and kind. Maybe because he was also a GP.

Nolan gave him a sincere smile. "It would be no trouble at all, and I'm glad to have them as our guests."

"I hate to interrupt this touching conversation, but we have a murder to solve." Mina gestured down the hallway. "I'll show you to the scene."

Dr. Osborne tsked. "You're always one to stick to the point. You never did grasp the idea of laid-back, small-town conversations. I was just enjoying a few moments of reminiscing before the ugly task at hand."

He spun and started down the hallway.

Mina faced Nolan. "You can return to the dining room, and please don't wander around on the way."

"I was hoping to accompany you and the doctor."

"No," she said, but her attention had drifted to a tall, lanky guy pushing a squeaky-wheeled gurney in their direction.

Nolan kept his focus on her, taking in details of her features that he'd forgotten. Details like her high cheekbones he'd traced the sun-soaked days they'd sprawled out on the beach.

Concentrate, man. You have a murder to solve. "I thought we were going to spend all of our time together."

"I never agreed to that, and if I do, it won't start until I can verify your alibi for the mayor's time of death. And I won't know the time of death until the ME does his job." She pivoted and hustled down the hallway, her booted footfalls reverberating against the plaster walls and ceiling.

He'd always liked her feistiness. She knew her own mind, knew what she wanted and how she was going to achieve it. So when he said he thought she would solve this investigation with or without him, he really believed that. But he wouldn't give up trying to help with the investigation.

He didn't want to spend time with her. Not with his residual pain from their breakup. Too bad. He needed to. If he didn't, he could very well find himself or one of his team members arrested and charged with murder.

5

Mina escorted Dr. Osborne into the escape room and stood back. "As you can see, they wedged Mayor Sutton into the locker on the end."

"How in the world did they fit him in there?" Osborne shook his head in bewilderment and set down his medical bag on the floor just inside the door.

"When you take a closer look, you'll see there's a cutout in the wall behind him, providing extra room."

Osborne crossed the room and pulled the locker door open further. "Oh, I see. Just like you said, there's space behind the locker." He studied the body from every angle possible.

"Can you determine any cause or time of death?" she asked, eager to move forward in her investigation, though she knew he would shoot her down.

"No." He turned, a frown on his face. "Just like with my conversation with Orr, you need to give this time. I'll have to extricate Ernie's body from the locker first, destroying as little evidence as possible, and then get him on the table for an autopsy."

The rattle of an off-balanced gurney sounded in the

hallway, signaling the arrival of his assistant, who Mina recognized from other body retrievals. Hands gripping the gurney, Kevin stopped at the doorway and peered at the doctor.

"Leave the gurney there," Dr. Osborne said. "We don't want to contaminate the scene. I'll need your help extracting the mayor."

Extract the mayor. Now that's a phrase Mina never expected to hear. She knew him as more than the mayor. He was the father of a woman who was four years behind Mina in high school. Becca Sutton still lived in town and was the mayor's next of kin. The person Mina would have to tell that her father had been murdered.

Mina's heart clenched. She'd made death calls before from car accidents, but she'd never had to tell someone a family member had been brutally murdered. That was a whole other type of notification. Both deaths were sudden and jarring to the survivors, but learning that someone had taken your loved one's life on purpose added a greater level of grief. One Mina couldn't imagine. Didn't want to imagine.

"Crazy that it's the mayor," Kevin said as he joined Dr. Osborne at the locker. "As far as I knew, he was a pretty all right dude. Not like the guy before him."

"You're right," Dr. Osborne said. "His reputation as a top-notch mayor was talked about all over the county. I almost regretted not living here in Lost Lake to see him in action."

"Yeah, but you could never run a practice in a town this small," Kevin said. "I know this dude will be missed."

When news got out of Mayor Sutton's death, conversations like this one would be had all across town. He really didn't have any enemies, as far as Mina knew, but he did have a lot of supporters. She could understand someone like Dr. Osborne thinking highly of him as he'd known the mayor for years, but when the lowly paid assistant who moved to town about a year ago sung the mayor's praises, she knew Sutton reached most every demographic in town.

"Gently now," Dr. Osborne said as he and Kevin eased the body out of the locker.

Kevin held the mayor's feet and Dr. Osborne his upper body as they crossed the room and laid him on the gurney. The mayor was a slender man and fit for his age. He was a runner and a golfer, which kept him active. Becca had held a big sixtieth birthday celebration for him last week.

She inched closer to the gurney and took in details. He wore dress slacks and shoes, along with a white, starched, long-sleeved shirt, the side that had been facing into the locker soaked with blood. A ring of shredded fabric sat directly above his heart.

"He was shot," she said.

"That looks like the case." Dr. Osborne unbuttoned Mayor Sutton's shirt. A circular wound appeared under the bloody area. "Yes, indeed. It looks like he was shot. Judging by the size of the hole, I would say it was a small caliber bullet. It wasn't at point-blank range but not a long-distance shot either."

"So he might've known his killer."

"Could be, or he was just taken by surprise by the shooter."

"Murder statistics say that odds are good that he knew the shooter, though."

"You're right." Dr. Osborne frowned. "A larger percent of people are killed by someone they know. Often someone they loved. Especially when the victim is female."

A very sad statistic, but it was true. It was rarer for someone to be killed by a complete stranger. It was a more common occurrence these days than it had been in the past, but the statistics still held. A greater percent of murders were committed during an argument or romantic triangle than any other circumstance, and by far, the majority of murders were committed by men wielding guns or strangulating their partner.

Using that theory, they were likely looking for a male who had known and argued with Mayor Sutton. Someone like Nolan Orr or his male teammates.

Dr. Osborne turned the body. "We have an exit wound, so you'll find the bullet that killed him somewhere at the scene."

"A through-and-through." She cruised around the room and examined it. "No extraneous blood, casings, bullet holes, or any other sign that he was shot here."

"Yes," Dr. Osborne said without glancing up. "The lack of blood in the room suggests he was killed elsewhere and placed in the locker. Or the killer cleaned up the blood."

"Then the forensic staff should be able to find traces of it." Suddenly hoping they *did* get the world-renowned Veritas forensic staff to process the room, she returned to the gurney. "Any idea on time of death?"

Dr. Osborne looked at his assistant. "Let's get the ambient temperature."

"On it." Kevin reached into the doctor's medical bag and lifted out a thermometer to measure the air temperature.

Osborne lifted the mayor's pant leg and pressed his finger into his purple skin. "Clear signs of lividity throughout body, but it's not fixed. Which tells me he's been dead for less than ten hours. Maybe less than six."

"Six to ten hours," she said. "Getting alibies for such a wide time frame could be tricky. Can you narrow that down further?"

"Maybe." Osborne lifted Mayor Sutton's right leg and then the left. He moved to his arms and followed suit. "No rigor mortis in larger muscles. It occurs in all the muscles in the body at the same time, but it can first be felt in the smaller muscles of the face, then the arms, and finally the legs."

She might not have worked a murder investigation before, but anybody who watched murder mysteries or movies on television or read much would know rigor mortis was the stiffening of muscles in the body that occurred after death.

He pressed his fingers on the mayor's face. "Rigor's present in the smaller muscles but not fixed. We're at least in the first five to seven hours since cessation of life."

Good. Now they had a two-hour window. "So we're talking this afternoon between two-thirty and four-thirty."

"Yes, and hopefully the temperature of his liver will help confirm that timeframe. If you're squeamish you might want to turn away." He grabbed his medical bag and removed a scalpel and what looked like a meat thermometer.

She wasn't squeamish, and even if she were, she wasn't about to look away at a very important moment in the investigation. After lifting the mayor's shirt, he sliced a small incision in the upper right abdomen and passed the thermometer into the liver.

"Ambient temperature is 72.4," Kevin called out.

The doctor kept his hand on the thermometer. "Get out your phone so you can determine the hours since death based on the liver temperature."

He tapped his foot for a while, then looked up. "We have a liver temp of 90.4."

Kevin thumbed his phone screen. "We're talking five and a half hours."

Mina looked at her watch. Nine-thirty p.m. minus the five and a half hours. "That would be four p.m."

"Yes," Dr. Osborne said. "But I won't state specifically that he died at four p.m. There are factors in my calculations that could change based on circumstances. And I won't declare an official time of death at this point, but I will suggest that it's between three and five p.m. today. That should give you a place to start. If I can be more specific after the autopsy, I'll let you know."

"Thank you," she said. "I should be able to obtain alibis in the interviews tonight for the people who found him."

She didn't mean to sound so eager, but apparently she was eager to prove Nolan had nothing to do with this murder. Why, she didn't know. Maybe it was simply because she knew him. The rest of the team too.

When she'd gotten to know his friends, she'd respected them and gotten along with them. They were a close-knit group. Been friends since college. By the time she'd met them, they were more like a tightly knit family. Despite that, they were also welcoming and inclusive. She appreciated that and had once looked forward to being part of their alternative family unit.

She resisted sighing. "I'll let you finish up here. Please let me know when the autopsy is scheduled."

She started down the hallway but stopped for a moment. She was in over her head. Not only in the investigation, but with Nolan and his team. She couldn't do it alone. Not at all. She lifted her head.

Please let all of these team members have a solid alibi for the time of death. The last thing I want to do is to charge one of them with murder. Especially not Nolan.

Nolan stood in the dining room, when all he wanted to do was pace up and down the hall as he waited for Mina to return. He'd taken a few strides, but the deputy in charge had given him a dirty look. No point in poking the bear. So he'd entered the dining room and leaned against the fireplace mantle. He tried to pay attention as his team talked about an upcoming town festival celebrating the founding of Lost Lake that they would participate in for community goodwill.

He didn't feel like small talk. Not at all. Especially not on the topic of goodwill. Many of the residents didn't like the fact that they'd converted the fifteen-room inn and light-house from a housing venue into their type of business.

How could they argue? The place had sat vacant for three years since the bank foreclosed on it, and no one wanted or had the money to buy it. Sure they were wishing it remained an inn in hopes that it would help the resort traffic, but it went out of business for a reason. And wasn't it better to have his team there, slowly restoring it to its former glory, than to have it sitting vacant and decaying into the ground?

Of course it was. But people in small towns like Lost Lake didn't always welcome progress. Nolan understood that. Kind of. He'd never lived it. He was born and raised in Portland and had always lived in cities.

His father was a top executive for Nike in Beaverton, and his mother a socialite who had more time for her groups and causes than for Nolan. He was basically raised by his nanny, who, God bless her, was a God-fearing Christian woman. His mother had allowed her to take him to church with her.

As far as he was concerned, he got the best end of the deal when his mother had little time for him. He got a chance to learn about Jesus and had faith in his life. Besides, he found family with his teammates. They each had reasons they weren't close to their birth parents, and they embraced everyone on the team, warts and all, as family.

Conversation down the hallway caught his attention. Mina was talking to someone, but he didn't know who and couldn't make out what she was saying. Probably talking to her deputy or the doctor.

He shook his head. Seeing her again had cut him in two —an almost visceral reaction. He knew he hadn't let their breakup go, but he had no clue he still had feelings for her. Or did he and he'd buried them?

Could be he was just upset that she was the one who got away. Or maybe he just wasn't sure he could believe her about not getting the note. There was nothing he could do about that. That was for sure.

Hurried footsteps coming their way echoed in the hall. He faced the door.

Mina whipped into the room as if on a mission, her expression tight. "I've set up a room down the hall to take individual statements. As usual, don't discuss the situation. I don't care who goes first. Any volunteers?"

"I'll go," Nolan said. "That is, if you still need a formal statement from me."

"I do. Follow me." She spun on her heel and marched down the hallway. She passed the crime scene where the medical examiner and his assistant were zipping the mayor's body into a black bag.

She stopped next to them. "Before you take him away, can we check for a cell phone?"

"Open the bag, Kevin," Dr. Osborne said.

The assistant sighed but pulled down the zipper, and they both patted the body down.

"Nothing here," the ME said. "If we find one when we get back to the morgue, I'll let you know."

"Let me dial his number to see if it rings." Mina got out her phone, tapped the screen, and lifted the device to her ear. She soon frowned. "Nothing. Thanks for taking the time to look."

Kevin pulled the zipper closed and then wheeled the body down the hall.

Nolan resisted shaking his head. He never imagined he would come to the sleepy town and become entangled in the first murder of his adult life. Much less be implicated in it because of the items in the escape room. Or have to deal with Mina Park in any capacity, not to mention her being the investigating officer.

She took off down the hall and stopped outside the door on the left. "In here. Have a seat." She didn't wait for him but stepped into the room.

The living area held a small round table and chairs at the far end. Bookshelves loaded with books and board games surrounded the room.

Mina had already taken a seat on the far side of the table and rested her hands on top.

He sat across from her and leaned back, acting relaxed when he was anything but at ease in her presence.

She took out a pen and notepad. "Start by recounting the events tonight again."

He took her through the evening, and she scribbled most of the time without looking up or asking clarifying questions. When he finished, he placed his hands on the table. "That's everything until you arrived."

"The same thing you told me earlier."

"Why would I deviate? It's what happened."

"Where were you today between three and five p.m.?" she asked, ignoring his question.

"The medical examiner gave you a window for time of death, I see."

"I didn't say that," she said, tapping her pen on her notepad. "Where were you?"

"That's simple. We had just finished an investigation,

and we were all in a debrief in our conference room at the inn."

She arched an eyebrow. "The whole team?"

"Well, no." His gut cramped. "All except Jude. He was on his way back from Portland but on the phone with us."

"That's convenient, isn't it?" That eyebrow rose even higher toward her hairline. "For all of you to alibi each other out for the time of death."

"I don't know if it's convenient, but it's what happened and where we were."

She laid her pen on the table. "Do you have any proof of your whereabouts other than vouching for each other?"

Did they? *Think, man.* Think like an investigator, not a former boyfriend. "We had food delivered. Not sure of the guy's name, but the food came from Submarine Burgers. You could contact them to confirm."

She wrote that in her notebook. "That doesn't help Jude."

"You could trace the whereabouts of his cell phone at that time."

"I could, but that would just mean Jude's cell phone was located in his car. Was he alone or did he have a passenger in his vehicle?"

"Alone," Nolan said, though he felt like he was ratting out a brother and fellow teammate. But he had to tell the truth, and they would have to find a way to prove Jude hadn't been near Mayor Sutton at that time.

He waited for her to comment on Jude's whereabouts, but she remained stone-faced, jotting notes in her book. She looked up. "Now that you've had some time to think about it, did you come up with anyone who would want to kill the mayor?"

"No." He left it at that. If they had been working together, he would suggest they speak to the mayor's assistant. Daisy Ellington knew everything about the mayor's work and daily schedule. But until Mina said she would let the team help, he would keep this lead to himself. And Daisy would be the first person he talked to.

His phone rang, and he glanced at caller ID. He looked up and made sure not to let his excitement over the name on his screen color his tone. "It's the Veritas Center. Want me to answer?"

"Absolutely." She leaned closer to him, not holding back her excitement.

He accepted the call. "Nolan Orr."

"This is Sierra Rice at the Veritas Center." Her businesslike tone didn't give away the reason for her call. "I'm the partner in charge of forensics for our center. Reid Maddox asked me to call you."

"Thank you for getting back to me so quickly. Sheriff Mina Park is here. She's in charge of the murder investigation. Do you mind if I put you on speaker?"

"That would be great," Sierra said. "You can bring me up-to-date on everything that's occurred tonight." Nolan placed his phone on the table and tapped the speaker button, then promptly told Sierra what had occurred. "Sheriff Park is currently conducting my initial interview and will be interviewing my teammates before the night is through."

"Is the scene secured and will remain so until we can arrive tomorrow?" Sierra asked.

"It's secure," Mina said. "And I can make sure it remains that way until further notice."

"Thank you for your cooperation, Sheriff Park," Sierra said.

"Please call me Mina," Mina smiled though this wasn't a video call. "Does this mean you're considering processing the forensics for us?"

"We're not considering it," Sierra said. "We've decided to do it, and before you ask, we have plenty of money left in our budget to handle the investigation pro bono."

"Thank you very much." Mina's tone was flooded with relief.

"Yes," Nolan said. "This is really good news."

"Our team will be departing Portland at eight a.m. At this point, I'll be arriving along with two of my assistants. Unless there are other needs beyond forensics."

"Our victim was shot, so we will need a firearms expert too." Mina tapped her finger on the table. "The ME confirmed the slug was a through-and-through, but the victim wasn't shot where we discovered him. We haven't looked for the murder scene yet, so we don't have anything to evaluate right now."

"Once you locate the actual scene where the victim was killed and the slug, we'll talk about that again." Sierra cleared her throat. "What other resources might you need?"

"I would foresee the need for a digital expert. Both to evaluate our victim's phone if we find it, and the computer at his office and home."

"That sounds to me like it could be handled at our facility if you can provide me with the devices. Nick may want to travel there to take the device and computers into inventory. He's a real stickler about making sure nothing is altered. If so, I'll let you know if you should expect him."

"It's wonderful to have such a professional team to work with." Mina sounded equally professional, and Nolan was oddly proud of her.

"It will take us at least a day to process your scene," Sierra said. "Then we'll have travel time. Means we'll need lodging for a minimum of one night. Is this something you can arrange and provide for us?"

"Yes," Mina answered right away. "I'll book you at the local hotel, and my department will pick up the cost."

"Excellent," Sierra said. "Nolan, I know you arranged for our services, but I'm assuming that all reporting will go to the county."

Nolan really didn't want that to happen. "Can't you report to both of us?"

Mina glared at him.

"Maybe," Sierra said. "If you want me to be able to access government databases, I'll need an official case number from you, Mina. Which means this investigation will be in your county's name. It will be up to you whether you allow Nolan access to those reports too."

Mina lifted her chin and pointed it at Nolan. "Let's just keep them directed to me at this time, and I can decide what I want to share with Nolan."

"Is that all right with you, Nolan?" Sierra asked.

No. Not at all. But did he have much choice? Not if they wanted Sierra to access fingerprint and DNA databases, and what good would either prints or DNA do them if they couldn't perform the searches? None.

"Yes," he answered reluctantly. He would have to find a way to persuade Mina to include him in the reporting and pray that she didn't withhold information from him. He sure didn't want to badger her. That would only serve to make their terrible relationship even worse.

6

Mina waited at the table as Nolan went to fetch the next teammate for interviewing. She couldn't help but think about him. Every spare moment. Her brain should be working on the murder, but it was full of Nolan instead. Now that he had an alibi, which she assumed would check out, she could involve him in the investigation. Question was, would it be more distracting to have him around all the time or be thinking about him?

If only she could prove Tommy had the note from Nolan and didn't give it to her, she might be able to put her past to rest and stop thinking about Nolan. But how would she do that? The bigger question was, why would Tommy have withheld the note from her?

Was there some reason he might not want her to get together with Nolan? Maybe he feared if she did, she would leave town and their friendship would be over. She knew he'd counted on her. He'd gone off to college and earned a degree in information technology, then landed a wonderful job in that field in Portland. But unfortunately, he started gambling online and got into serious debt. His parents had to bail him out to the tune of fifty grand.

Their conditions for providing the money were that he was no longer to use a computer, had to join a gambler's anonymous support group, and had to move back home with them to save money and pay off the debt. He took the first job he could get, assistant manager at the hotel. He hated every minute of it, but it gave him some spending money and money to start paying his parents back.

He'd gotten a bit depressed and often talked to her to find the light of day. Now that she thought about it, he'd become somewhat dependent on her. So maybe he *had* feared she was going to move to D.C. with Nolan, and he would have no one in town to help make his life better. But was that motive enough for him to ruin her life?

"I'm your next victim." Abby laughed as she stepped into the room and took a seat. "Seriously, I've been in your shoes, and I'm more than willing to cooperate in any way I can."

Mina appreciated her good mood and cooperation. "How about starting with telling me what happened tonight?"

"I'm sure you've heard the story from Nolan, but here goes." Abby leaned back in her chair and started from the time she arrived at the location.

Mina didn't disturb her with questions. No reason, when Abby was recounting the same thing as Nolan, though she did add a bit more of a nostalgic feel to speaking about her academy days.

"That's it." She let out a long breath. "This was my first escape room, and I never want to do one again."

"That's understandable." Mina set down her pen. "Can you tell me where you were between three and five p.m. today?"

"Ah, you have an approximate time of death, I see." Abby's eyes narrowed. "I was in a meeting with the rest of the team. We were debriefing from our most recent investigation. Everyone was there but Jude."

"And where was he?" Mina asked.

"On his way back from Portland, but he was on the phone with us the whole time. And before you ask, we had burgers delivered, so you can check with the Submarine delivery guy. He can confirm five of us were present."

"Did you know the mayor very well?"

"Not at all. I'd only met him once when he and his daughter came to our open house." She smiled. "He seemed like a real friendly guy. His daughter too. So friendly that she had a date with Jude before she left."

"That was fast," Mina said, but took a moment to link Jude to several parts of the crime. His locker held the body. He didn't have a solid alibi. He'd dated the mayor's daughter. Could be coincidence, but like most law enforcement officers, she didn't believe in coincidences.

"Yeah," Abby said. "I don't know anything about her, but Jude's a real charmer."

"Have they gone out yet?"

"Two times, in fact, but I don't get the sense from Jude that it's very serious. He's not really looking for a steady relationship."

"Did she seem upset by that?"

"Not that Jude has said."

"Is there anything else you can tell me about the mayor or about who might want to harm him?"

"That's all I know. I joined the team later than the others, so maybe they have more information about him than I do. Nolan has been here the longest, so if you haven't asked him —which I suspect you have—you should do so."

"Do you remember the Smythe fellow well enough to be able to provide a description for an artist?"

"Oh yeah. He treated me like a princess during dinner,

and I'm not about to forget any man who treats me that well." Abby laughed.

"I don't have any further questions. Is there anything I haven't touched on that you think I need to know?"

She sat up straight. "About the investigation, no. About Nolan, yes."

Mina took her time closing her notebook and laying her pen on top of it. "What exactly do you think I need to know about Nolan?"

"He told us that you never got the note he left you that spring break."

Mina didn't expect this to be personal, and she wanted to shut it down. "That's really between Nolan and me."

"I agree, but when Nolan won't stand up for himself, I'm going to do it for him."

"What do you mean stand up for himself?"

Abby crossed her arms. "We all know he left that note for you."

"How do you know? Were you there when he did it?"

"No, but he told us immediately after he did."

"He can tell you anything, but that doesn't mean he did it." Mina folded her hands on the table. "Besides, even if he left a note, that didn't have to be the end. He could've followed up."

"And that's what he didn't tell you. He did follow up. A week later he called the desk clerk to see if he gave you the note. He said he couldn't find you, but would keep trying. So a week later Nolan called the clerk, and he said he'd given you the note. Nolan asked how you reacted to it. The clerk said you just took it and left. So Nolan asked him to find you again to ask if you'd read it. He promised to do that."

Mina slumped back into her chair. "I had no idea."

"That wasn't all. After a week, he called the clerk back. The clerk told him you tore up the note and said you wanted nothing to do with him. But Nolan didn't stop at that either. He came back to town as soon as he could get leave from his job and located your parents. He went to their house. They said you no longer lived there, and he'd hurt you badly. They wouldn't tell him where you went."

"I'd moved to Portland to get some experience in city policing, but they never mentioned that to me." And the first moment she got, she was going to ask them about it.

"He did everything he could to tell you where he'd gone and why he had to leave so abruptly."

"Why didn't he tell me any of that?"

Abby shrugged. "Only he knows that. But maybe he wondered what the point was. Too many years have passed. Or maybe he thought he looked too desperate, and if you'd wanted to be with him, you would've found a way to tell him."

Mina didn't know what to think now. She'd like to race to her parents' house and question them, but how could she? Her top priority had to be finding Mayor Sutton's killer, and she could talk to her parents in her downtime.

But then, was there any downtime when hunting for a killer? She'd never had to find one before, but she was certain her every waking moment needed to be spent on bringing the killer to justice.

Nolan had no idea why he was being summoned along with Jude to speak to Mina again. Sure Jude still had to give his statement, but Nolan didn't need to be there. Maybe something the others said made her want to clarify his statement.

He entered the room behind Jude. She had her back to them, facing the window. Perfect. She wasn't looking, and he took a moment to study the curves of her body evident even in the nondescript county uniform.

She rested her hand on her sidearm, and the manicured nails painted a delicate lilac were a contrast to the weapon. To her rough and tumble personality too. Reece was the only other woman he'd seen so at home in both the tough law enforcement environment and as a feminine single woman. He hadn't just seen it in Mina, but he loved it. He'd always been a sucker for a woman with a gun.

She turned and ran her gaze over them. "Have a seat, Jude."

"You want me to sit too?"

"That's up to you." She stepped to the table. "I thought since Jude's the only one without an alibi, he might want you with him for the interview."

Jude's eyes flashed up. "Am I a suspect?"

"Yes, until I can rule you out."

"Come on, now." He narrowed his eyes. "I've only met the guy once at our grand opening. Why would I want to kill him?"

"Maybe he didn't like you dating Becca."

"Seriously?" Jude blinked at her. "We only went out twice. I don't think he even knew about me."

"Were you planning on a third date?"

He shook his head.

Mina's eyebrow rose. "Why not?"

"No spark." He held up a hand. "Before you think she was upset by that, it was a two-way street. A mutual decision."

"So if I ask her about it, she'll tell me the same thing?"

"Absolutely."

Nolan took a step. "Do you want me to hang out here, Jude?"

He crossed his arms. "Probably wouldn't be a bad idea

since it seems like Mina has forgotten everything she knows about me."

Mina lifted her shoulders. "That's not fair and you know it. If you were still an FBI agent and handling this investigation, you would be doing the same thing. Even if you knew and respected the primary suspect."

Nolan leaned against the wall. "She does have a point. I think we'd all be doing the same thing and should give her a break. And be honest with her, as I know you will. The more you tell her, the sooner she can rule you out."

Jude eyed Mina. "What else do you want to know?"

"You were on the way back from Portland when the mayor was killed, is that right?"

"Correct."

"What were you doing in Portland?"

"Not that it's related to the investigation in any way, but I had just come from the Multnomah County Courthouse where I was looking up records for our investigation."

"He's being modest," Nolan said. "He had a lead on a property that we couldn't get detailed owner information about online, and he got the clerk to give him the owner's name, which led us to find our missing girl in time."

"The Jennings girl from Seaside Harbor."

"Yeah," Jude said. "That's her."

"Congratulations on finding her."

"We were glad to bring her home." Nolan smiled as he recalled the moment she'd reunited with her parents.

She smiled back at him. "Always a good day when a missing person case turns out that well."

He loved feeling the warmth of her genuine smile again. "Which is why we do what we do, even if we sometimes step on law enforcement's toes in the process."

Her smile vanished. She probably realized a day could come when she would butt heads with him over such an investigation. She shifted her focus back to Jude. "Did you stop along the way where anyone could've seen you?"

"No."

"Make any video phone calls?"

He arched a dark eyebrow. "Why video in particular?"

As a former FBI agent, he knew the answer to her question, and for some reason, was playing dumb with her. Why, Nolan didn't know. Maybe testing her skills.

She didn't miss a beat. "You know we can trace any calls you made on the drive, triangulating your location. A video call proves that you were with the phone when the call was made. Otherwise, if you texted or made a regular call, it only proves that your phone was in that location."

"No video calls." Jude's expression was deadpan. "In fact, no calls at all after I left Portland other than with the team while I ate a granola bar or ten and drooled over their burgers."

Jude had probably hoped for a laugh with the burger comment, but she didn't crack a smile. His rejection by his parents when he'd gone into law enforcement had done a number on him, and he'd taken to using humor to cover up his emotions.

"Do you know who invited you to this party tonight?" Mina asked.

"No." He flexed his fingers but kept a blank expression. "Just like the rest of the team, I was surprised by the invitation."

"How about the property? Know who owns it?"

"No."

"What about Smythe? Do you know his full name or anything else about him?"

"No. Tonight was the first time I've ever seen him."

"Why do you think the locker you opened was the one that contained the mayor's body?"

Jude sat up straighter. "I have no idea."

"One of your trophies is present in the room too. Do you have any idea why that might be?"

"Not my trophy." He stared at her, looking like her endless questions might be getting to him. "Just one made to look like I got it. Unless it's a plot to make me look guilty of something."

"You mean you're being set up?"

"I can't think of any other reason for the mayor to be in the locker assigned to me or for a trophy with my name on it." He clamped his hands on his knees. "Although I have to say there were trophies from other of our teammates too. Not that I'm throwing them under the bus because I know none of them are guilty."

She took a long breath, pausing as if regrouping. "Do you know why anyone would have motive to kill the mayor?"

"Like I said, I didn't know the mayor, so I wouldn't have a clue as to why someone would want to kill him. His daughter spoke highly of him, and it was clear that she respected him."

"If there's anything else you would like me to know about your involvement in this murder, now would be the time to tell me."

"I have nothing else to say." Jude stood. "I didn't kill the mayor, I had nothing to do with this night at this place, and I'm innocent of all charges."

He strode toward the door without waiting to be dismissed.

"You can go," Mina called after him. "But don't leave the area without letting me know."

Jude snarled and exited the room.

Nolan pushed off the wall. "You honestly don't think Jude killed the mayor, do you?"

"Put on your law enforcement hat, Nolan. You would see that he has to remain a suspect until proven otherwise. So whether I believe in what he has done or not done is irrelevant."

He didn't like that answer. Not at all. "You know we're going to do our very best to prove his innocence. To prove the innocence of our entire team."

She locked gazes with him. "I can't have you go off half-cocked and interfere with my investigation."

Nolan wouldn't be told what to do when it came to defending his family. Sure, many people thought the team members were just friends, but they were more than that. More than most families. Connected. Caring. Protective. A strong unit. One that couldn't be destroyed. No matter their circumstances.

He pulled his shoulders back. "Unless we break the law, I can't really see how you can stop us."

She looked down and ran a hand through her hair. He recognized her expression. She was thinking, and he imagined thoughts pinging through her brain. She suddenly looked up. "I have a proposition for you. Something that will benefit both of us."

"I'm listening."

"You served as a deputy before the Secret Service and are familiar with the proper investigative procedure. I can deputize you, and you can work directly with me."

He almost sputtered and had to work hard to keep his mouth from falling open. "I can see how that would benefit you. After all, you can keep tabs on me and boss me around, but I sure don't see how it would benefit me or my team."

"Of course it will. You'll have access to all of the information and reports about the investigation. Official law enforcement officers will have your back, and you'll have the right to make arrests."

She was right. That *was* appealing, but appealing enough to give up his independence and work for her? Work for the woman who he'd never wanted to see again? Despite the fact he still had feelings for her, was this the way to move forward in the investigation?

He just didn't know.

He needed to clear Jude's name and, because of their association with him, the team's reputation so people would continue to hire them. Just having any whiff of impropriety connected to the team could be the end of the business they'd just started—sunk all of their money into. Being officially connected to the investigation gave Nolan a stamp of approval, and they could likely clear their names faster.

But he wouldn't just roll over and let her use him. He held out his hand. "As long as you promise not to stonewall me or keep me out of pertinent details of the investigation, you've got a deal."

She grabbed his hand. "I promise. And you promise too. No going behind my back with your team. Before you do anything, you'll discuss it with me."

"Then we have a deal," he said and hoped he wasn't making the biggest mistake of his life.

7

In the hallway outside the escape room, Mina watched Harmony's expression as she and Nolan questioned her about the rental. She said she'd worn noise-cancelling headphones to watch television in the second-floor sitting room and had been oblivious to the events on the first floor. It was only when she saw the patrol car lights strobing in the window that she came out to investigate. Or so she said.

"And you're sure you didn't leave that room?" Nolan asked.

"Why would I?" Harmony's surly tone grated on Mina. "My contract with Palmer says I have to be present when the building is leased, but it doesn't say I have to babysit the occupants."

Harmony was known to have an attitude. Which is why Mina had been surprised when she learned Cody Palmer had hired her to manage the leasing business. She could certainly do the cleaning and organizing, but when it came to being pleasant to customers, that wasn't the woman's forte. Hopefully for Palmer's sake, she was pleasant with customers, and if she copped an attitude, she didn't do so until after the contracts were signed.

"What can you tell us about the person who leased the space tonight?" Mina asked.

"First of all, it wasn't just leased for tonight. The contract was for a full five days starting on Thursday."

Nolan tilted his head. "So you had to be here for the entire five days?"

"That's the weird thing about it all," Harmony said. "The only time they came to the building was this afternoon to set up the dining room and then the event tonight."

"Let me clarify. The escape room would've taken time to prepare. They didn't arrive earlier in the week to set it up?"

Harmony's eyes creased. "I don't know what you're talking about."

Mina pushed open the door. "Have a look."

"That's a new lock. I don't know how it got there." Harmony poked her head into the room and spun around. "Man, oh, man. I wasn't here when they did all of this. Palmer is going to kill me if I can't get this room back to normal."

"If you weren't here, how did they get in?" Mina asked.

Harmony tapped a finger against her narrow chin. "I dunno. Must've broken in or something."

"I checked the door locks when we were looking for Smythe," Nolan said. "No sign of a forced entry."

She crossed her arms. "Like I said. I didn't let them in except today. So I don't know how they got in here. Maybe through a window. Did you check all of those too?"

He shook his head. "But that can be easily remedied. How about the building keys? Was there any time that your master key was left unprotected, and they might've had a copy made of it?"

"No, I keep them on this ring on my belt." Harmony patted a keyring clipped to the belt at her ample waist. "And you're not going to try to pin this on me. I didn't do it."

Mina didn't doubt her answer, but she could just be a good liar. "So where were you between three and five p.m. today?"

"Here, like I said." She fired an irritated glare at Mina.

"Is there anyone who can corroborate that?" Nolan asked.

Harmony tightened her arms. "If by using a big fancy word like *corroborate* to mean vouch for me being here, then yeah, this Smythe fellow. He brought me up a snack around three o'clock, just as I was falling asleep watching the Road Runner. That show really cracks me up."

For some reason, this woman wasn't getting the gravity of the situation, and Mina needed to make sure she got the point. She propped her hands on her hips. "You better get serious about this. You could be in trouble. We don't know how to find Smythe right now, which means you don't have an alibi for the time of the mayor's death."

"Don't need no stinking alibi." Harmony glared at her. "I didn't do it, and that's all you need to know."

She resisted sighing. "That's not how it works, Harmony. If you watch enough television, like it sounds like you do, you've probably watched crime shows. You should know better."

"I don't watch them kind of serious things." She scoffed. "I'm a comedy person myself."

Maybe in your television viewing, but the humor doesn't extend to your personality, Mina wanted to say but kept it to herself. "Are there security cameras on the property that could confirm your arrival and departure?"

"Nope. I wanted to install some for my safety, but Palmer wouldn't allow them. Said he had guests who didn't want to be seen, and he didn't want to infringe on their privacy." She sniffed as if the air were suddenly foul. "Maybe this will show him, and he'll decide to put some in."

This Palmer guy didn't seem like he cared much about Harmony's safety, otherwise he would've installed security cameras despite the cost of providing a private retreat. "Before I let you go, tell me about the person who leased the building."

"Never met the guy. He made the reservation online. I can look up the information for you, but when he made the reservation his notes said a man named Smythe would meet me here and be in charge of the evening."

Nolan described Smythe. "Is this the man you're calling Smythe?"

"Yeah. Yeah. Sounds like him. I let him in and watched for a few minutes while he brought supplies into the dining room, then I went upstairs. My only other contact with him was the snack and dinner. I liked the guy. He's the first person who's ever brought me food. Didn't much care for the meal, though. Too fancy for me. Especially that kale salad. That stuff belongs in a recycle bin, not on a table."

After hearing what was served, Mina could see how Harmony might dislike it. But most importantly she could describe the food, lending credence to her statement. "Okay, then, we're done here. I need you to go directly to your computer and print out the rental agreement for the property and any contact information you have. Include Cody Palmer's address and phone number too. Drop it off at my office tonight."

"Okay." She lowered her arms like she was lowering her defenses.

Mina eyed her. "You're to talk to no one about this. Are my instructions clear?"

"Crystal," Harmony said and stomped down the hallway. "So much for sleeping."

Mina tracked her departure.

Nolan kept his focus on her too. "Nice woman. Unless

she just behaves this way when questioned by law enforcement."

"She's known for her attitude." Mina shifted to look at him. "Which doesn't make her a good match for this job. She must really have snowed Cody Palmer in the interview."

Nolan turned. "Do you think she's telling the truth?"

"I do. She might be a character and often times an unpleasant person, but she's more known for being straightforward than lying. Besides, I can't see a motive for her to want the mayor dead."

"You'll still keep her on a suspect list, though, right?" Nolan asked.

"Absolutely, and I'll have my team check her out to see if there's a connection to the mayor that I'm missing." Mina stowed her notebook and pen in a cargo pocket. "I need to get to Becca's house before Harmony blabs."

"You think she'll tell someone even though you told her not to."

"I know she will."

"Before we go, I'd like to check the building to see if I can find a place of entry," Nolan said.

She appreciated him telling her of his plans instead of just demanding to do it. "You should have time to do that while I give my deputies instructions. Don't get sidetracked because we still need you to do the description of Smythe with my digital artist. Meet me at the door."

As he walked away, Mina tugged the escape room door closed, then did just as she'd told Nolan she would do. She gave all three of her deputies instructions, ending with the guy outside, finishing before Nolan arrived. She texted her sergeant to let him know that these deputies would be assigned at this location for the foreseeable future, which took almost half the force away. He would have to figure out a schedule without them. They would have to pay overtime to handle this incident, but protecting the scene was top priority right now in finding the murderer.

Nolan stepped outside, and they hurried to her patrol car. She got them on the road. Neither spoke. She actually preferred that so she could think about what had occurred.

If someone had told her she would be on her way to notify the mayor's daughter that he'd been killed and that Nolan Orr would be sitting in the passenger seat next to her, she would've laughed. But here she was, the bearer of horrendous news, driving at midnight down the quaint streets of Lost Lake, heading for Becca's secluded house near the harbor. She could only hope Becca was still awake and she wouldn't have to pull her from sleep to deliver the news.

"Have you done this before?" Nolan asked. "I mean a death notification call."

"For traffic fatalities, yes. Not for a murder. This is my first murder investigation as a sheriff."

He glanced at her. "But you were involved in murder investigations when you served in Portland, right?"

"Right, but not as a detective, just as a patrol officer arriving first on the scene and taking statements, then running down a few leads for the detectives."

"It's not the same," he said, his tone somber. "The notification. At least that's what I've heard. I've never handled traffic fatalities like you, but when I was on the governor's detail before I moved up to D.C., I did have to notify a good friend's family that their son had been killed protecting him."

"Oh, I remember that assassination. That was your friend, huh? The guy who threw himself in front of the governor to save his life?"

"It was. Great guy. We served together on the governor's detail for a few years and had a lot in common."

She could only imagine how hard a notification like that might be. "Why did you have to make the call instead of the lead detective?"

"I didn't have to. I asked to." Nolan drew in a deep breath. "For some reason, I thought it might be better if they heard it from me. From someone who was there when he died. A friend who held his hand and told him things were going to be okay when they'd gone horribly wrong. To be able to tell them how brave he was. What an amazing person and true patriot he was. The detective didn't know him. He couldn't share those things."

"Do you think it helped?"

He shrugged. "I think so, or at least I hope so. When someone is suddenly taken from you, like in a car fatality, that's one thing, but to have someone actually be a victim of violence? To be gunned down? That's a whole other thing, and I'm not sure anything can make it easier."

"Yeah, I could see that," she said, thinking ahead to her upcoming task. "Becca's mom died a few years ago. She's bound to take this hard."

He sat silently for a moment. "You sure you don't want me to come in with you? You know. For moral support."

"I appreciate the offer," she said, and despite their differences she did think having him at her side would help. "But I think it might be harder on her with a stranger in the room."

"Makes sense." He looked out the window again. "Do you know if she has any close friends we can call to be with her?"

"I don't know her that well, but I'll ask when I see her." She didn't want to talk about this anymore as the closer they came to the house, the more nervous she got about sharing such difficult news with someone she knew. "Thank you again for getting the Veritas team on board with this investigation. I'm sure it will make a big difference."

"You're welcome," he said, and if she was right, she detected a note of thankfulness at the change of topic. "As an official deputy now, I assume I'll have access to those reports when you get them."

"I want to review them first, but then…" She stopped as she really hadn't had time to think this through.

"Then what?" he asked. "I got into this whole deputy thing because I expected you would share every report."

"I will," she said and hoped she didn't have to withhold anything. "I just want to process the news first."

She turned the corner onto Becca's street and pulled onto the narrow lane that led to her secluded property, not as brightly lit as the main road. Trees on the property ahead cast ominous-feeling shadows.

Nolan glanced at her. "I'd love to see this in the daylight. I'll bet it's beautiful back here. I'm surprised someone as young as Becca could afford this place."

"The property has been in the family since this town was founded. She inherited it from her maternal grandparents."

"Looks impressive from what I can see."

"It really is something. Despite all the trees lining the driveway, the entire back wall of the house is filled with windows overlooking the cove."

As Nolan leaned forward to look ahead, she pulled into the circular driveway and up to the house. The outside lights burned brightly as if Becca was expecting visitors or someone was already visiting. But there were no cars in the drive ahead or on the road. Lights shone out from the first floor, even at this time of night.

Mina couldn't be more thankful. It was looking like she wasn't going to have to wake Becca up. She might not even be there. "No car in the driveway."

"It's likely in the garage," Nolan said.

Mina shifted into park and looked at him. "Wait here. I might be gone awhile, but please don't come looking for me."

"Are you planning to question her about her father's death?"

"Maybe," she said, though she hadn't thought that far ahead yet. "It'll depend on the situation and how Becca responds."

She got out of the vehicle and headed toward the garage. The scent of pine filled the crisp night air, and an owl hooted from nearby. She looked through the garage windows.

No car. Not home? She turned to face Nolan and shook her head to let him know Becca hadn't parked in the garage. Could be she wasn't home and this trip was for no reason.

She started for the solid oak door. It stood open about three inches.

Her steps faltered and goosebumps prickled across her back.

Moving slowly forward, she rested her hand on her firearm and resisted pushing the door open farther. "Becca! It's Sheriff Park! Are you here?"

Mina waited for a response. Counted in her head.

One one thousand. Two one thousand. Three one thousand. Four one thousand. Five one thousand.

No response. Deadly silence surrounded her.

She nudged the door open with her elbow. She didn't want to touch anything in case something terrible had happened here. The door groaned inward, revealing a small entry area that led directly into a large open-concept family room.

She took a few steps, her gaze sweeping over the space, traveling across the floor and landing near the stairway.

She halted. Stopped. Abruptly.

A large pool of blood glistened from the tile. The scarlet red color stark against white marble tiles. The metallic smell scenting the air.

She swallowed hard. Gulped in a breath.

Was she looking at the mayor's murder scene? And if she was, where was Becca? Or was this Becca's blood, and she was dead too?

8

Nolan didn't like being left behind. Sitting in the car like a flunky instead of the partner Mina claimed him to be. But he understood her reasoning for talking to Becca alone. They had to do whatever was best for Becca right now. She was the only person who mattered at the moment. But he sure didn't want to miss out on any questioning Mina might conduct. He had to hope she would share all the information she learned.

Movement on the drive caught his attention. Mina raced toward him. The tight set to her face raised his angst.

No. No. Something had happened.

Something bad.

He was out of the vehicle before she could reach his door. "What's wrong?"

"There's a large pool of blood in her entryway."

"And Becca. Is she—"

Mina gave a tight shake of her head. "No sign of her, and she's not responding when I call out."

"Did you go in?" he asked, though it would be foolhardy to do so without backup if whoever caused the blood pool was still in the house.

"A few steps inside." She shook her head in wide side-to-side movements. "I saw the blood and stopped. Called my sergeant for backup."

Okay, so maybe they weren't partners after all. Or she didn't trust him. "I'm capable of backing you up."

"I know. I assume you're carrying."

He pulled back his tuxedo jacket, revealing his holster. He drew his sidearm. "Let's go."

She held up a hand. "We wait for backup. For someone to mitigate the threat at the door while we go inside."

She was following sound procedure, but... "Becca could be injured. Needing our help."

"What good will we be to her if we're dead?" Mina gave him a pointed look. "My sergeant is on a call only a few minutes out. We wait."

"Fine." He tried not to sound surly as he knew she was right. "Did you try calling her?"

"I don't have her number." She went around to the driver's side of her vehicle and lifted the radio through the open door. "I need a phone number for Becca Sutton. Preferably cell."

She got out her phone, but tapped the rooftop with her finger until dispatch broke through the silence and offered Becca's information. Mina quickly entered the number in her cell. Nolan could hear it ringing from across the vehicle. In the distance, sirens blared in the night, and he prepared himself for going into the house.

"No answer." Mina stowed her phone and nodded at the swirling lights flashing ahead. "It's go time."

A burst of adrenaline pushed him down the street to meet her sergeant. Mina joined him and handed him a flashlight, which he would definitely use in their exterior search.

The sergeant climbed from his patrol car beneath a

streetlight, and the six-foot-tall beefy man with buzzed blond hair planted his booted feet. "Sheriff."

"Sergeant Abell meet Nolan Orr," Mina said. "He's former law enforcement, and I've deputized him to help in this investigation."

Surprise flashed in the sergeant's eyes, but it quickly washed away. "Everybody calls me Abe."

Mina pointed a finger at the house. "Nolan and I'll secure the inside in case Becca is here and injured. I'll take lead in the house. Abe, you have the door unless I call out."

"Roger that," Abe said, not questioning being left behind and having a temporary deputy get in on the potential action.

Maybe he'd been a sergeant long enough to know that protecting the exit was a vital job and one that took skill to handle should an assailant try to flee. More likely he was a good sergeant and swallowing down any frustration he might have.

Mina, not waiting for compliance, set off with clipped but urgent footsteps, her weapon drawn and held in front of her. Nolan rushed after her, taking in every inch of the luxurious property including the glow of outside lights falling softly on the sidewalk, hinting at a peaceful scene, not a place where a murder had likely occurred. The lights illuminated the foundation shrubs, too, the view calm and also belying the danger inside.

Mina slowed on her approach to the front door. The solid wood that looked original to the older home stood open, and she stepped over the threshold, then paused.

Looking over her shoulder and around her, Nolan caught sight of the viscous pool of blood she'd mentioned. Memories flooded his brain. His gut cramped. He'd only seen this quantity of blood once. His buddy. Lying on the ground. His lifeblood oozing around him until he lost his life in protection of their governor.

No, stop. Don't let your mind go there. He was charged with having Mina's back, and she needed him clearheaded.

They approached the bloody pool. No one could survive this level of loss. At least, not likely. He wasn't an expert, but he suspected he was right. "We'll have to get Veritas to run a sample. See whose blood this is."

Please don't let another person have died.

"Stick right on my tail," Mina said, keeping her focus pinned ahead. "I'm counting on you to have my back."

She shouldn't have had to say that to him. Was it because she thought he'd deserted her once, and she feared he would do it again? No way he would abandon her here unless he was dead. No law enforcement officer worth their grain of salt would leave another officer vulnerable.

Nolan followed her under a wide arch into a formal living room. The nearest window was marred with telltale bullet holes and fissions in the glass extending outward. She stopped to take a look, and he moved closer to her.

"Looks like a bullet bullseye," he said. "Since the mayor was shot this could mean the entryway blood is his."

"Could be," she said, getting closer and eyeing the glass. "The bullet had to come from the outside."

He moved into place beside her for a better look. "The holes confirm that. A double pane window. Outside hole is smaller than the inside, so it would be the point of entry for the bullet." He looked around for blood, but found none. He turned and put himself in the line of sight that a bullet could have traveled. *Could have*, as the glass would alter a shot somewhat. But the pool of blood in the hallway was in direct range.

"We move on," Mina said and advanced further into the space.

He followed, his mind swirling with questions. The biggest still was, had the mayor or Becca been shot from this window? Seemed highly likely to him that one of them had been, but they would need a professional to trace the trajectory of the bullet. He would have to call Sierra back and ask her to process this scene too and have their weapons expert join them on scene.

He trailed Mina through the open doorway into a large dining room with a table and chairs for twelve people. The dark walnut gleamed as if it had recently been polished. He passed through the next doorway and reached the kitchen where Mina stood.

She turned to look at him. "Notice anything else?"

He shook his head. "I'll ask for the Veritas team to come here too. Now that we have a likely murder scene, we should request they also perform a bullet trajectory. That will confirm that a bullet fired from this window could've struck the mayor or Becca."

"We finish clearing the place before making that call." She turned toward the opening in the wall. "Back to the entry for the main stairwell."

He didn't question but trailed her down the hallway, skirting the sticky pool of blood, to the front stairs. A slight trail of blood about a foot long appeared where a body could've been picked up out of the blood pool and then removed via the front door. Or they'd cleaned up other residual trails.

Made no sense, though. Why bother to clean up any of the blood, then leave a massive pool in the entry? He took a closer look. A footprint in the blood. If the killer cleaned up, they surely wouldn't leave the footprint for forensics to evaluate.

"Coming?" Mina asked from the stairs.

He hurried ahead to a striped carpet runner covering

original treads. He searched it for any bloody footprints but found none. They climbed the stairs and silently checked out two massive bedrooms with ensuite bathrooms.

"All clear," he said, though she'd been with him on the search.

"No sign of a disturbance or struggle at all," she said, already turning toward the stairway again. "Time for a perimeter search, and then we can really look at this place without fear of a shooter remaining on the property."

They jogged down the stairs and out the front door.

"All clear out here," Abe said.

She nodded. "We'll head to the right. I'd like to get a look at that window from the outside. See if any tracks or other evidence were left behind."

She started down a concrete walkway highlighted by ground floodlights and leading to the side of the house. She moved slowly, her gaze roving over the area like a searchlight.

Nolan eased behind her, looking into the lushly land-scaped beds surrounding the home. Some of the rhododendrons and azaleas that grew so well in Oregon reached halfway up the wall, and they had to step out further to get around their girth.

She stopped near the broken window. "Looks like we have some fresh prints in the sand here."

Nolan took as close of a look at the window as he could from his distance. "The glass is still fairly intact. Had to be a small caliber."

"Likely a handgun," Mina said. "The most common would be a 9mm."

"The Veritas expert will be able to tell us for sure."

Mina moved ahead. He followed again. At the gate and fence securing the backyard, she used her sleeve to undo the latch. Large hanging lanterns fully lit a backyard that opened into a wide expanse overlooking the cove from up high. A glass-and-metal fence illuminated by more accent lights secured the rear of the property but didn't obstruct the view. A wide stone patio held casual furniture, and a large deck contained a massive teak dining table and chairs.

Nolan fought back a shiver. If Becca was living, they would change her whole world by telling her of her murdered father. No longer would she come back to this amazing backyard the same person she was before her father died. Everything was going to change for her, and he hated that. He hadn't lost family members, but after losing his buddy, he knew the agony of loss. That was bad enough, he couldn't imagine losing a father. He wasn't close to his father, but by all accounts, her dad meant a lot to her.

Mina ran her weaponed hand and flashlight over the shadowed perimeter and lowered them. "I'm glad there's no immediate threat, but it would've been nice if we'd found the shooter tonight."

"That would be too easy."

She glanced over her shoulder. "Additional backup should be here any minute, and they can secure the scene for evidence collection. Then we need to get over to the mayor's house to see if Becca's there or if we have a second crime scene."

He nodded. "I'll call Veritas on the drive, but mind if I take a closer look inside while we wait?"

"I'll grab some booties and gloves from my car." She bolted back toward the sidewalk, and he followed. He took a moment at the window to look in. Why, he didn't know because they both had come to an agreement of what had happened, and now it would be up to an expert to determine the caliber of the weapon and the trajectory of the bullet.

She'd returned to the front door with her supplies and was talking to Abe. "Let me know when backup arrives."

She held booties and gloves out to Nolan and put on a set of her own. A siren sounded at the main road as they entered the building together.

He moved to the doorway where the bullet would have come from and looked straight ahead. "Dr. Osborne said the bullet exited the mayor's body. If in fact the bullet fired through that window hit the mayor, we should find the slug in the wall over there." He pointed across the room, but Mina was already moving in that direction.

She stopped to examine the drywall. "Looks like we have an embedded slug. Small caliber. I still think a handgun is likely."

Nolan joined her, his booties whispering over the tile floor as he walked. "It's times like this that I wish Oregon had a gun registration law, and we had a database we could search for handgun owners in the area."

"I agree, but it might not matter. The gun could've been stolen."

"True," he said and stared at the hole in the wall. "Maybe our shooter has a concealed carry permit. Everyone on the team had to get new permits through your office when we moved here. Have you issued any others lately?"

She shook her head.

"You're sure? I mean you weren't involved in issuing our permits, so maybe someone got one without you knowing about it."

"Not possible." She rested a hand on her sidearm. "I review every application before the permit is issued. Besides, no telling if the shooter even had a concealed permit. Most gun owners don't. And who knows if he even resides in our county."

He leaned closer to the wall. "Looks like our shooter has skills and one shot was all it took."

She frowned. "Looks like he has skills in body removal too, because unless our shooter was strong, there should be some sort of trail from moving the body. Be it Becca or the mayor."

"There is that one little comma on the circle of blood, which could suggest the body was dragged in that direction." Nolan crossed the room and squatted. "There's a faint dirt line that looks like it outlines a large rug. Our victim could've fallen half on the rug and half on the floor, and the shooter only had to slide the body down the rug, roll it up, and take him or her away."

She joined him and squatted too. "Looks like you could be right. If so, the shooter's clothing would've been soaked with blood as he held the victim to move him. We find the bloody clothing, we find the killer."

"Same might be true of the footprint outside. We find the shoe…"

A car door slammed outside. Mina stood. "That'll be my deputy. Let me give him instructions, and we can be on our way to the mayor's house."

Nolan nodded and stood. His night had started with an invitation promising a killer of an evening. The discovery of the mayor's body had fulfilled the invitation's promise. But had the invitation underplayed the evening? Did this pool of blood belong to Becca, and they were going to find another crime scene at the mayor's house? Had two people lost their lives that evening?

9

Two streetlights at the road cast weak beams down on Mayor Sutton's house as Mina approached. Lights didn't shine from his windows nor was the outside one on to welcome them. The place was in direct contrast to his daughter's home, casting a dark and gloomy feel.

"Doesn't look like anyone is here," Nolan said.

Meaning Becca wasn't here either. She could be dead too.

He released the latch on his seatbelt. "You don't think Becca killed her father, do you?"

"What?" She gaped at him. "No. Not at all. She loved her dad, and they spent a lot of time together."

"The together thing I knew about." He let the belt slip through his hand until it rested against the door. "That was one of the reasons Jude stopped dating her. It was hard to schedule a date because she often had plans with her dad. He found that kind of odd."

"It is unusual, I'll grant you that. Could be from losing her mom. They were really close. It seems as if after her mom died, Becca let time with her dad take over."

"So on the surface, it looks like she couldn't possibly kill her father, but as law enforcement officers, we can't rule that out until we have a solid alibi for the time of death."

Mina nodded but didn't want to agree. "Believing something bad about people you interact with every day is one of the hardest parts of small-town policing." She killed the engine. "But, as you said, as law enforcement officers, we have to keep our minds open." She met his gaze and held it. "And that includes considering Jude as a possible suspect."

He flinched. "I know you're wrong about that, but I also know we have to prove that he didn't kill the mayor or find out who did."

She hadn't brought it up to discuss, just to remind him that Jude was their prime suspect at this point. Reaching over him, she opened the glove compartment and handed him a flashlight. "You might want this again."

She pushed out of the vehicle and marched up to ring the doorbell, then pounded on the door in case Becca slept inside. Tapping her foot, she waited for someone to answer. A few seconds passed. Silence and no lights turning on inside. She knocked again, harder this time, using the side of her fist.

No reply.

She put on a pair of disposable gloves and checked the doorknob. "Locked."

"Let's check the perimeter, and see if we can find a way in," Nolan suggested.

"Follow me and don't touch anything without gloves on." She chose the easy way to go, the side of the fence that held the gate. Maybe the other side had a gate, too, but that would be unusual. Using her gloved hand, she lifted the latch and slipped into the backyard. Nolan's body blocked light coming from the street. The gate slammed shut behind him and most all of the light vanished.

She turned on her flashlight. The beam caught on moss

and small ferns in the cracks of the cobblestone walkway that led her toward the back of the house. She flashed the light up to three large and closed windows. She tugged on the first one. Locked tight.

"Partially open window over here." Nolan stood shining the beam of the borrowed flashlight at the third window.

She assessed the window. "You'll have to damage the screen to get in, but with the mayor's death and blood at Becca's house, this definitely falls under exigent circumstances." With a quick glance at the disposable gloves on his hands, she said, "Go for it. I'll hold the light for you."

She took it from him. He fished a small knife from his pocket, then sliced through the screen and ripped it from the window.

"You wouldn't be a subtle burglar," she said, trying to add some lightness to the heavy feeling in the air.

"Trust me. If I didn't want to get caught I could be far more subtle." He raised the window and climbed in.

She followed, landing in the mayor's study. Once, when Mina was here, he'd proudly walked her through his sports memorabilia collection.

A sweet aroma snaked into her nostrils. "Do you smell that?"

He nodded. "Air freshener?"

"No. Perfume. Chanel N°5, to be exact."

He whipped his head around to look at her. "How do you know that?"

"It's what my mom wears."

"So Becca's perfume, then?"

"Doubt it. It's not a young woman's choice. This is a classic powdery and soapy scent that I didn't pick up on at Becca's house. Besides, I saw a bottle of Versace Bright Crystal on her dresser. My mom gave me a bottle of that for Christmas, hoping if I started wearing perfume, I might

94

snare a man and settle down to give her grandchildren. It doesn't smell anything like this."

He opened his mouth, but then he closed it and took a long breath. Did he plan to say something about her comment on snaring a man? Maybe or maybe she was still being overly sensitive to him.

"Okay," he said. "Could the scent still be lingering from his wife's things?"

"Not likely. She passed away two years ago, and this is too strong, too recent." Mina paused to think. "Unless he still sprayed it to remember her."

"That's possible, I suppose." Nolan ran his light over the room. "Or another woman has recently been in his house. Was he dating?"

"Not that I've heard."

"Maybe a secret relationship. An affair with a married woman?"

"I don't think Mayor Sutton was that kind of person, but then we don't ever know what goes on behind closed doors until something like this brings it out into the open."

Nolan nodded. "We really need to talk to Becca, but until we find her, the next closest person to the mayor would be his assistant. If he was dating someone, Daisy would know."

"First thing in the morning, then. We'll interview her about that and everything else going on in the mayor's life that might've gotten him killed." And hopefully find something to go on because right now they had nothing. Absolutely nothing.

Outside Becca's front door, Nolan put on a pair of booties and gloves. Since they hadn't found her in immediate need of assistance, they'd returned to her house to do a more thorough search. Mina gloved up, too, but she was more proficient at it, which made sense since she handled crime scenes all the time. Not murder scenes like this one, but burglaries, auto accidents, assaults, and other minor scenes.

Was she up to managing a murder scene? He would assist her, but he'd never run a murder investigation. Since he'd formed the agency, he'd headed up several missing persons investigations. Meant he would be better off looking for Becca and not working the murder investigation.

Something he felt compelled to tell Mina.

He stepped inside and waited for her to enter. "Looks like we have two investigations going on now. Murder and a missing person. I think it would be a good idea to turn Becca's investigation over to my team."

She cocked a hip. "I can't turn over any investigation to a civilian team."

Her posture was meant to reinforce her statement, but he just found it cute. "You could deputize all of the team. Or even a few of them. They could then do what we are exceptional at doing, and you can focus on the murder investigation. You would of course be in charge, and we could give you daily or even more frequent updates."

"I don't know." She put her hands on her hips. "That would be like publicly declaring that my team wasn't up to the job. I don't want to do that to them."

"Realistically, how many deputies can you afford to assign to either investigation and not compromise your patrols?"

"One, maybe two at the most."

"So assign them to the murder investigation. Or you could even embed someone in our office who could be your eyes and ears."

She tilted her head. "Embedding someone might work. Question is, who to have do it. I could assign Abe, but he's really needed in day-to-day operations. I have one detective on staff, and I believe she would be most put out if I took her off the murder investigation. I do have a deputy who just passed his sergeant's exam, so maybe he's the one to include. I'll think about it. But for now, we need to look at the scene in regards to both this murder and a missing person."

"Agreed."

She proceeded into the room and squatted near the pool of blood. "Footprint is small. Narrow."

He crouched next to her. "Woman's?"

"Could be Becca's."

"So maybe we're wrong. Maybe she's not missing, but she was shot here and her body taken."

"Or she was standing with the mayor when he was shot. Or she simply came through the room and stepped in the blood on her way out the door."

"If so, there should be a bloody footprint heading toward the door."

"You're right, and there isn't one."

"What if the rug suggested by the dirt outline was used for Becca? Or used for the mayor, then brought back for Becca or the other way around?" He stood. "Or if they're both dead, both of them at one time?"

"Any of those scenarios could be possible. All we can do at this time is speculate. We don't have enough evidence to make a determination."

"One thing is sure," he said, "Becca's missing person case could also be a murder investigation, and we have to look at it both ways."

"You're right again." Mina narrowed her gaze. "Maybe I *should* put my detective on your team after all. I can handle the mayor's murder investigation without her, and if we do determine the mayor was killed here, then it's likely our leads and forensics will intersect with each other."

Nolan nodded. "First step is to find out whose blood we're looking at. We should be able to get a sample for the mayor from his place for a DNA test. Same for Becca, but it'll take time to get the results back, and we don't want to sit around waiting for days."

"Then let's give the house a good once-over to see where we go from here." Mina moved around the blood pool to survey the room. "Pay particular attention to locating her phone and purse."

"You could try calling her again," Nolan said. "See if her phone rings here or even vibrates."

Mina got out her phone and tapped the screen. "It's ringing. Hear anything?"

"Nah, nothing. The phone's likely with Becca." He approached a small entryway table where someone might drop their belongings on the way into the house. "No purse on the table, but there's a set of keys."

Mina studied the table. "Could be a sign that she left involuntarily."

"Or we could go with Occam's razor and look for the simplest answer."

She transferred her gaze to Nolan. "Which is what, in your opinion?"

"That she's out of town, and her father was housesitting. Perhaps he surprised an armed burglar who thought the place was empty and was attempting to enter, and the burglar shot him."

"That's a plausible theory and one we need to pursue. Maybe the review of the property will answer our questions." She continued on the same path they'd taken earlier.

He trailed her. "FYI, Sierra mentioned arriving by helicopter to save travel time and to move samples back to their lab faster. She said they would touch down around ten a.m. I told her they could land on the old airstrip on my property.

It's technically designated for helicopter use, or at least it once was, so it should meet Oregon law."

He waited for her to argue about the airstrip not being current, but she really couldn't protest. They'd used it for medivacs lately, and if she argued today, they wouldn't be able to use it to save lives in the future.

"Let me know when they arrive," she said. "And I can supply an unmarked vehicle or two for use."

He gave her a tight smile for her easy agreement. "They've got that covered. Their assistants will leave early in the morning to drive their vans down here with all of their supplies and equipment."

"Ah." She sighed. "Assistant. I could use one of those."

He hated to see her so stressed, but he suspected that's how she was going to be until they concluded both of these investigations. "Sierra did say they would need six rooms reserved for the night, though they might not all stay over. All depends on how fast things go."

"I'll check with the hotel to see if they can handle it."

"If not, the rooms we aren't using at the inn still have beds in them, and we could work something out, though I'd hate to take the time to clean right now."

She nodded. "It's off-season, so the hotel should be fine."

"Let me know if it isn't."

"Let's finish our review of this place, get over to my office for the electronic sketch of Smythe, and call it a night. I can make that call to the hotel first thing in the morning, and we'll meet at the mayor's office at eight to interview his assistant."

Her phone rang. She looked at the screen and frowned but answered. "Sheriff Park."

She looked at her feet and paced. "So she hung up before you could triangulate the call, and we have no idea who the caller might be."

What in the world was she talking about? Did it even relate to their investigations? He moved closer in hopes of picking up information, but all he heard was a muffled female voice.

"Right, yeah." Mina blew out a frustrated breath. "Considering the murder and missing person investigation you were right to call me. Thanks for letting me know."

She hung up and looked at Nolan. "That was the 911 dispatch supervisor. They had an unidentified female caller at 4:07 who ended the call within ten seconds and before they could get a location."

Becca? Nolan's heart skipped a beat. "What did she say?"

"'He's gone crazy. Has a gun.'" She shook her head. "That's all. Nothing we could act on. Still, the dispatcher shouldn't have kept the call to herself instead of notifying her supervisor. She's already on probation, and this will be the end for her. I feel bad about it, but we have to make sure patrol is notified in the future of even an abbreviated call like this."

"So you're thinking this could've been Becca calling in her father's murder, and she really was present to see it."

"Could be. If so, she knows who the killer is. Finding her is already our number one priority in case she might still be alive, but this makes it even more important, if that's possible."

"What's your decision on turning Becca's investigation over to us?"

"Let me talk to my detective. If she agrees to be embedded with your team, then I'll approve it."

"And my role? Are you still wanting me to work the murder investigation with you?"

She nodded, but her sour expression said she would rather shake her head. "You can help me figure out what your team's past has to do with the mayor's death. Because, honestly, Nolan, I don't have any idea where to begin on that."

"Then I'm glad to help you." He gave what he hoped was a confident look when he had no clue why someone would kill the mayor and try to pin it on him or one of the people he cared most about in this world.

10

A killer of an evening. Yeah, the invitation had come through as promised. The strain lingered in his teammates' eyes as they gathered in their conference room late that night. Or should he say early the next morning. Once the inn's dining area, the oversized space had a huge commercial kitchen with stainless steel everything connected through a set of swinging doors at the end of the room.

After Nolan had gone to the sheriff's office to get a reasonably good digital sketch made of Smythe, Mina agreed to let his team, with the help of her detective, take on Becca's disappearance. He didn't want to wait to gather the team, so he had a patrol deputy drive him to the mansion to pick up his SUV while she'd updated her sergeant and detective.

Nolan had brewed a large urn of coffee and dug a chunk of cake from their grand opening out of the freezer. He sliced the nearly frozen cake and handed the small plates down the table.

Memories of the day came back. Not a big celebration, it was more of an event for the team to mark the day. But the mayor had insisted on providing a cake from Stella's Bakery downtown, along with a big bowl of punch. He had come to cut the ribbon at their front door. Becca had accompanied him, and that's where Jude had met her, putting him in his precarious place as a murder suspect.

Grinning, Jude held out his hand. "Give me the biggest piece you've got. If I'm a condemned man, I might as well get some cake in before I'm incarcerated."

Reece swatted at him. "I don't know how you can laugh at a time like this."

She might have commented on his misplaced sense of humor when someone had lost their life, but no one else thought anything of it. He simply employed a coping mechanism that law enforcement officers often used to get through difficult situations, and Nolan suspected that she'd used it a time or two in her career as well.

After handing out the last piece, Nolan sat at the small table they'd shoved together with several of the old dining room tables to form one large conference table and shoved a fork into the cake. The utensil came away with a bite of vanilla cake, raspberry filling, and creamy white frosting. He let the sweet goodness melt in his mouth. "I thought this might've tasted old by now, but it's almost as good as the day it was baked."

"You might be exaggerating just a teeny bit." Reece laughed.

Nolan laughed with her, but it was short-lived as the point of their meeting wouldn't let go of his brain. "Before I start, I told Mina I would ask if anyone kept their envelope from the invitation. Anyone have one?"

"Mine should still be in my trash," Gabe said. "Haven't emptied the can in my office area for a while."

Hayden snorted.

"What?" Gabe mocked an innocent pose. "Many more

exciting things to do along the coast than waste time with trash."

He spoke the truth, but if they only did things they liked, they wouldn't be able to successfully run the business.

But trash wasn't something Nolan wanted to waste time discussing. "If you can retrieve the envelope when we get done here, that would be great. Keep the fingerprints to a minimum."

"No problem, but after fishing it out of the trashcan, I don't know what else might be on it." He laughed.

Nolan shook his head and looked around the team. "Thanks for dropping everything to meet."

Abby frowned. "With Becca missing, it's the least we can do, boss."

Nolan might've founded Lost Lake Locators, and the team had voted for him to be the leader, but he wasn't the boss, and being called that reminded him of his father, a memory he'd rather not have. Besides, each member of the team had an equal financial partnership and equal say in everything.

He ran his gaze around the table. "What's it going to take to get you to let go of the *boss* thing?"

"Well, you are kind of bossy." Reece laughed.

"That could be said of everyone at this table." Nolan took another bite of cake.

"Someone's gotta take charge," Jude said. "And we tasked you with the job, so that's how we think of you."

"Sorry if you don't like it." Hayden stabbed up a bite of cake but held the fork midair. "But you also own this property, so it's only fitting that you're the boss."

Nolan ran his gaze over the group again. "But you all have the freedom to remodel and decorate your suites as you see fit. If I was really bossy, I would tell you what to do there too."

"Nah," Abby said. "You know better than that. You'd have a mutiny if you did."

They all joined her in a good-natured laugh, but the subject wasn't over as far as Nolan was concerned. He didn't want to tell them about the connection between the word and his dad, but maybe that's what it would take.

A loud knock sounded on the outside door and rang down the hallway.

"That'll be Mina and her detective." Nolan left the room and wound down the long hallway that led to the front door. The old mahogany door had a beautiful finish on the inside, but when he opened it, he saw the work they would have to do to restore the weatherworn exterior—one of a hundred, maybe thousands of tasks to be done to bring this property back to its original glory.

Another topic for another day.

He turned his attention to the detective and gave her a thorough once-over. She stood at five-eight or so but didn't wear any makeup and had her hair severely pulled back, leaving a few strands dangling on each side. Severe look or not, she was an attractive woman. She wore a nondescript brown suit and collared blouse. It was as if she was trying not to be noticed as a woman. Maybe she needed to be taken seriously in what was still a man's world in a lot of ways.

"Nolan Orr," Mina said. "Meet Detective Elaina Lyons."

She shoved out a hand.

"Detective." Nolan took her firm grip for a moment, then stepped back. "Follow me to the conference room. The team is waiting."

The door rubbed against the frame as it latched, but he didn't bother to see if the women were following him. In the conference room, he paused at the head of the table.

"This is Detective Elaina Lyons," Nolan said and stopped

there, purposely not sharing the team members' names to save time.

"Elaina is my great grandmother, so please call me El," Elaina said as an unpleasant look crossed her face before she gave a tight smile he was sure she offered to suspects before interviewing them.

"Go ahead and have a seat," Nolan said. "Instead of long intros, everyone can identify themselves when they speak. We're having coffee with leftover cake from our grand opening. Fair warning before you grab a slice. It's been in the freezer for over a year."

"No worries for me." El reached for a plate with the biggest slice of cake. "Sugar in any form goes well with coffee, and I need something after a long shift that doesn't look like it's going to end anytime soon."

"No sugar for me, but the coffee is much appreciated." Mina poured a cup.

It steamed from one of the old mugs stamped with a Portside Inn logo Nolan had inherited when he'd bought the place. She sat in a chair near the head of the table. El took a seat between Gabe and Hayden. Gabe cleared his throat and ran his finger around the neckband of his T-shirt. One of his tells for showing his discomfort.

Was there something about El he didn't like? Or was it just the opposite? He liked what he saw too much to be comfortable sitting so close to her. Only time would tell, but Nolan would keep an eye on it.

He remained standing at the head of the table and grabbed a blue dry-erase marker. "We might all be getting our sugar high, but we have serious business ahead of us. I think we can agree that it's looking like Becca isn't simply a woman who doesn't want to be found, but this is a case of foul play, and we need to locate her ASAP."

He received nods and murmurs of agreement from the group.

"However," Mina said. "She could just be away from home, and we have to keep that on the table until we rule it out."

"Agreed," Nolan said. "With that in mind, let's start by listing our tasks on the whiteboard. You can weigh in on your preferred job as we go along or choose one at the end."

"We start where we always start," Hayden said. "We do a deep dive on Becca and the mayor too. Like you said, she could just be gone, but it's more likely the mayor's murder is linked to her disappearance. We include finances and see if she has used a credit or debit card after the mayor was killed."

"This would be Hayden Kraus who didn't identify himself," Nolan said for El as he jotted the note on the board.

"Oh, right, yeah. Like he said." Hayden laughed. "Former Customs and Border Protection, and I handle most IT related items for the team. All we'll need are Becca's date of birth and social security number, and we're on our way."

"I'll go ahead and put your name down as we all know that's what you would've volunteered for, and in fact, what we want you to volunteer for." Nolan grinned at his teammate and added his name next to the item. "Since we didn't locate either Becca's or the mayor's phones, we'll also want cell phone records from the providers."

"I'll see what I can do," Hayden said.

"Let's make this a top priority," Mina said. "And if you need a warrant for these, I'm sure we have enough probable cause to get one. At least for the mayor. So check in with Detective Lyons for that."

Hayden nodded.

Gabe shifted away from El. "Gabe Irving. Former state

trooper. You got a theory and need a hole shot in it, I'm your guy."

"I remember that about you," Mina said.

"We need to contact her employer," Gabe said. "Her friends, family, and acquaintances too. See if she's visiting any of them or find out when they saw her last or if they know anything about the murder."

"Or if they know of a reason why anyone would want to hurt her." El dropped her fork on the plate. "We should especially be aware that the majority of women who go missing and are found murdered are killed by someone they know or are having a romantic relationship with."

"If she's typical of someone her age," Hayden said. "she'll have social media accounts. I can review those and make a list of people we should contact."

"Also," El said. "If she's simply out of town and unaware of what's going on, her socials could give us an instant take on what she's doing right now."

"I'll make the friends list," Hayden said. "But it would be best if someone else reviewed her posts so I can concentrate on the deep dives."

"You're the resident charmer, Jude," Reece said. "You should follow up on the list in person or on a phone call. You might as well check the posts too."

"That would be my dear friend Reece Waters calling me out." Jude laughed. "She was with ATF. I'm Jude French, once an FBI agent. You already heard that I can be charming, but you should know Reece is our go-to weapons expert, so you don't want to make her mad."

Reece punched him in the arm. "Trust me. He's far more dangerous than I am. He'll charm you into something before you know what hit you or make a joke of it."

He beamed a smile at Reece. "And yet you love me."

"I do, but I'm not proud of it and will deny it outside of this room." She laughed.

Nolan was about to apologize for his team's banter at such a serious time, but the group, including Mina and El, laughed too.

When the laughter died down, Reece cleared her throat. "Becca could be on a business trip. Who does she work for?"

"The county as a social worker," Mina said. "So it's not likely she's out of town unless it's for training."

"I'd be glad to see what her supervisor knows," Reece offered.

Nolan recorded that on the board.

"Something no one has mentioned," Gabe said. "What if she saw her father gunned down, and she took off, fearing for her own life? Went into hiding somewhere."

"Good point," Nolan said. "Hayden, search for any connected properties where she might've gone into hiding."

"The mayor doesn't own any other property," Mina said. "Or if he does, he's never mentioned it, and I've never heard anyone else talk about it."

"Still, look into it, Hayden," Nolan said. "And then look for secluded properties belonging to any friends or family that she might've gone to in the past or when she was a kid. Somewhere she might feel safe."

"There'll be friends, maybe family, who won't be on social media who might know her whereabouts," Mina said. "I think the best person to make a list like that would be the mayor's assistant, Daisy. I'll ask her to give us the same list for Mayor Sutton."

"We have, of course, put out an alert for her and her vehicle," El said. "And I've already checked with hospitals. No one fitting her description."

"How likely do we really think it is that she's just away?" Hayden asked.

"Her car is gone, but her suitcases are in her closet," Nolan answered, thinking back to his search of her bedroom. "But she could just be gone for the night and took a tote bag or backpack. And if abducted, her captor could've taken her car."

"So fifty-fifty odds, you think?" Hayden asked.

"I'm more leaning toward abduction," Mina said and shared the 911 call. "The call came in the window of the mayor's time of death. The female caller said, 'He's gone crazy. Has a gun,' which could easily apply here."

Hayden scowled. "If it was from her that *does* change things."

"But we can't prove it, so it's just speculation again," Gabe said.

"So back to the hospitals." Abby leaned forward. "Abby Day, former sheriff. Did your hospital check include the morgue?"

El nodded, but looked a bit put out over the suggestion that she wouldn't have been thorough.

"We should also canvass the neighborhood," Mina said. "Not that Becca lives in much of a neighborhood—her property is very secluded—but perhaps someone on the roads nearby caught the killer on their security camera. And we need to do a detailed daylight search of the area too."

Nolan added that item to the board.

"I can handle that," Gabe said. "I did my fair share of door-knocking and bush-beating in the past."

"I was going to volunteer Detective Lyons for that," Mina said. "She knows the residents and area. Plus, she's an official member of our team."

"What if they pair up?" Nolan asked. "We could get a better read on the neighbors' truthfulness with two people observing their responses."

Mina nodded and offered a tight smile. "Sounds like a good compromise."

"I'll put down both names." Before recording the action item, Nolan kept his gaze on Gabe. He shifted uncomfortably in his chair.

El sat straighter. "When it gets light out, I'll head up a search party. Then we can knock on doors."

Gabe's sharp nod and lack of comment was more telling than anything. He rarely held back like this.

"I'm not sure if now is the time to mention this," El continued, "but I'll be heading up this investigation. All reports and information will come to me, and I'll keep Sheriff Park in the loop."

She looked around the table as if waiting for someone to argue, but no one did. Surprising, as far as Nolan was concerned. His team was rarely silent when someone tried to take control of what they believed to be their investigation. But they'd already been notified that Veritas would be reporting all of their findings to Mina's office, so it probably came as no surprise that Mina and El would control the rest of the information too.

"Thank you for understanding." Mina glanced around the table. "Nolan and I'll be interviewing Daisy later in the morning. We'll ask her to make that friends list, and we'll also question her regarding Becca's disappearance and the mayor's murder."

"I'm assuming two investigations will overwhelm your records clerk," Abby said. "With my background, I know exactly what you need in your files for a successful prosecution. I could handle the recordkeeping for you, if you want."

Mina nodded. "I'll be glad of that, but all documents will come through my office first, then we'll pass them along to you." She stood and looked around the room, pausing to let her gaze linger on each team member. "I want to be sure that point is understood and complied with. We're very thankful for your team's expertise and help, but you're civilians and this is a law enforcement matter. I hope you're all on board with working within these parameters."

Gabe grinned. "Promise me a Frenzy Burger at Submarine Burgers, and I'll make sure to keep these goofballs in line."

"I guess it's true then." Jude eyed his teammate. "You'll do anything for a burger."

"You gotta admit a great burger alone is worth so much." Gabe's grin widened. "But eating one in an old submarine? Wouldn't that be the highlight of everyone's day?"

"Not that I think your team will need anyone to spy on them," Mina said. "But El loves burgers, too, and I'm sure she'd be glad to take you there if necessary."

Normally Gabe would've laughed. Maybe even give Mina a high five, but his jaw tightened. Had he finally met the woman who might challenge his single-for-life philosophy? Or was Nolan just reading something into it so he could keep his focus off his own relationship—or lack of one—with Mina?

Problem was, later that morning he would be alone with her, except when interviewing people, and Gabe wouldn't be around to distract them. Nolan would just have to ensure every moment together was packed with interviews. If not, he might find himself with the same uncomfortable expression plaguing Gabe.

11

Nearing eight a.m., Mina stepped into the outer area of the mayor's office, Nolan accompanying her. Daisy Ellington sat behind her wide, wooden desk, the top neat and tidy and still holding an old-fashioned Rolodex. The fifty-something woman was perfectly groomed, as usual. She'd slicked her dyed blond hair back in a bun and wore a flowery dress with a fitted waist, much like the ones she often wore.

Mina had known Daisy for years. Exactly how many, she wasn't sure. She'd first met the mayor's assistant when she was in grade school. Daisy and her husband had left Georgia for him to take the job as Lost Lake's local sanitation and waterworks expert. They lived five houses down from Mina's family home, and within the first two weeks of arriving, Daisy had called on everyone on the block, bringing her famous poundcake and southern charm with her.

It had taken only six months before she went to work for the mayor where she received the report listing every new person who'd moved into town. She baked and delivered a poundcake each to them, welcoming them on behalf of the mayor and town. She continued that warm welcome to this day, knew most everyone in the area, and was a deep well of information.

She literally was Lost Lake's form of Google. If anyone would know who killed the mayor, it would be Daisy.

She looked up, and a broad smile crossed her face. "Sheriff and Nolan. I don't have you on Mayor Sutton's calendar today."

"We're not here to see him." Mina approached the desk but didn't sit. "We've come to see you."

She raised her hand to clutch her short strand of pearls. "Me? Whatever could you want from me?"

"It's about the mayor."

"Ernie?" She blinked mascara-coated lashes. "Is he okay?"

Mina took a seat across the desk.

"He's been shot," she said, unable to say right off the bat that he'd been murdered.

Daisy leapt to her feet. "So he's in the hospital? I need to get over there."

Nolan held up his hand. "Wait. He's not at the hospital."

"He's not de..." Her eyes flashed open. "Oh my goodness. He's dead, right?"

"Yes," Mina said, wishing there had been a better way to deliver this shocking news.

Daisy fell back in her chair. "But that can't be. Who would want to shoot him? Everybody loves Ernie. Just everybody."

"Apparently not." Nolan offered a sincere look. "I'm so sorry for your loss, Daisy. I know you were close to Mayor Sutton."

"Close?" Her voice rose. "He was like family. He and my Roger were best friends. How am I going to tell Roger?"

"I know you'll find a way," Mina said.

"Yes, I suppose I'll have to." She seemed to deflate in resignation of the news.

Mina hated to push her at a time like this, but Daisy would want the mayor's killer brought to justice. "We have a few questions for you, and then you should go home to tell Roger before he hears about it via the grapevine. If you're not up to driving, we can escort you home, if you'd like."

"Yes. Yes." Tears glistened in her eyes, and she reached for a tissue on her desk, but they were too far away.

Nolan grabbed the box and walked around the back of the desk. He squatted next to her and held them out. She wiped the tears now rolling over wrinkled cheeks, then lowered her hands to the arms of her antique wooden chair.

"I really am sorry, Daisy." Nolan patted her hand. "Is there anything else I can do to help besides take you home?"

"Aren't you just the sweetest." She offered a wobbly smile and looked up at Mina. "Isn't he just the best?"

Mina nodded, and she really meant it. As he and Daisy chatted about ways to break the news to Roger, Mina drifted off to the past. The Nolan she'd known that summer was exactly the kind of guy who would take Daisy's hand and offer to help her. To offer her advice and let her talk through her pain. But the Nolan who walked out on her wasn't that kind of person. So which one was he really?

Could she trust him? Could she believe that he'd left her a note?

She had to do something to regain her ability to trust men. Even with a father and two brothers who were faithful husbands, she couldn't find it in her heart to trust any guy who wanted to date her.

If she didn't find a way to get over the betrayal, she would remain single for the rest of her life. Maybe a good thing. For her career anyway. Being a sheriff and a mom at the same time could have its challenges.

Or not. She just didn't know.

She could go over to Tommy's house and ask to look through his things. If Nolan really had given the note to Tommy, maybe he'd kept it for some reason. She wouldn't want to stir up any pain for his mother, but surely she would allow Mina to search his room.

Not now though. When she had some free time. Right now she had a killer, perhaps an abductor to find. That meant they had to question Daisy, but she was fragile, and Mina had to be sensitive.

"When was the last time you saw the mayor?" she asked.

Daisy didn't hesitate. "Yesterday afternoon around one o'clock. He left for a late lunch but didn't come back to the office."

Nolan released her hand and stood. "Was he supposed to return?"

"No. He didn't have any additional appointments and said he wouldn't be back for the rest of the day."

"Was that unusual for him to leave so early?" Nolan asked.

"Normally I would say yes. He was usually still here at five-thirty when I left for the day, five days a week." Daisy sniffled. "Many days even later. There were times I've gone out to dinner with Roger and saw the lights on here when we drove by on the way home." She shook her head. "We'll never have another mayor as dedicated as Ernie was."

Mina agreed, but she couldn't let that distract her. "But that changed lately?"

Daisy nodded. "He left early at least one day a week for... I don't know...the past two months, I'd say. He made it clear that I shouldn't question where he was going. Out of respect for him, I never did."

Nolan returned to his chair. "Do you have a theory about what he was doing on these days?"

Daisy didn't respond but twisted the tissue in her hands.

"It's okay, Daisy," Mina said to encourage her. "You can tell us."

She swiped a tear from her cheek. "I don't want to speak ill of Ernie, especially when he can't defend himself."

Mina leaned closer and lowered her voice. "Whatever you say will go no further than the three of us."

She bit her lip, gnawing off peach-colored lipstick. "I thought he might be having an affair with a married woman."

"Why would you think that?" Nolan asked.

Good thing he'd asked. If Mina had questioned Daisy, her tone of voice would've given away her shock at the comment and perhaps troubled Daisy.

Daisy pressed her hands out on the desk and raised her shoulders. "I don't pay bills as part of my job, but I do open the mail when it comes in. That includes his work credit card. I happened to see the charges for a hotel in Portland on one of the statements. The date matched one of the days he was out of the office. I didn't look any further because I certainly would never spy on him, but it made me wonder. Not only about that, but wonder why he would charge something personal on his work card."

"And that's it?" Mina asked. "Just one day at a hotel left you curious? Maybe he was attending a conference."

"He would've told me about something like that," she said. "And that's not all. He took several phone calls recently on his cell phone, and when I had stepped into his office, he tried to hide the conversation from me. He's never done that in the past, no matter who he was talking to, so I figured it could be the woman."

Daisy twisted her hands together. "We also share a calendar, and one day I discovered he had a separate calendar on his computer. None of the events were spelled out but were listed in cryptic notations. I access his computer all the time, and he obviously didn't want me to know what was going on. Again, out of respect for him I didn't ask. But then the last thing was that he'd lost weight lately, and I figured he was more cognizant about his appearance and wanted to look good for this woman."

Mina had to agree with Daisy's assessment. These things could mean he was having an affair, and an affair could also explain other things.

"What about perfume?" Mina asked. "Are you familiar with the scent of Chanel N°5?"

She nodded. "My mom wore it. I did too for a while."

"Has any woman come into the office wearing that scent?" Nolan asked.

"I don't know." Daisy tilted her head. "Not that I'm aware of anyway."

"Do you know who he was meeting for lunch yesterday?" Mina asked in hopes that he really had gone to lunch.

She shook her head. "He said it was personal."

Mina needed better answers, but Daisy could only speak to what she knew. "What about his daughter, Becca? Do you know if she's out of town or on vacation? Maybe Mayor Sutton was housesitting?"

"He didn't mention it. They're—they were—so close he would've said something about her being gone."

"When was the last time you saw her?" Mina asked.

Alarm shone from Daisy's watery eyes. "I don't like these questions. Don't tell me she's dead too?"

Mina lifted her hands. "No. No. But we haven't been able to locate her."

Daisy blinked a few times. "I saw her on Wednesday evening at a fundraiser for Ukrainian refugees who've settled in our state. She's heading up the local committee to get needed supplies for these families."

Mina had heard good things about their organization. "I know she's done a wonderful job, but can you think of anyone who might want to hurt or take her?"

"This is all just so surreal." Daisy shivered and rubbed her hands over her upper arms. "You're talking about Lost Lake here. Our tiny little town. Who wants to hurt anyone here? I mean sure, we all have our quarrels and disagreements, but nobody wants to murder or abduct someone."

"Any normal day I would agree with you, but a murder has occurred. Someone we all care about." Mina let that comment hang in the air for a moment. "Becca could be the key. So can you think of anyone who disagreed with her?"

Daisy stared off into the distance, then shook her head. "There are some folks who don't believe refugees should be coming to our country. Ernie was also a staunch supporter of the effort to relocate them here too. But again, is that enough of a reason to kill?"

A wavering smile crossed Nolan's lips. "You can never tell what could cause a person to break and commit murder. I've seen some pretty bizarre threats to the president's life over the years, and it seemed like if these people could actually get to him, they would follow through."

Daisy frowned. "I suppose that's true."

"Would you be willing to make a list of local friends and family Becca might have?" Mina asked. "The mayor's close friends too. We'd like to follow up with them to see if they know where she is or would know a reason someone might want to kill the mayor."

"I'll get to it the moment you leave." Daisy scribbled something on a pad next to her. "You should know. Ernie didn't have many friends. No close ones that I can even think of. He hung out with his birdwatching club, but otherwise it was just Becca. Me and Roger, too, but we really didn't do that much together."

"He was such a social guy, that surprises me," Mina said.

"He said he spent his entire day catering to people, and when he was off the clock, he just wanted to be alone or with Becca."

"That makes sense." Nolan laid a business card on her desk. "Can you take a picture of the list and text it to me at this phone number as soon as you complete it?"

"Of course."

He rested his hands on the arms of the chair, but gripped them tightly. "Another strong motive behind murder is money. Did the mayor need money or borrow money from someone?"

Daisy puckered her lips. "I don't know anything about that. He managed all of his personal affairs. Now if you want to know about the city finances, I can tell you all about that."

That's an area Mina hadn't considered. "Is it possible that someone in a city office has been embezzling or siphoning money and the mayor discovered it?"

"Not that I know of." Daisy tapped her finger on the desk. "I can't think of anyone who had access to the funds who would be misusing them, but I suppose it's possible."

"Who has access to the money?" Nolan asked.

"Our treasurer, of course, and then our accountant." She sat silently, her head tilted in question. "We have separation of duties to keep theft at bay. Our treasurer deposits the money and our accountant disperses it and pays the bills."

"Has Mayor Sutton met with either of these people recently?" Nolan asked.

"Now that you mention it," Daisy's eyes brightened, and she sat forward, "He did have an appointment with our accountant early in the week. It seemed amiable though."

"Could I get a copy of the last six months of budget reports for the city?" Mina asked, but didn't add or even hint at the fact that she wanted them in case the mayor himself was dipping into the money.

"I'll print them for you right now." She clicked her computer mouse, tapped on the keyboard, and soon, the printer behind her was humming. "Anything else?"

"Has the mayor seemed off or out of sorts recently?" Nolan asked.

"Um, no." She shook her head. "Not really. Everything seemed normal."

"Has he had any unusual visitors lately or anyone you didn't know or someone acting suspiciously?" Mina asked.

Daisy sighed and flipped through an appointment book. "I wish I could be more help, but no. No one in here that I didn't know and everyone seemed normal."

She shoved her chair back with extra force as if frustrated and grabbed the reports from the printer. She straightened the pages with a vigorous tap, then laid them on the corner of her desk. "The reports you want. If you need anything else, just ask."

Mina swiped to the sketch of Smythe on her phone and held it out. "Has this man been in here or have you seen him before?"

Daisy gave the screen a careful study. "I'm sure I haven't seen him here, and I don't remember seeing him out on the street or anything." She furrowed her brow. "Since he's not one of the locals, are you also looking outside of town for the person who killed him?"

"We are," Mina said. "Is there someone outside of Lost Lake who you might consider a suspect?"

She opened her mouth, then closed it to tap her finger on the desk again. "Maybe, but not really. Still, I should mention that Ernie dealt with mayors from other cities and of course other county officials. He seemed to have a good relationship with all of them, except for the mayor of

Seaside Harbor. They had a rivalry going, but far as I know, it was friendly."

Mina jotted down *Seaside Harbor Mayor.* "Do you know of any locals who own handguns and are proficient in shooting them?"

Daisy shook her head. "You would know more about it than me. I stay away from things like that."

"We might as well rule you out as a suspect right now," Mina said. "Where were you yesterday between three and five?"

"Here. A few people stopped by during that time and can vouch for the fact that I was here. Not that I need anyone to vouch for me. You know I would never kill Ernie." She wrinkled her nose. "Lands' end! What am I saying? I'd never kill *anyone.*"

"I believe you. Of course I do." Mina slid her notebook across the desk to Daisy. "But I need you to jot down the names of the people who saw you yesterday afternoon."

"Gladly." She grabbed a pen and wrote quickly before passing the book back to Mina. "They're all local, so you shouldn't have a hard time finding them."

"Did Mayor Sutton happen to leave his phone here?" Nolan asked.

"Not that I know of, but I haven't been in his office this morning. Let me call it to see." She picked up her desktop handset and punched a speed dial number. "It's ringing but not from here."

Daisy sagged as if this was getting too much for her, but Mina had to press on. For Becca's sake. "The mayor was famous for his social media posts. Have you noticed anything unusual in his posts lately?"

"Actually, he didn't do his own posts." She gave a half smile. "He didn't have a personal account, and it was our little secret, but I did all of the social media and other promotions for his job."

Mina thought about the creative, often humorous posts and smiled. "Then you're a very talented social media creator."

Blushing bright red, she waved a hand. "I'm not sure I'm proud of that fact, but I find it very easy to do. Maybe it's so easy because I respected Ernie so much."

"If you generated the content," Mina said, "there's no point in looking at his posts, but has anyone left negative replies that we should consider?"

"Oh, yes!" She sat up in her seat. "One person in particular likes to post negative comments on everything I put out there. Even on best wishes on holidays. He goes by the name Patriotic Puzzle." She wrote *@patrioticpuzzle* on a Post-It note and slapped it on top of her list of those who could vouch for her. "He really doesn't have anything in the description on his account and has zero posts of his own. I don't know what the name is supposed to mean other than he might like politics and puzzles."

Mina shared a look with Nolan. He gave a brief nod. Yeah, he'd caught the connection between puzzle and cipher and the mystery room.

"I wanted to block him," Daisy continued. "But Ernie wouldn't let me. He said it would just infuriate the guy and make him escalate into something other than leaving negative replies. Besides, Ernie said, all positive comments on a post isn't realistic, and he wanted to come across as realistic to his constituents."

"He was a real down-to-earth man," Mina said sincerely, and the three of them fell silent enough to hear the hammers pounding outside on Main Street.

Daisy's focus shifted to the window. "Founder's Day. It won't be the same without Ernie."

"Do you think we should cancel it?" Mina asked.

"No. No." Daisy leaned closer. "That's the last thing Ernie would want. He loved that day, and he loved his town. He wouldn't want anything to interfere with it."

"Maybe we could do something special to honor him," Nolan suggested.

"Yes!" Daisy grabbed her pen and paper. "I'll get ahold of the council members, and we'll plan something."

"Can you please hold off on that?" Mina said. "I don't want word getting around about the murder until we have a better handle on the investigation."

Daisy dropped her pen. "Just tell me when I'm cleared to take care of it, and we'll do something special."

"I know you will." Mina smiled at the amazing woman and wanted to stop here, but she had additional questions. "He was also once a partner in a charter fishing boat. Was he still involved in that?"

Daisy frowned. "He has a boat with his brother-in-law, Wade Collins."

"You don't think that was a good thing?" Nolan asked.

"Wade is kind of a freeloader." Daisy shook her head. "I don't need to speak badly of anyone, but he didn't work very hard, and when he ran out of money because he didn't sign up enough clients, he always hit Ernie up. Of course Ernie gave the money to him out of his share of the business profits."

"So the mayor didn't make any profit from this fishing venture then," Mina said.

"Again, I don't know his finances, but on the surface it didn't seem like he could have. When his wife was alive, I heard him tell her he wanted to get out of the fishing business, but he stayed in it for her sake."

Mina made a note of that. "And yet two years after she passed away, he was still involved with her brother."

Daisy wrinkled her nose. "It makes no sense to me, but it must've made sense to Ernie."

"Do you know if they both owned the boat?" Nolan asked.

"That I don't know, but I've lived here long enough to know fishing boats like that one are pricey. I doubt there was any way Wade could've owned it outright."

Mina glanced at Nolan to see if he was thinking along the same lines as she was—if Wade needed a quick infusion of cash, he might have killed the mayor so he could sell the boat.

Nolan's furrowed brow and knowing look told her it was likely they were of the same mind. It also told her they might just have their first viable suspect for murder.

12

Nolan didn't want to seem excited about a strong suspect, so he schooled his emotions as they headed for her car. Excited really wasn't the right word. How could a person be excited over finding a potential murder suspect? Eager to question the guy might be more appropriate.

Mina got behind the wheel, and he slid into the passenger seat. He should wait to speak until she had the vehicle on the road, but he clicked on his seatbelt and turned to look at her. "I know we have to meet with the Veritas team soon and you want to talk to Palmer, but then we need to talk to Wade Collins."

"I agree." She shoved the key into the ignition, but her phone rang. She grabbed it. "Putting you on speaker, Abe. Nolan is with me."

"Harmony finally dropped off the rental agreement," Abe said. "And information on the building owner."

"And?" Nolan sat breathless in hopes of a strong lead.

"I reviewed the agreement," Abe said, sounding a bit defensive. "The name on it is Smythe Fitzwilliam."

"Smythe Fitzwilliam." Nolan echoed. "Seems like a bogus name to me."

"Me too," Abe said, "but I searched for it anyway. Found no one. Called the phone number listed on the application. It's disconnected."

"At least there was once a phone connected to that number," Mina said. "But not surprising that it was disconnected now that Smythe's role in the murder seems to be over."

"We can't let it go, though," Abe said. "I'll run down call logs for the number. I'm guessing we'll find out it was a prepaid phone, but still, if we can discover where Smythe bought it, security footage could give us an actual photo of the man, and we can search databases."

"That would be most helpful." Mina shifted in her seat. "And phone numbers he called or who called him could be helpful as well."

"Agreed," Abe said. "The contract also has an address listed in Seaside Harbor. Turns out it's the address for the local library. I'll visit them to see if they've heard of this guy, but I feel fairly certain that will be a negative."

"You should still show them Smythe's sketch," Mina said. "Just in case it's an employee or a regular visitor masquerading under the name Smythe Fitzwilliam."

"Already in my plans." Abe's tone was definitely surly now. "Will let you know what I locate."

The call went dead, and Mina turned her full focus on getting them on the road. Nolan wanted to ask about Abe's behavior and why Mina didn't say anything about it, but it was none of his business to interfere with how she ran her department.

They raced through the foggy, rainy streets of Lost Lake, out into the country, and then into the seaside section of Seaside Harbor where Palmer lived.

Cody Palmer's extravagant house overlooked the hilly terrain, where the sun was just breaking through early morning fog and clouds. If they weren't there to interview a potential murder suspect, Nolan would stop to admire God's creation as it unfolded over the landscape.

One of the unexpected joys he'd found in living at an inn perched on a cliff overlooking the ocean was seeing God's beauty day in and day out. Nothing in his life had prepared him for the calm evenings he now experienced, erasing some of the horror and strife from the day and giving him a new perspective to begin his day.

But he was at this home for an ugly reason today. Murder.

He climbed the steps with Mina and looked over the two-story building. It boasted double-height windows in the front and a wide expanse of manicured lawn.

He let out a low whistle. "Guy's got money. Fitting for someone who could afford to own a mansion. Especially not as his main residence."

"Yeah, it looks like he's made of money and investing in property is generally a sound decision." Mina stabbed the doorbell.

The chime rang in the house, and Nolan half expected Smythe Fitzwilliam to answer as the butler. Instead, a tall man with a thick head of dark hair, a wide jaw, and a well-built body pulled the door open and stared at them. "Help you?"

Mina displayed her badge and introduced them. "Did you speak to Harmony Vance last night?"

He arched an eyebrow. "No, but I had a text from her telling me to call her. It was after business hours, and she usually has trivial things she needs help with, so I haven't given her a call."

"This isn't trivial," Nolan said, not liking the off-hand way he was responding. "It's about the contract signed for your Tidewater Mansion last night."

He raised his chin. "I don't handle those little details and don't know anything about it. You'll have to talk to Harmony. She manages the reservations." He started to close the door.

Mina stuck her foot in it to stop him. "It's not quite that simple, Mr. Palmer. The Lost Lake mayor was murdered, and his body was found in your mansion last night."

Palmer took a step back but otherwise seemed unfazed by the shocking news. "I guess that's why she was calling me then."

"Seems so," Mina said. "I've reviewed the contract. It's in the name of Smythe Fitzwilliam. Does that name ring a bell with you?"

Palmer shook his head.

Mina displayed the sketch of Smythe. "Have you ever seen this man before?"

Looking bored now, Palmer shook his head again. Nolan itched to tell him an honorable man had been murdered and demand Palmer pay better attention. That wouldn't end well if they wanted his cooperation, so he shoved his hands into his pockets instead.

"All of the information in the contract is bogus," Mina stated. "What do you do to confirm contracts, if anything?"

"After the credit card for a reservation deposit goes through, Harmony calls the provided contact number to confirm they're the signed renters. She then talks with the renter about their specific needs."

"But you don't do any kind of background check to be sure they're legitimate?" Nolan asked, trying not to sound testy.

"As long as their credit card goes through and the balance is paid before the event begins, we're good."

Mina let out a long breath, her frustration obvious. "We'll be needing the credit card information for this reservation."

"Like I said, Harmony handles all of that. You'll have to get it from her."

Mina took a hard stance in front of the man and handed him her business card. "You don't seem to understand. *You'll* get that credit card information for me and text it to my phone number within an hour, or I'll arrest you for obstruction of justice."

Nolan knew she couldn't do that as Palmer had given her a way to get the information. For that matter, he could demand a warrant for it, but if this worked, Nolan was all for it.

He sniffed the air as if it was foul, but nodded. "Have your little tantrum, but I assure you it isn't necessary. I'll be sure you have the information within the hour."

"And you need to stop by my office before noon for fingerprinting and a DNA swab so we can eliminate you from any prints and DNA we recover at your property."

He looked down on her with hard eyes. "Fine. Anything else?"

"Not at the moment." She glared up at him. "But a better attitude might be nice."

He rolled his eyes and pushed the door closed.

"Nice man," Nolan said on the way to the car. "I loved your comment about a better attitude."

"No wonder he hired Harmony." Mina climbed behind the wheel. "They're two of a kind."

"We still need to figure out other things for the night." He closed his door. "Like where the trophies were bought and engraved and who provided the food. Was there a caterer?"

"Already have Abe looking into that among other things. He'll let me know if he finds anything helpful." She flipped on a blinker and glanced at him. "I've been so focused on the murder I haven't asked if you have any updates on Becca from your team."

They could use some positive news right about now, and he wished he had some to share. "They're working every angle, but nothing yet."

Mina sighed. "I keep praying that she's simply taking the week off or a long weekend, and she'll show up today."

"Me too," Nolan said, his prayers echoing her thoughts.

Mina fell silent, and Nolan used the rest of the drive to the airstrip at the inn to review and reply to a long list of emails.

He looked up as the inn and surrounding property came into view. He rarely approached while not driving and was free to take it all in. Majestic. His gaze traveled to the airstrip. An airstrip he owned. Him. A former civil servant. How crazy was that?

"Looks like some of the team has arrived." Mina lifted her hand from the steering wheel to gesture at the runway.

Four vans holding the Veritas logo on the side door had parked near the edge.

She shook her head. "I'd love to have the resources they have at their disposal."

"I hear you."

"But you have *this* place." She clenched the wheel.

"I never imagined I'd be able to afford any property, let alone an inn on the coast with panoramic views."

"So how *did* you afford it?"

Her suspicion was well deserved as she'd known he had little money. "One of my great aunts died and left it to me. Which is really odd. You know I wasn't close to my family, and that hasn't changed. I didn't really even know my aunt. I saw her a few times when I was a kid but that was it."

"You must've made quite an impression."

The grim look on her face said something, but he didn't know what. Maybe she thought he'd made the same impression on her and then didn't see her again. But that was a whole other thing. His family skated on the edge of breaking the law to earn a living. Maybe crossed the line, too, but he didn't want to know those details. As soon as he was old enough to realize what was going on, he couldn't abide being part of it.

He'd gotten a job in high school and worked every free minute to save money for college. He'd also made sure his grades were good enough for a scholarship so he could walk away from them.

Didn't matter. Not anymore. His so-called adoptive family was here with him. Had been with him since college. Honest. Caring. Responsible men and women who held God and His commandments in high esteem. They landed firmly on the side of legal enterprises and would never even contemplate profiting from illegal ventures.

Mina pulled into the parking lot as rotors thumped from offshore, the wind just starting to buffet the vehicle.

Her phone rang, and she answered it on speaker.

"Go ahead, El," she spoke loudly to be heard over the chopper.

"Our daylight search of Becca's property paid off," El said. "We found a female shoe under the bushes at the front door. The bottom is covered in blood. What do you want me to do with it?"

Mina cast a bright look at Nolan. "Leave it where you found it for the Veritas team to photograph and take into evidence. Make sure whoever is stationed at the front door is aware of the shoe's location and no one disturbs it."

"Roger that," El said. "Now that our search is complete, I'll be meeting Gabe to do the neighborhood door-to-door canvass."

"Let me know if you learn anything." Mina ended the call.

Nolan raised his voice over the approaching helicopter noise. "The shoe suggests she was at the scene when her father died and someone took her." He let that thought settle in. "I suppose she could've been afraid the shooter was coming for her, too, fled, and lost her shoe as she took off. Either way, she was there."

"Yeah." Mina shifted into park. "But your earlier suggestion that she killed her father and ran could be right too. I still don't buy it, but you could be right."

"Neither do I, but we can't rule it out." He opened his door.

The chopper approached the shoreline, the increasing *thwack-thwack-thwack* of the rotors and whine from the chopper's engine getting louder. He slid out to watch the landing. It hovered above, sending sand swirling in the air.

He lowered his head and narrowed his eyes.

Nice one. He should've stayed in the car to watch the chopper land, but since he'd gotten out, he waited in place. At the slowing whirr of rotors, he lifted his head again to see the large chopper on the ground and the side door slide open. Mina exited the car, and they rushed forward.

He expected Sierra as his contact to get out first, but the first person jumping down was a clean-shaven man with dark hair. He wore black tactical pants and a team shirt. Nolan put him in his late thirties. He carried himself with assurance as he made his way over to Nolan and Mina.

He stuck out his hand. "Blake Jenkins. I coordinate all the multi-disciplined law enforcement investigations for the Veritas Center. Since this project has grown from one crime scene to three, all perhaps connected, coordination will be priority."

"Then welcome." Nolan gripped his hand and accepted the firm shake. "I wasn't expecting you."

"My fault." A woman with shoulder-length blond hair and bangs called out as she approached them. She also offered her hand. "Sierra Rice. I head up the trace evidence group. We spoke on the phone."

Nolan and Mina introduced themselves as other team members piled out of both the vans and the helicopter, all converging on their location and looking expectantly at Sierra and Blake.

"Let me start by introducing you to everyone." Sierra placed a hand on Blake's arm. "I'm sure Blake has told you what he does for us, but you should know about his past as well. Sheriff Park, you'll be particularly interested to know he was a former sheriff as well."

"Please call me Mina." She shifted her attention to Blake. "And Blake, we'll have to find some time to compare notes and trade horror stories."

He gave a sharp nod.

Sierra moved her hand to a tall, well-built man with red hair who had an arm around the woman next to him. With her dark brown ponytail, she looked far too young to be on this top-notch team.

"This is Grady Houston." Sierra waved a hand toward the redhead.

"You have something go boom, I'm your guy." Grady grinned, and the woman next to him rolled her eyes.

Sierra shook her head. "He's our ballistics, firearms, and explosives expert. The ever patient woman next to him is his wife, Ainslie, one of our forensic photographers. And next to her is our other photographer, Chelsea Vale."

They didn't offer their hands, so Nolan nodded and smiled.

Sierra stepped down the line. "Last, but not least are my assistants, Chad Powell and Jeremiah Paulson."

Nolan shook hands with Chad, who had thinning dark hair and a slight build, then with Jeremiah, who was tall and wiry. His red hair outshone Grady's.

A sudden commotion behind them took Nolan's attention. An average-height, but well-built, guy with jet-black hair bounded from the pilot's door and jogged across the tarmac. He had a twinkle in his almond-shaped eyes. "I'm here. Let the party begin."

Sierra groaned. "Meet Dylan Wix, our most recent partner addition. He's an IT expert, and as you can see, also a pilot. He'll be collecting all of the electronics."

"I mean, not just *any* pilot." He blew his fingers and brushed them across his chest. "One of the top pilots in the area."

"Based on what rating?" Grady's tone was liberally laced with sarcasm. "The Dylan Wix rating scale?"

"I could say according to a recent internet poll, but I assume you'd think I fixed the voting." Dylan belted out a laugh.

"As you can see," Sierra said. "He's the life of our party."

"Yeah," Nolan said. "We have one of those on our team as well."

"Doesn't most every team?" Mina asked. "I know I've met a lot of life-of-the-party people on the teams I served on over the years."

"An insecure guy might infer that you mean this in a derogatory way," Dylan said. "But I always say we only have one life to live. Why live a dull one?"

"Be that as it may," Sierra said. "Today is all about the minutia of a crime scene. Actually, three crime scenes."

"To that end," Blake, a guy who seemed all business all

the time, said, "Sierra and I'll visit each scene with you while our team gets the vans in place and prepares to work."

"I'll take charge of one scene," Sierra said. "Then assign the others to Chad and Jeremiah so we can process them simultaneously. I'll review all the findings and the scenes again before we conclude our work. Any questions?"

"I just want to confirm that all of the results will come to me," Mina said.

Blake nodded and lifted an iPad from under his arm. "I have a contract here that we'll sign stipulating that very thing. You can also authorize us to share with anyone you might want to be included in this document as well."

"Just me for now," she said. "If that changes, I'll let you know."

Nolan wanted to say something. To argue. But he gritted his teeth and stood quietly while the Veritas staff eyed him and Mina, likely looking for any tension that might exist. He didn't want to communicate any unease. Mina had every right to get the forensic reports delivered to her, and she had every right not to share them with him. She said she would, and he hoped she did, but he knew she would only give him information she thought pertinent for him to know.

Not that he could do the same thing with her. Everything his team learned had already been shared with her, and everything they learned in the future would go via El as well.

Sierra clapped her hands. "Then let's get to the first crime scene. We have the address of the escape room, and we'll meet you there." She started off, and Blake followed her.

Mina and Nolan caught up to them.

"We have an envelope that needs processing too," Mina said. "It once held one of the escape room invitations sent to the team. Unfortunately, all of the invitations were surrendered to the man in charge of the evening and the other envelopes destroyed, so this is the only remaining one. It's in my car."

"And you should know," Nolan added, "it was thrown in the trash, so you might find interesting residue that has nothing to do with the mail delivery or origination."

"We'll mark that as exhibit one," Blake said.

"One of many things we'll be collecting today," Sierra added.

At their vehicles, Nolan stared at her. "Let's hope something you find leads us to the killer, because as of this moment, we have few promising leads."

13

The moment they arrived at the mansion, Sierra took charge of the scene, allowing Mina to stand back and observe. Maybe notice things she'd missed last night. Things that could move this investigation forward.

They checked in with the deputy on duty, and as they walked up the big, wide steps, Nolan described the details from the night before to Sierra and Blake.

Inside the large foyer, Sierra turned to Nolan. "So you don't think Smythe cooked the food on site?"

Nolan shook his head. "First of all, the house didn't smell like anything had been cooking. There were some pleasant food aromas, but only when he uncovered the serving dishes. Nothing as intense as if he'd cooked here. Second, I don't think he could've cleaned up the entire kitchen and packed up his supplies in the time we were in the escape room."

Sierra frowned. "So he likely didn't leave prints in the kitchen, but you can at least check with local caterers to see who might have supplied the food."

"Not many caterers in the area," Mina said. "And the meal wasn't your typical chicken dish, so I'm confident my sergeant will track that down."

Sierra shifted her attention back to Nolan. "You mentioned that you put your phones in a Faraday bag. Where is that bag now?"

"I'll show you." He took off down the hallway to the dining room, then stood back and pointed at the gleaming mahogany buffet. "We found them here after we got out of the escape room."

"Any thoughts that your phone was cloned while you were inside?" Blake asked.

Nolan blinked a few times. "Now that's something I didn't really think of. I'll have Hayden check that out."

Sierra got out a small notebook much like police officers carry and wrote something down. "We'll be sure to check the bag for Smythe's DNA."

"But he wore gloves," Nolan said.

"Now this is where you're underestimating Sierra's skills." Blake cracked the first smile they'd seen.

"We transfer DNA in many ways other than fingerprints. For example, he could have dry skin, scratched his face or his eyebrows and released flaky skin onto the gloves. Or brushed his arm or his face. All are good possibilities."

"Which is why we're so thankful you're here," Mina said.

Sierra smiled. "So, where is this escape room?"

"Follow me." Nolan strode down the hall and stopped outside the closed door.

"Has the door been closed the entire time?" Sierra asked.

Nolan shook his head. "Smythe unlocked it and it remained closed while we were inside the room, but we left it open when we went to search for him and to call 911."

Mina rested her hand on her sidearm. "If you're worried the scene was contaminated, I can assure you it's been protected from the moment one of my deputies arrived."

Sierra waved her hand. "I'm sure you took care of that,

and I'm not concerned. I'm just questioning the air quality inside, if we can retrieve DNA from an air sample."

"From the air?" Nolan gaped at her. "If that's possible, then forensics have changed a lot since I attended police academy."

"That it has, and it's changing all the time." Sierra retrieved gloves from her pocket and put them on. "It's not possible in all instances an air sample will give us DNA, but once I see the size of the room, I'll know more."

She bent down to the box of booties sitting by the door and slipped on a pair. "Please come into the room and close the door, but stay by the entrance while I get a good look at the scene."

She entered, Mina followed, and Nolan and Blake came behind. When Nolan closed the door, Mina understood what it must've been like to be trapped in this room with the mayor's body. Her gaze went directly to the locker where they'd found him, and she fought off a shiver. She considered herself a tough law enforcement officer, but no one ever got used to finding a murder victim. If they claimed they had, they were probably lying.

Sierra looked over her shoulder. "Which locker held the mayor's body?"

"The first one as you're entering the room," Nolan said. "If you look inside, you'll see the back is cut out, providing extra room for his body."

She peeked into the locker, then started down the room toward the punching bag, turning around to come back down the other side. She took notes as she walked and stood scribbling for a few moments before looking up. "This room will take considerable resources and time. It's likely the killer, or this Smythe fellow if he's not the killer, touched every item in this room. And like I mentioned with the

Faraday bag, DNA could be left in many forms in here. Think of it. One of them could simply have sneezed."

"Surely they would've wiped the object off," Mina said.

"They might have indeed, but even if they wiped it off, they likely still left DNA behind." Sierra turned to survey the room and shifted her stance as if fortifying herself for the task at hand. "Each removable item in here will have to be photographed and bagged. The fixed items and furniture will be processed in place, though I would like to see if the lockers can be dismantled to bring the one that held the mayor back to the lab."

"Do you need help with that?" Mina asked.

"Thank you, but no." Blake planted his hands on his hips. "Our team has taken apart far more challenging items than this, and they can handle it. After today we don't want anyone outside of our team in this room without our knowledge until the scene is finished."

"If you need to see this scene or the other two, just let me know, and I can arrange to escort you." Sierra moved her hands to encompass the space. "A room map will have to be created. In addition to copious photos. I'd also like to do a 3-D video so we can refer back to it if we need to."

Blake looked Mina directly in the eye. "And like she said, that will take time."

"How much time?" Mina asked, starting to wonder how long this killer would go free.

Sierra studied them as if she expected an argument. "This room alone will probably take one forensic expert plus a full-time photographer two days to complete."

"And don't forget the time on the other end in the lab." Blake let his hands fall to his side. "The items will have to be processed for DNA and fingerprints. Sierra will handle fingerprinting, and my wife, Emory, will process the DNA."

"Dare I ask how long we'll have to wait for that?" Nolan asked before Mina had a chance to voice the same question.

Sierra nipped her lower lip. "The actual DNA processing requires a full twenty-four hours, but locating, extracting, and quantifying it could eat up days. Honestly, with extensive potential evidence to process, it could be weeks. However, if you would like to prioritize the items we collect, that could speed things along."

Nolan let out a long breath. "I can give you a list of items that helped us solve the escape room mystery. Maybe we could start with those things."

"That sounds like a good idea," Mina said. "If our killer touched anything in this room, he likely touched those objects."

"Then I'll text you a list as soon as we finish up here," Nolan said.

Sierra nodded. "With your permission, I'd like to hold off on processing the kitchen and dining room until after we see what we locate here."

"I've already searched the kitchen for any takeout containers or other leads," Mina said. "And I've looked for trash taken out to the bins. We found nothing, so he must've taken it all with him."

"Makes sense," Blake said. "From what I've seen so far and heard from you all, we could be looking for a person with serious skills in evading law enforcement."

"We could even be looking for someone who once was in law enforcement," Nolan said.

Blake looked at Mina. "It might be worth investigating prior members of the local force, if you haven't already done that. Especially someone who was let go."

"That would be a short list," she said, but he was right. "I'll certainly look into it."

"There could be someone on that list who had a grievance with the mayor."

"I can't speak to the time when I didn't live here," she said. "But local politics can always play a role in hiring and firing. I suppose someone could've made the mayor mad and the sheriff terminated the employee."

"Then let's move on to Becca's house." Sierra changed the subject. "Maybe we'll find something there that will jump out as a strong lead, and we can get it handled quickly."

Mina could only hope so, but investigations didn't work that way. Leads weren't handed to law enforcement. Finding a killer required detached, diligent work. She only hoped she could put aside the fact that someone under her watch, someone she knew and liked, had been murdered and find the strength to lead such an investigation.

Nolan led Sierra and Blake toward Becca's main door. He was impressed with the Veritas staff, to say the least, and looked forward to their take on this crime scene. They were both very knowledgeable about crime and crime scenes, and Sierra seemed to have cutting-edge knowledge and skills in forensics. He didn't know how he was going to repay them for their kindness, but he would try to find a way.

His phone rang. Seeing Jude's name he answered. "Hold on a second."

He looked at Blake and Sierra. "I have to take this. Mina can show you around, and I'll be right in."

They departed, and Nolan turned his attention to his call. "Please tell me you have something about Becca to report."

"Not really. It's more like what I don't have to report. I

reviewed all of her social media accounts, and there's no mention of her going out of town."

Nolan wanted to pound something, anything, but he shoved his free hand into his hair instead. "Was there anything of interest in her accounts at all?"

"She was close to her dad, as we suspected. Lots of pictures of them doing things together. Not many friends. Two who seemed really close. I'll interview them in person this morning. The others were more like acquaintances. I'll get their phone numbers and give them a call after the interviews."

"Anything else?" Nolan asked, as his phone sounded a text that he ignored for now.

"Not for me, but Hayden's about to call you with an update. So stay tuned."

"Roger that," Nolan said and ended the call. So they couldn't confirm that Becca *was* out of town, but they also couldn't confirm that she hadn't gone out of town. They were really still stuck on square one.

He checked the text to find the list of family and friends that Daisy promised to provide. He replied with a *thank you* and then forwarded the list to Reece to begin researching.

He stowed his phone and entered the house. All three of the occupants turned to look at him. He shared the information from Jude.

"Mina has updated us on this situation," Sierra said. "I'm sorry that you weren't able to confirm good news on Becca."

"Then we move forward with the forensics and prove where this pool of blood came from." Nolan stopped to the left of the blood. "The footprint outside the window along with the bull's-eye in the window says the shooter was outside when he fired his weapon."

"Grady can confirm that for us." Blake pointed at the

slug in the wall. "Of course he'll also give you the ballistics information for that bullet too."

"The mayor's fatal wound was a through-and-through," Nolan said. "We're suspecting that's the bullet that killed him."

Sierra gave a firm nod. "We could potentially get DNA from the bullet. Not only the mayor's, but the shooter's as well. After Grady removes it, we'll be sure it's top priority for processing."

Odd. "Grady has to do it?"

"Removing a bullet from the item it's lodged in without damaging it can be tricky." Sierra lifted her shoulders. "We want to be sure we take every opportunity to preserve the slug so Grady can analyze it and we can try to locate that DNA. And since he's here, we should let him handle it."

"How likely is it that you'll get DNA?" Nolan asked.

"It happens, but not as often as we would like. Grady can give you more information on that." Sierra frowned. "The thing that we have to keep in mind here, is that even if we locate DNA samples, that doesn't mean they'll match to anyone in the CODIS database."

Nolan was familiar with the Combined DNA Index System, the FBI's national database that stored DNA profiles to help solve crimes and identify missing persons. He'd used it when hunting down the suspect who'd tried to kill the governor. He wished he had access to it for his missing persons work, but only law enforcement officers and labs like the Veritas Center could access it.

Blake's expression tightened. "Odds of matching to the database are better if a random burglar committed the murder."

Mina nodded. "He's most likely to have his DNA in the system."

"So true," Sierra said.

Nolan didn't like being the only person in the room who didn't understand this conversation, but he wasn't going to let his lack of knowledge embarrass him. Not when he needed to know this information. "I don't follow."

"Unless a murder is a crime of passion," Mina said, "it's likely that the shooter is someone who has been involved in other crimes before that. Criminals don't generally start right out committing murder but have a list of lesser crimes that escalate to a level where they're comfortable with taking someone's life."

"Oh. Right. Gotcha," Nolan said. "So the odds are good that they were busted somewhere along the line and their DNA will be in the system."

Blake nodded. "You should be proud of your sheriff. She's looking at all avenues and not forming a single theory, then setting out to prove her theory."

Mina blushed under his compliment, but Nolan was indeed proud of her.

Sierra jotted a note on her pad and stepped deeper into the room. She turned to face them. "Was this portable air conditioner unit running when you arrived or was it turned on later?"

A flash of something crossed Mina's face. Sierra's implication that someone modified the crime scene probably didn't sit too well with her, but also, she might be wondering if someone on her team had turned it on.

Nolan could end that worry. "It was on when we arrived."

"Are you sure?" Sierra asked.

"Positive," he said. "I remember thinking it was a bit early in the season to be running the AC, but then we've had some unseasonably warm weather, and it's been humid too. So I assumed they were cleaning the humidity out of the house."

"Is that a problem for forensics?" Mina asked.

"Problem." Sierra shook her head hard. "Not at all. In fact it's a good thing. Remember when I mentioned getting DNA samples from the air in the escape room? The same can be true in a home, but due to the large size of rooms open to one another, it makes it more difficult. However, we can find DNA on the surfaces of the air conditioner units for the usual users of a room as well as visitors."

"So if the killer came in the house to verify the mayor was dead and take his body, then his DNA might be on that AC unit?" Nolan clarified.

Sierra smiled. "Exactly. We'll still take air samples as they most likely denote the more recent occupants, where the air conditioning unit will more likely represent previous occupants."

Nolan shook his head. "It still surprises me where DNA can be located these days."

Her eyes lit up. "There are a number of research projects going on now, and it's an exciting time in environmental DNA. Seems like there's a new development every day. eDNA—environmental DNA shed from sources like skin and saliva—can be detected in so many places in the environment. That includes water, ice, air, soil. Even dust."

"A word of caution, though." Blake took a wide stance. "As of now, some of it's too experimental to use as evidence in a court of law, but it's enough information to give you a suspect to pursue."

"We'll take any help we can get," Mina said.

"Okay, so we'll process this entire room, plus the outside, making sure we get that shoe into evidence. Do you want us to handle the rest of the house too?"

"No," Mina said. "We gave it a thorough search and didn't see any indication of a disturbance or struggle. If that changes, I'll let you know."

Sierra closed her notepad and shoved it in her pocket. "The next stop is the mayor's house. It doesn't sound like you've found any forensics in his house at all. Am I right?"

"That's right," Mina said. "Since we can't yet prove that this was the murder scene for the mayor, Becca could've been killed here as far as we know. I was hoping you could use your special lights to search for blood that someone might have tried to clean up in his house."

"That we can do." Sierra clapped her hands, the sharp sound reverberating off the high ceiling. "So this is what we'll do. I, along with Ainslie and Jeremiah, will go to the escape room. I'll take air samples and process the fixtures in the room. This is where the work is more complicated, so I'll handle that. Then since there's so much in the room to be taken into evidence, and it isn't a very complicated task, I'll have Jeremy package the evidence after Ainslie photographs it."

"That sounds like a good plan," Nolan said. "What about this scene and the mayor's house?"

"Chad is a very skilled forensic technician, so I'll have him process this house and have Chelsea take photographs. Since that's the entire staff I brought with me assigned to duties, once I complete my work at the escape room, I'll go to the mayor's house and search for blood evidence."

"And of course, she'll oversee everything to make sure it's done correctly," Blake said. "Our team is quite capable of doing their jobs, but that's just who Sierra is."

"Aside from lives depending on us to do everything correctly, we also have to maintain our reputation as a premiere agency," Sierra said. "That means making sure our work is above reproach."

Blake nodded. "I'll see that Grady does the bullet trajectory along with removing the slug from this wall. He won't begin work until Chad has finished the forensics in the area so he doesn't disturb the evidence. I can notify you when he begins, if you like, so you can ask any questions you might have."

"That would be great." Mina smiled at Blake.

"From what you've told us," Blake said. "There's a computer at the mayor's office, his home, and one here that Dylan will need to image. Is that correct?"

"Image?" Nolan asked. "Does that mean making a copy of the computer's hard drive?"

Blake nodded. "Exactly. We need to do that to maintain the state of the computers for evidence. Any searches Dylan conducts, he'll do on the image."

"How long does that take?" Mina asked.

"Depends on the size of the hard drive and the complexity of it," Blake said. "Would you like me to get Dylan on the phone to give you more details?"

"That would be great," Mina said. "I was hoping once he took the computers into evidence that he might have time to search for information that I'm sure he could locate far faster than my one-man IT staff."

Blake got out his phone and made a video call. After Dylan answered, Blake held the phone out so Mina and Nolan could see the screen. "We have three computers to take into evidence and as far as I know no cell phones."

"That's right," Nolan said. "We haven't located any cell phones."

"How long would it take you to image the three computers?" Blake asked.

"We talking laptops or desktops?"

"Two laptops and one desktop," Mina said.

"Likely a couple of hours then," Dylan said. "I can take the laptops to the desktop location and image them all at the same time. Why do you ask?"

"Mina was hoping you would have time to search for information for them," Blake said.

"Yeah, sure. I don't have the computing power I'd have at the lab at my fingertips, but I should still be able to get more information than most people around here."

"Modest much?" Sierra asked.

"Why be modest when you're telling the truth?"

"And here I thought Nick was the team superstar." Nolan joked.

"He's good for an OG."

"Old guy?" Nolan asked. "He's at most in his late thirties. Just a few years older than us."

"Exactly. An old guy." Dylan laughed.

"Looks like we can't take you out of the office." Blake stared at his phone.

"Oops, better start to be on my best behavior as my mom always said." He chuckled again. "Anything else? If not send me the address to come retrieve the computers."

"I'll text you," Blake said, not seeming too happy with the new young guy, but he turned to them with a tight smile on his face. "I'll coordinate all of the staff and evidence collection, so if you have any questions while we're in town, would you please direct them to me so the techs can continue to do their jobs to the best of their abilities?"

"Of course," Mina said.

Blake gave a firm nod. "Also, we'll be sending the helicopter back to Portland at the end of the day with today's evidence so our staff there can begin processing it."

"That's wonderful." Mina gave a big smile.

The smile hadn't been directed at Nolan, but he felt his mouth turning up too. "I second Mina's comment and thank you for coming. Without you, I'm not sure we would be able to find Becca or solve this murder."

14

Mina didn't know what to expect when she and Nolan reached the marina and laid eyes on the boat owned by Mayor Sutton and his brother-in-law. But she had to admit surprise when she spotted Wade standing on such a fancy boat. She squinted to read the name painted on the back. *Off the Hook.* Yep, they had the right boat.

Having just finished his text to Sierra with the info he'd promised, Nolan let out a low whistle. "That's not just your basic fishing boat. That's more like a yacht. I'd say it's a fifty-footer or more."

She watched the shiny white boat bob in the slip. It was by far the largest boat in the marina. Boasting wood accents, it had a large deck with fishing poles mounted along the side.

Nolan held his hand over his eyes to block the sun. "Looks like he's got living quarters on the bottom and the helm is on top."

Wade sat in a recliner in the back, his head laid back and a hat over his face as if he were asleep.

"I'm actually surprised to see him out here at this time of year," she said.

Nolan nodded. "It doesn't make sense, based on what we learned on the internet."

On the drive over, he'd looked up the fishing seasons in this part of the country, and right now lingcod were the only fish that could be caught. That coupled with the usual bad weather in the spring wouldn't make for many tourists wanting to fish.

"Maybe he's just taking advantage of the nice weather," she said.

"One way to find out." He held his hand out, gesturing at the dock leading to Wade. "After you."

She started down the bouncy planks toward his boat. The sun shone radiantly, and a soft breeze blew over the rippling water. An ideal day to be on a boat, but they weren't here for pleasure boating. They had a job to do. She suspected it would be a death notification call as word wouldn't likely have reached Wade in a location away from Lost Lake. Unless of course someone had called and told him.

She stopped near the boat.

"Wade Collins," she called out to be heard above the seagulls chattering at the end of the dock.

His head snapped up. He turned to look at her and blinked several times. His nonexistent chin and wideset eyes gave him a shifty look. Or maybe she was pre-judging him based on what Daisy had to say about him. Still, it was hard to see someone like him alive and kicking when the man who had dedicated himself to helping others had been murdered.

"Who wants to know?" He stood and looked down on her. "Oh wait, right. I know you. You're the pretty lady sheriff for our county."

"This is my associate, Nolan Orr," she said, ignoring the

pretty lady comment. "Do we have permission to come aboard to talk to you for a moment?"

"I didn't do anything wrong." He scowled at her, giving her a moment's unease. He might be partners with the mayor, but he seemed to have a mean streak that Mayor Sutton didn't have.

"We didn't say you did." Nolan stepped close to her. "We just have something we need to talk to you about."

"Fine," he said. "But make it quick. I've got things to do."

Mina boarded the bobbing craft, forcing herself not to comment on what he had to do when they'd found him sleeping in the sun.

"So what's this about?" he asked.

Mina kept eye contact with him. "We're here to talk about your brother-in-law, Ernie."

"What about him?"

"So you haven't heard?"

"Heard what?"

"I'm sorry to tell you but we found his body last night. Someone shot him."

Wade gaped at her. "He's dead?"

"Yes," she said. "I'm sorry for your loss, Mr. Collins."

He slapped his wide-brimmed hat on his leg and ran a hand over his shiny bald head. "So someone shot him. Killed him. But who?"

"That's what we were hoping you could tell us," Nolan said.

Wade flashed his gaze to Nolan. "You don't mean me, do you? Think *I* killed him?"

"Where were you yesterday between three and five p.m.?" Nolan asked.

"Here." He gestured at his boat. "Just like today. The weather was too good to do anything but come out here."

Nolan arched an eyebrow. "Can anyone vouch for that?"

He nodded toward the land. "Check with the office. I signed in and out on the marina books. Got here around one o'clock and stayed until the sun set, so that was about seven o'clock."

"And you stayed in the marina?" Nolan asked. "Didn't take the boat out?"

"Well, yeah... I mean... I went for a little cruise, but that was all."

Mina kept her gaze pinned on him. "You could've put in at another marina and gone to see your brother-in-law from there."

"No, that's not possible. Not with a boat this big. I need to have permission to dock, and I don't have permission at other marinas." He shuffled his feet. "Think of these places like private parking lots. The public isn't allowed in and you have to gain access somehow."

"What about anchoring off the coast, putting on a wetsuit, and swimming to shore?" Mina asked. "Do you have a wetsuit onboard?"

"Only for emergencies, and I didn't put one on yesterday and swim to shore to kill Ernie. Why would you think I'd do that anyway? What reason would I have?"

"Who owns the boat?" Nolan asked.

"Ernie does now."

"Now?" she asked.

"We bought it together, but I've had some bad luck in getting enough clients for the business and needed money to live on. So he fronted me the money for my salary and took it off my share of the boat. By now, I figure he has to own all of it, or at least most of it."

Something a solid businessman would know. "Did you buy the boat outright when you got it or did you finance it?"

"Finance, man. This baby cost more than two hundred grand, and I've never had that kind of cash. Or even half of it. So Ernie paid the deposit and financed it in his name. But we drew up a legal agreement stating our ownership details. I helped make the payment whenever the business income exceeded the salary we agreed on."

"What happens to the boat in the event of Ernie's death?" she asked.

"Now wait a minute." He scowled. "You don't mean you think I killed him so I could get the boat. Well, I didn't. I don't even know what's in his will."

"Were the two of you close?" Mina asked.

"Close? No, I wouldn't say that. I saw him more when my sister was alive. After she died, we still got together for a beer every now and then, but we didn't have much in common."

"Not even fishing?" Nolan asked.

"Nope. Ernie didn't like to fish."

Unbelievable. "Then why in the world did he agree to buy a boat with you?"

"It was a business investment. A good one. Just a few miles offshore, we've got forty to a hundred twenty-five feet of water offering the best ocean-bottom fishing opportunities on the Oregon Coast. We were supposed to both make money on the deal. Wasn't my fault that we haven't. Just hasn't gone my way."

He clearly didn't take responsibility for the business failure, but she didn't think he killed his brother-in-law. "Do you have any idea of who might want to kill Ernie?"

He scratched his belly hanging over a tight belt. "Nah, everybody loved him. I suppose some nutso psycho who didn't like his politics might've gone after him. After all, that's happening all over the world today."

He could have a valid point.

Mina got out her phone and displayed Smythe's digital

image. "Have you ever seen this man or do you know who he is?"

He studied the picture. "Nope. Never seen the guy before."

"When was the last time you saw Ernie?"

"Hmm, I don't remember exactly. Was one day a few weeks ago when I went into his office to talk about my finances."

"Did he seem unusually concerned or preoccupied by anything?" she asked.

"Maybe a little, but he had a lot on his plate with his job, so I didn't think much of it."

"Do you know if he was dating anyone?" Nolan asked.

"Ernie?" Wade let out a boisterous laugh. "Nah, he was a one-woman man, and I don't think he'd yet moved on from my sister. I can't wrap my head around the fact that he's gone." Wade swung his head. "Guess I better find out about that will to see if I still have a job."

And there, the man showed his true colors. More worried about his job than mourning the loss of his brother-in-law.

"We haven't been able to contact Becca to let her know. Have you seen her lately?"

"Bex? Yeah. Last week. On our usual Wednesday night date that we've had since she was a kid. We had dinner together at the Rusty Hull. I can't get enough of those hush puppies."

"Did she mention that she was going on a trip, or did she seem to be troubled by anything?" Mina asked.

"No trip and no troubles." Worry took over his expression, the first honest emotion she'd seen from him. "Is she okay?"

"Like I said. We haven't been able to find her."

"You're looking for her though, right? I mean, yeah, you

wanna find Ernie's killer, but he isn't going to get more dead. She could be hurt and need you."

Ah, such sensitivity.

"My team is investigating," Nolan said. "We're working on it full-time and doing everything we can to locate her."

"You'll let me know the minute you find her?" He worried his lower lip between his teeth. "I mean, I ain't never gonna have any kids, and she's the closest thing I'll ever get. I couldn't lose her."

"We'll let you know," Mina said. "If there's nothing else you think we should know about Becca's disappearance or the mayor's death, we'll be going."

"Nothing that I can think of. But I think I might head home in case Bex has shown up there for some reason."

Mina got out her business card and handed it to him. "Call me if she's there. And if she is, it's up to you whether you want to tell her about her father or if you want us to."

"Man. Man." He ran a hand over his head and clamped it on the back of his neck. "I've never much liked you cops, but now I see you have a tough job telling people that someone they love has died. Still, I think I'd like to tell her. She'll take it better from me than from you."

Mina nodded and climbed over the side of the boat to the dock. Wade Collins wasn't a man that she could highly respect, but at least in the end, he showed that he wasn't in everything for himself alone. He appeared to care about his niece, and perhaps that said more about the likelihood of him being a killer than anything else.

Nolan had never attended an autopsy, so he wasn't certain how he would react. He thought he could handle it, but then he couldn't be sure. Mina, on the other hand, didn't seem to be nervous at all and marched right through the doorway of the hospital morgue. She paused in the vestibule outside the exam room. Nolan kept at a slower pace, adding the facial shield to his white suit provided by Dr. Osborne.

Nolan wasn't eager to enter the autopsy suite. His phone rang, giving him a reprieve. "Hold up."

He dug his phone out from inside the white suit and looked at the screen. "Hayden. Good!" He accepted the call. "Putting you on speaker so Mina can hear what you have to report."

"I did a background check on both Becca and the mayor," Hayden said. "There was nothing in either one to suggest something troublesome. Unfortunately, I don't have anything to report that can help find Becca. She hasn't used a credit card or debit card since the mayor's death."

"But you have something to report, or you wouldn't waste time calling me," Nolan said.

"Yeah, the mayor's finances are sketchy."

"Sketchy how?" Mina asked.

"He's deposited large sums of money for the last four months. Most of it coming from an auction house in Medford. Other deposits are electronic payments from PayPal for what looks like the sale of eBay items."

Mina blinked. "He's selling things off?"

"Looks like it. Then he's turning around and taking the money out in multiple cash withdrawals just below ten grand. Likely to stay under the threshold over which banks must report cash withdrawals to the feds."

"So he didn't want Uncle Sam to know about the money and perhaps question it," Mina said. "But he needed cash."

"That's the odd part," Hayden said. "He has a healthy balance in both his savings and checking account, and if you add up all the money he's received and withdrawn, it wouldn't even touch the amount in his accounts."

"So he didn't need to sell things to get this money that he was using for something." Nolan shook his head. "What if someone was blackmailing him?"

"Over what?" Mina asked. "He was squeaky clean, and no one likely had anything to blackmail him about."

"Everyone has secrets," Nolan answered.

"And I just have to find out what his are, but nothing as of yet." Hayden sighed. "I have several algorithms that are scraping the internet right now. Maybe they'll turn up something actionable. Also should reveal any properties he might own that we don't know about, but so far that's been a bust too."

"Thanks for your diligence," Mina said.

"Have you thought about checking out our phones to see if Smythe put trackers or cloned them?" Nolan asked.

"Already checked mine out and a few of the other ones. Nothing, but I'd like to examine them all."

"Perfect. I'll give you mine when I see you again. Let us know what else you find." He ended the call.

Mina looked at him. "Maybe the autopsy will give us the insight we need."

She entered the room. Nolan lowered his shield as if it could protect himself from the upcoming sight and trailed her into the sterile space. An antiseptic smell laden with death hit him, and he swallowed hard to keep nausea at bay.

He averted his gaze from the two stainless steel tables in the middle of the space to take in a wall of stainless steel sinks and another one with large drawers used to hold bodies. He eased out a long breath and shifted to face the mayor lying on the closest table, his insides splayed open. The doctor stood over him.

Nolan's stomach turned, and he wished he hadn't eaten lunch. Not that he thought he was going to lose it, but his stomach roiled in queasy waves.

Mina strode right up to the table, and Nolan trailed behind her.

Dr. Osborne looked up. "Better late than never I guess."

Mina apologized. "We got sidetracked in an update meeting for locating Becca."

Dr. Osborne's frustrated look melted into a soft expression. "Any luck in finding her?"

Mina shook her head.

He gave one of his hard nods that seemed designed to handle difficult news and turned his attention to the body. "I've completed my initial assessment. As you can see, he has various bruises on his head, but they were made postmortem."

"Could they have been made while moving the body to the locker?" Nolan asked.

"Most definitely," Dr. Osborne said. "In fact, that was what I was going to suggest. I've also made the cut. There's nothing under his nails and no broken nails either. No perimortem bruising or other marks on the body. So the man didn't struggle or fight for his life."

"That wouldn't be unusual, though, right?" Mina asked. "Not when it appears as if he was shot from a distance."

"I'm not sure where you're getting the information that he was shot at a distance, but I can tell you from looking at the lack of stippling on the wound, that you're correct."

"We believe he was gunned down at Becca's house from outside, through a window," Mina said. "I'd say from about twenty-five feet."

"That would be fitting for the size of the entry wound." Dr. Osborne shifted on his feet.

"Any thoughts on ammo used?" Nolan asked.

Osborne nodded. "The wound and my experience as a field doctor suggests 9mm."

Mina changed her focus to Nolan. "Dr. Osborne served in the Iraq war."

Osborne frowned. "Army medical corps. I saw more bullet holes in bodies than you can imagine." He stiffened his shoulders and peered at the body. "I've also confirmed that the bullet exited his back as we suspected when we retrieved him."

"Is there anything else you can tell us at this point?" Nolan asked.

"I've reviewed his stomach contents." He held up a bowl with sloshing liquid which brought Nolan closer to hurling than anything else. "His last meal consisted of salmon, coleslaw, and hush puppies."

"He ate at the Rusty Hull." Mina's eyes sparked with the enthusiasm of a lead. "The only restaurant in town that serves hush puppies. And it's the right time of year for fresh Chinook salmon from the Rogue."

"My thoughts too," Dr. Osborne said. "Based on food digestion I observed, he would've had lunch there."

Mina's mouth turned down. "They require reservations for dinner in every season but not lunch, so they won't have a record of him dining there except for a credit card."

"Sounds like you eat there often," Nolan said.

"Best seafood in town, and mostly it's takeout for me." She gave him an awkward glance. "Hopefully, they'll remember the mayor coming in and know who he dined with, if anyone."

"That would be great," Nolan said.

Osborne cleared his throat. "You should also know I ran a rapid drug test."

Mina gaped at him. "For the mayor? Surely you're not looking for illegal drugs."

"Not exactly," he said. "I run the test for anyone who dies

under suspicious circumstances, and you don't get more suspicious than a bullet to the heart."

Nolan agreed. "But you didn't find anything, right?"

"Actually, I did. Not illegal anymore, but the report showed marijuana in his system."

"Really?" Mina asked. "The mayor was high at lunch?"

"I wouldn't say he was high, but I would say he was taking marijuana for pain."

"What kind of pain?" Nolan asked.

The doctor pointed to the mayor's abdomen. "His body is riddled with cancer. In my opinion, he had, at most, a couple of months left to live."

"Man, that's hard news to take." Mina ran a hand around the back of her neck. "I wonder if he told anyone? I mean, if he told Daisy, she didn't mention it. If she knew, I think she would've said something."

Nolan processed the news. "It could explain the times he was away from the office when Daisy didn't know where he went. He might've been undergoing chemo or radiation or just going to doctors' appointments."

"I suppose he could've done all of that without anyone knowing it," Osborne said. "Even if he lost his hair."

"Right, because he already shaved his head." Nolan gave the situation more thought. "We need to follow up with Daisy. See if she knew about this, then take some time to figure out what it could mean for his murder."

"You think the cancer could be playing a part?" Mina blinked up at him. "Like maybe he hired someone to end his life so he didn't have to go through the decline in dying?"

Could that be it, and they weren't looking for a cold-blooded murderer? "I hadn't thought of that, but now that you mention it, it's a possibility."

"It would be an odd way to do it, though," Osborne said. "So violent."

"Very odd, and why hire someone when he could simply have turned a gun on himself?" she asked.

"Maybe he didn't want anyone to know he committed suicide," Nolan said. "Maybe he has an insurance policy that pays out to Becca, and he wanted to make sure she got that money."

Mina gave a vigorous nod. "We'll have to check for that policy, then, won't we?"

They would. Without a doubt.

Was this invasive cancer actually linked to their investigation? Nolan didn't know, but it was a possibility, and one they couldn't ignore if they were to bring his killer to justice.

15

Nolan had eaten at the Rusty Hull a few times, and he highly recommended the food. He also recommended the atmosphere. The laid-back, dimly lit, remodeled fishery had multiple rooms, all decorated with nautical items. Not in-your-face kinds of things, but rusty old items that looked like they'd been at the bottom of the ocean for years.

Nolan stopped to inhale the savory scent of fried seafood mixed with the pungent smell of today's fresh catch lingering in the air. His queasiness had subsided on the drive over, and his stomach gave a loud growl of approval.

If Mina noticed, she didn't let on, but went straight to the greeter. He hung back to observe.

The greeter stand was positioned near the door. Fresh fish and oysters on the half shell in refrigerated cases stood next to a tank with live lobsters. Diners could pick up their seafood of choice on the way in and have it cooked to their specifications, or as in the case of the oysters, served raw on the half shell.

"Afternoon, Amy," Mina said.

"Hey, Sheriff." The young blond woman in a white blouse and black pants fidgeted with her hands sitting on the wooden stand. "Take out as usual, or are you wanting a table today?"

"I'm here for information about Mayor Sutton," Mina said, skipping any social niceties.

"Ernie?" A broad smile lifted Amy's mouth. "He's one of our regulars. The sweetest guy ever. What can I tell you?"

"Did he have lunch here yesterday?"

Amy put a finger on her chin. "You know, he comes in so often I'm not sure."

"Is there anyone here who could confirm it for us?" Mina asked.

"Paisley." She smiled again. "He has a regular table, and she's always his server. She would know."

"Then please take me to Paisley."

"This way." Amy traveled to the end of the small room and turned left.

Nolan let Mina go first, and they kept up with Amy until she stopped in the middle of the room beside a plush booth. "This is Ernie's favorite spot. Go ahead and have a seat, and I'll send Paisley out to you."

She rushed off, and Mina and Nolan slid into the booth on opposite sides of the table.

Mina's focus remained on Amy as she disappeared through swinging doors. "Obviously, they haven't heard about the mayor's death. I'm glad it hasn't made the grapevine yet."

"Surprising for this town." His proximity to Mina in the small booth left him uncomfortable, and he clamped his hands on his knees to keep from fidgeting. "Which is one of the reasons I found it hard to believe that the hotel clerk couldn't find you that summer."

She whipped her head around to study him. "Abby told me you followed up with Tommy."

He wasn't sure if now was a good time to talk about it,

but they didn't have anything else to do. "I didn't give up until I talked to your parents."

She locked gazes with him. "They never told me."

He worked hard to keep his mouth from falling open. "All this time, I thought you were blowing me off."

Her eyes softened, and she rested her hands on the table. "Just the opposite. For a very long time, I hoped you would come back. But when you didn't, I had to move on, and that meant leaving town. Too many memories with you here."

He wanted to take her hands, but didn't know how she would react, so he resisted the urge. "I thought coming back here would be easy. That the beauty of the area and the scenery would take over. Enjoy the friendliness of the residents."

"But it hasn't been that way?" She looked like she was holding her breath as she waited for his answer.

"No," he all but whispered. "I see you at every turn and remember the amazing week we had together." He gave in and placed his hand over hers, the touch going straight to his heart. "Since this was all a misunderstanding, maybe we should give things between us another chance."

"I don't know." She closed her eyes for a long moment. When she opened them he could see the doubt lodged there.

He tightened his hand on hers. "You still don't believe me. Don't trust me."

She didn't answer right away but took a deep breath and let it out slowly. "I've believed the worst of you for five years. It's going to take me more than a day to change that."

He studied her expression and found something else. Something he couldn't decipher. But he would take a stab at it. "You need to talk to your parents, don't you? You need to be sure that I did indeed go to their house back then."

She jerked her hands free. "I'm sorry. I do."

He wanted to keep pushing. To win her trust, but he could do no more for now. He had to give her time and space. Let her work things out for herself.

A short, dark-haired woman wearing a white blouse, black pants, and white apron approached the table. "Hi, Sheriff. Amy says you need to talk to me."

Mina shifted to face the server. "Thank you for seeing us, Paisley. We have some questions about Mayor Sutton."

Paisley's eyes narrowed. "What do you need to know?"

"Did he have lunch here yesterday?"

"He did."

"Was he alone?"

Paisley shook her head, and her ponytail swung in arcs behind her. "He was with a man I didn't recognize. Usually Ernie introduces me to his guests, but this time he didn't say a word."

"Was it a business meal?" Nolan asked.

Paisley narrowed her gaze. "Didn't seem like it."

"Were they friendly?" Mina asked.

She swung that ponytail again. "Actually, they were arguing about something."

Mina leaned closer to the server. "Did you hear what they were talking about?"

"No," she said with certainty. "They clammed up every time I came close to the table. I did hear what sounded like the word 'taxes'."

Taxes. Unexpected. "And you're sure you don't know this man?"

"I don't." She pressed her hands down her apron as if wiping off a distasteful thought. "It wasn't like Ernie to argue with people, so I asked the others if they knew him. No one did."

Could they be on to something? Was this man blackmailing the mayor, and was he the recipient of the money Mayor Sutton had been withdrawing from his account?

Mina got out her phone and displayed the digital sketch of Smythe. "Was this the man?"

Paisley studied it, her forehead creasing. "No. Definitely not."

"Have you ever seen the guy in here before?" Mina stowed her phone.

"No."

The perfume smell at the mayor's house came to Nolan's mind. "Did the mayor ever have lunch with a woman he seemed romantically involved with?"

Paisley gnawed on her lower lip. "I don't know about romantically involved, but he had lunch with the same woman a few times lately. They've huddled together, talking and whispering. It's not normal for the mayor to try to keep his conversation so quiet, and it's unusual for him to be meeting with a woman I've never seen before."

"And he didn't introduce you to this woman either?" Mina asked.

"No, and just like the guy yesterday, I asked the others and no one knew her. I hinted around a few times for an introduction, but Ernie just sidestepped it. I figured it was none of my business, so I left it alone."

"Can you describe her for us?" Nolan asked.

"An older woman probably around Ernie's age. She dressed expensively. Tailored suits. Pearls. She had gray hair with white streaks in a blunt cut and always wore large diamond stud earrings." Paisley got a sour look on her face. "But she also had a big honking diamond ring on her finger, so she was likely married. I figured that's why Ernie wasn't introducing me."

"You mean you thought he was having an affair with her?" Nolan clarified.

"Yeah." Her gaze ping-ponged around the room as if unable to look at them. "I didn't see Ernie as the kind of guy who would have an affair with a married woman, but then none of us are perfect."

"Did she wear perfume?" Mina asked. "Specifically Chanel N°5?"

"Oh man, yeah. She laid her perfume on heavy, but I don't know what brand it was."

Mina slid closer to Paisley. "Has the mayor seemed off or worried lately?"

She frowned. "His appetite has been off, but he's been his cheerful self all the time. I asked him about his appetite, but he said he had some bug that he couldn't seem to shake. Still, at lunch yesterday, he was able to eat his salmon and hush puppies with no problem. Even asked for seconds on the hush puppies."

"Did he always pay for the meals with this woman?" Nolan asked.

"I don't ever remember a time he let anyone else pay. Even the guy he argued with." Paisley's eyes narrowed. "What's this all about, anyway?"

Mina leaned close to Paisley. "I'm sorry to say that Mayor Sutton has been murdered."

"Murdered!" Paisley grabbed hold of the table. "Who would want to kill Ernie?"

"That's what I was hoping to ask you." She kept her attention on Paisley. "Is there anyone you've seen the mayor dining with who you think might be out to get him? Other than the guy he argued with?"

"I mean, he's had some good-natured political discussions with people, and he always argued with his brother-in-law before Wade stomped out. There didn't seem to be any love loss there, but Ernie didn't seem to give up on the deadbeat. Just kept giving the guy money and buying his lunch on top of it."

"The mayor really was a top-notch guy," Mina said, her tone ringing with sincerity. "Anyone else you can think of who he might've had a negative interaction with?"

"There was never anyone who seemed really angry with him until yesterday." Her eyes flashed open. "Wait. Do you think that's the man who killed him? A killer was in here yesterday? Oh my gosh!"

Mina took Paisley's hand. "Now don't jump to conclusions. We don't know this man had anything to do with his death."

Paisley stood staring at Mina. "But he could've, right?"

"Of course, he could've." Mina released the server's hand and glanced around. "I don't suppose you have any security cameras on the property."

Paisley shook her head. "Folks around here don't much like them, and we respect their privacy."

Mina let out a breath that sounded like it carried all of her frustration with it. "Would you be willing to come down to the office and describe him and the woman Mayor Sutton had lunches with so my artist can make sketches of them?"

"Of course. If you think that will help, I'm glad to do it for Ernie." She rubbed her hands over her forearms. "I can't believe he was murdered. Not only that it was Ernie, but that anyone was murdered in our small town. This world. What's it coming to?"

Nolan couldn't agree more, but didn't go there to distract from the point of the interview.

"If you'd make your way to the office now," Mina said. "I'll have my deputy waiting."

"I'm on my way." Paisley started untying her apron.

"One more thing," Mina said. "I need you to keep this

information to yourself. No mentioning his murder to anyone. It's important for our investigation."

"It'll be hard, but I can do it." She rushed towards the swinging doors.

Nolan looked at Mina. "Do you think this man could be our killer?"

She slid out of the booth. "It never pays to jump to conclusions in this business."

"Agreed," he said, making strong eye contact. "But if I were a jump-to-conclusions kind of person, I sure think he's the man we're looking for."

"But what about the woman?" Mina asked, taking off for the exit. "She sounds like she could be behind the Chanel N°5 we smelled at the mayor's house."

He hurried to keep up with her. "I suppose she could've killed him, but then using a gun to murder someone is not a woman's typical way to commit murder."

Mina looked over her shoulder at him. "You're right. Women prefer less violent methods, and they tend to kill inside and men outside, so that fits."

"That's assuming the blood at Becca's house belongs to the mayor."

"Yes," she said, holding the door open. "But this woman is high on my suspect list along with the man Ernie had lunch with."

They stepped into the late afternoon, sunshine slowly fading but still adding warmth to the spring day.

"We need to check in with Abe and El," she said. "See what progress they've made, and then the Veritas team too. Maybe they have something to report."

Nolan nodded and followed her to her vehicle. He thought both teams would've shared any big leads they found as they located them, but he could be wrong, and it wouldn't hurt to check in. After all, the sergeant or detective might have news. A good thing, as he and Mina would need a direction to head in after this interview with Paisley left them with more questions than answers.

16

Mina nodded a greeting at Grace, the uniformed desk clerk in her office, but didn't take the time to introduce Nolan. She hurried straight to the small bullpen where Sergeant Abell and Detective Lyons occupied large cubicles. El investigated all crimes, and Abe was responsible for staffing and patrol schedules. Plus, he was first on scene when an unusual problem arose. Unless he was off duty—like last night—when she took charge.

He sat at his desk, his focus on his computer screen. He'd run against her in the sheriff's election, and she'd thought it would be tough to manage him, but he'd been a team player most of the time, albeit one with an attitude. She kept her eyes open for any unrest he might start in the ranks.

El was at her desk, too, but she'd arranged her computer on the outer L of her setup so she wouldn't have her back to people. She looked up and offered a tight smile. "Boss."

Abe spun.

"How's it going?" she asked stopping in the walkway between the two cubicles, Nolan posting up beside her.

"We've made progress," Abe said before El could speak.

"We've made progress too, but then hit a brick wall," Mina said and looked at El. "You should join in with us in case any of this information relates to Becca's investigation."

"Sure." El stood and rested against the end of her cubicle, her posture relaxed but her gaze sharp.

Mina shared their morning conversations with Palmer, Daisy, Wade, and Paisley. "One thing we can determine with the escape room set up is that we're dealing with premeditated murder and not a murder of passion. It's likely one of our suspects has it out not only for the mayor but the LLL team too as the killer has tried to pin the murder on them."

"Or they could simply have killed the mayor just to get one of the LLL team put away for murder," Abe said.

"You could be right, but as of now, we don't have any reason anyone might have it out for them."

Abe stared at Nolan. "Since you opened your business, have you failed to bring someone home alive?"

Nolan shook his head. "I know odds say it's going to happen, but we've been spared that outcome so far."

"Could mean it's not related to any past cases, but we should still look into them," Abe said.

"I think it's a waste of time, but you're right. We have to look at every possibility." Nolan gave Abe a tight smile. "I can have my team take care of that."

"As long as it's not Jude doing the looking," Mina said.

"Point taken," Nolan agreed.

She shifted her attention back to Abe. "We have nine suspects, and I'll need your help to narrow that list down."

"Nine?" El asked. "Mind listing them out for me?"

"In no particular order," Mina said, "we have the Smythe fella who we keep striking out on his true identity and where to find him. Number two is Jude."

"Not really a viable suspect," Nolan said.

Mina agreed. "But he's the only team member who has a

personal connection to the mayor and needs to remain on our list until we can somehow confirm his alibi. Same thing with Harmony's alibi. She stays on the list until we're sure she's not involved. My gut says Patriotic Puzzle could be our guy. He's the first person who's been overtly negative about the mayor other than the guy the mayor argued with at lunch."

"Trouble is, we don't know either of their identities," Nolan said.

Mina resisted offering a frustrated comeback that wouldn't help at all. "Next up is the mayor of Seaside Harbor, then the brother-in-law, Wade. We have Becca, and lastly, the woman he had lunch with whose perfume may be lingering in his house."

"Long list." Abe creased his forehead. "Especially for a force our size to pin down."

"We'll just have to do the best we can with the resources we have." Mina gestured at Nolan. "At least we have Nolan and his team to help us."

Abe started to roll his eyes, but Mina stared him down.

He stopped. "Before we go any further, I should tell you that Deputy Gibbs said he saw Mayor Sutton about a month ago at around three a.m. with a woman in his car. He turned onto the street for his private residence, so Gibbs thought the woman was Becca and didn't think anything more of it."

Mina raised an eyebrow. "Why didn't he mention that last night when I saw him at her house?"

"He'd forgotten about it, but then I specifically asked every deputy if they'd seen the mayor acting out of character."

"Good thinking," Mina said.

Abe thrust his chest out. "Yeah, well, it's a good idea because when I asked Gibbs, he remembered seeing the mayor."

"Might not have been Becca, though," Nolan said. "If not, that could reinforce our affair theory, though bringing a married girlfriend to his favorite restaurant where he's well-known and visible wouldn't be a wise move."

Mina nodded. "What about his phone records? They could help give us her identity. Any progress on getting them from the phone company?"

"I served the warrant." Abe's chest deflated. "But we haven't heard back from the provider. I'll put pressure on them today."

"And what about his financial records?"

"Same thing. I'll keep after the bank."

"Hayden's looking into them both," she said. "Has he been in touch with you?"

Abe nodded. "He's struck out so far on the phone records, so I told him about the warrants. He said he had the finances well in hand. I figured I'd concentrate on the phones."

"Yes, he called to tell us that he's been able to get into the mayor's finances." She explained what Hayden had learned.

"Maybe Dylan can help figure out what he's been selling," Nolan said.

"Dylan?" Abe stared at him as if he were an alien.

"The Veritas Center's IT person." Nolan explained about Dylan agreeing to help search for information that afternoon.

Abe's expression turned testy. "Anything he gets won't be legal. Same thing with your Hayden guy."

"That's not necessarily true," Nolan said. "But even if it is, the information they provide will move us along faster. Then you can produce the documents we need for any future trial."

Abe crossed his arms. "That's not how it's done, and you know it. A good defense lawyer will call into question how you could act on information before we even had it in hand."

"I'll instruct Dylan on the subject," Mina said. "Which I don't think he'll need as he does forensic information searches for investigations all the time."

Abe rocked his chair forward and planted his feet on the floor. "If it comes back to bite us, it's all on you."

"That's right," Mina glared right back at him, though she shouldn't let him get to her. "I'm the sheriff. If I get ousted for using unusual methods to find a killer, then you can step into the role you've wanted since you lost the election."

Abe whipped back in his chair as if he'd been slapped.

"I'm sorry. That was uncalled for." Mina said right away. "I let the stress of two major investigations get to me, and I took it out on you. I hope you'll accept my apology and not let this interfere with your work on the investigation."

He gave a sharp nod. "What specifically do you want me to do?"

"Paisley will come in to complete the sketches for the man who the mayor had lunch with yesterday and also the woman," Mina said. "When they're finished, be sure you send a copy to me. Then I want you to put out an alert for both of them and get it circulating around Lost Lake. Maybe someone has seen them or knows them. Wouldn't hurt to have it distributed to law enforcement in nearby counties as well. Let me know the minute anyone identifies them."

"I'll distribute them everywhere." Abe sat stone-faced.

She couldn't tell if he was holding her outburst against her or not. Not something she could waste any bandwidth on now. "I'll be sure to check my emails when they come in, and let you know if there's a problem."

"And when I'm done with that?"

"I'll give you a list of people who saw Daisy in the office

during the time of the mayor's murder. I need you to follow up with them to confirm her alibi."

"I can do that in my sleep." Abe frowned. "Is there something more challenging you want me to do?"

"Interview the mayor of Seaside Harbor. See if he and Mayor Sutton simply had a friendly rivalry or if there was more to it. Be sure to get his alibi for the time of death." She took a deep breath. He wouldn't like this one. "You're more familiar with deputies who worked here in the past. Since it seems like we're looking for someone with weapons experience, we might be looking at someone in our own office. Especially someone who was let go and has an interest in guns. Maybe a grudge against the mayor."

Abe shot forward in his seat. "You can't seriously think it's one of us."

"I don't, but we have to keep an open mind. You'll need to forget you're looking at people you know, or might've known, and be thorough."

He shook his head. "It's a waste of time if you ask me. We have more viable suspects we should be looking into."

She opened her mouth to respond but thought better of it to keep from getting into an argument. "I imagine you don't yet have any updates on the trophies, caterer, or phone Smythe listed on the contract, but thought I'd ask."

"Phone is a burner," he said, his tone sharp. "I'm trying for the records, but have to wait. I'll let you know when I know more on any of these things."

"Thank you," she said and meant it. "Lastly, can you check into Harmony Vance. See if there's a hidden connection between her and the mayor, giving her a motive to want to kill him."

"Finally, something interesting." Abe jotted some notes on the legal pad on his desk.

Her phone rang, and seeing the Veritas Center's name

flash on her screen, she quickly answered the call. "I'm with my team and am putting you on speaker."

"Glad I caught you," Sierra said. "I decided to quickly type the blood from the large pool in the entryway instead of waiting for the DNA results. I figured if we have a blood type you might be able to match it to Becca's or to her father's blood type."

"Great idea," Mina said, excitement building over potentially having an answer to where the murder scene was located. "So do you have a type?"

"Yes. Blood sample is type O. I tested several locations to be sure we weren't looking at a mixed blood pool, and we're not."

"So if I can get the mayor's and Becca's blood types, we could determine if this was the murder scene."

"Exactly," Sierra said. "Blood typing is routinely done at an autopsy. Maybe your medical examiner can provide you with the victim's type."

"He didn't mention it at the autopsy, but that doesn't mean he didn't do it," Mina said.

"You'll want to check back with him then," Sierra said. "Also, Grady will be doing his ballistics tests in about an hour if you have any questions for him."

"Thank you," Mina said. "We'll be there for sure."

She ended the call and dialed Dr. Osborne as others watched. She didn't care that they were waiting on her. This was too important to put off. She wanted to know for sure if they'd found the mayor's murder scene.

"Voicemail," she told the others and left a message for Dr. Osborne to call her back about the blood typing. She looked at Abe. "Find the name of the mayor's doctor and request a warrant for his medical records."

"It's possible he has the record at his house or at his work," Abe suggested.

"We have to go back to see Daisy this afternoon anyway," Nolan said. "If Dr. Osborne hasn't completed the blood typing, maybe she knows the mayor's type or where we can get it."

"We should request Becca's medical records too," El said.

"Not as easily done," Mina said. "We haven't proved she's missing or come to any harm, and I can't see a judge approving a warrant request. Our best bet is to search her home for that."

"I can take care of it this afternoon," El said. "Also, I'm meeting with the LLL team for a dinner meeting for an update on Becca's investigation. Nothing fancy for dinner. Just salad and pizza. Can you join us?"

"We'll make time for it," Mina said, looking at Nolan to see if he would argue with that.

He nodded. "Any response to the alert on Becca or her car?"

"Not really," Abe said. "We've had a couple of similar cars reported, but the plates don't match. Once we open it up to the public, I have no doubt we'll get our share of usual prank calls. I'll keep you informed of any genuine leads."

"Then we're done here," Mina said. "We'll be heading back to Becca's house to meet Grady. Call me the moment you get the mayor's blood type." Mina ran her gaze from one person to the next. "And be thinking. The biggest thing we need to answer is which one of these people has the most to gain by killing the mayor."

"We figure that out," Nolan held her gaze, "and we figure out our killer's identity."

She couldn't agree more. But it was too early in the investigation to determine who had the best motive to commit murder.

17

Nolan entered Becca's house, his shoe coverings brushing on the tile floor. Mina came to a stop next to him as he paused to look for Grady. She pointed to the room with the broken window. "He's over there."

Grady stood behind a tripod, holding an instrument that Nolan wasn't familiar with. They picked their way around the blood pool and evidence markers toward the weapons expert. He looked up, a grim expression on his face.

"I hope you have information for us," Mina said.

"I do. I've removed the bullet from the wall." He bent down to pick up a plastic evidence bag resting in a large tote filled with a variety of supplies. Inside the bag lay a mangled bullet. "It's a 9mm slug, copper-jacketed ball and supersonic. Most likely a 9mm +P with 115 to 124 grain, which I will confirm in the lab."

Interesting info, but Nolan wasn't a gun enthusiast, so he didn't know the implications of it all. He did know the copper jacketed ball and supersonic meant the lead bullet was encased with copper, which enabled the slug to maintain its shape at high velocities, making it suitable for supersonic speeds. But the other bit? Nah, he had no clue. The team used whatever ammo Reece recommended and left it up to her to know what they needed.

"And the shot that killed the mayor was taken through that window from the outside?" Mina asked.

"I can definitively say a shot was taken from there. At this point though, I can't tell you this bullet killed your mayor. The slug does appear to have blood and tissue residue on it, but again, that's something I'll have to confirm in the lab, and if so, have DNA run."

"The caliber you mentioned," Mina said, "is it something that's sufficient to have gone through the mayor's body?"

"Yes, that combined with the angle of the shot tells me it is."

"Is that what your thing on the tripod is for?" Nolan asked.

Grady nodded. "My trajectory calculations tell me the gun was fired reasonably close to perpendicular—ninety degrees—to the glass. At least within plus or minus fifteen degrees. That coupled with the caliber and special characteristics of the bullet is why we have a through-and-through. Anything less might not have exited the body."

"You said, *at this point* you can't tell us that it's the bullet that killed the mayor," Nolan said. "But will you at some point be able to tell us that it's the one that passed through his body?"

"Certainly, if there's blood and tissue residue that's positive for the mayor's DNA. But it also contains ground glass, which I can match to the window."

That seemed to strike Mina's interest. "How?"

He used a long tweezer to take the bullet out of the bag and display it for them. "Can you see the white glass embedded between the lead slug and the copper metal jacket?"

Mina leaned close to his hand. "Oh, yeah. I see it."

"We can take a sample of the window glass and compare the chemical makeup to the glass in the bullet."

"Thus proving the slug in the wall was fired through that window," Nolan said. "That, along with having the mayor's DNA, would prove it's the bullet that killed him and this is the murder scene."

Grady nodded, then frowned. "Until we have the DNA results or proof Becca is alive and unharmed, this bullet could've passed through her as well."

He secured the slug, then held up another bag. "We also recovered a spent cartridge casing outside the window by the footprint. We can process the casing for prints and DNA, too, leading to our shooter's ID. Any questions?"

Mina gave a slight shake of her head.

"We're good," Nolan said.

"Then that's all I have for now." Grady dropped the casing bag back into his kit. "I'll be returning to the lab tonight with all the logged evidence, and we'll get going with the DNA as soon as possible."

"I can't begin to thank you for your help," Mina said.

Grady waved a gloved hand. "No worries. It's what we do."

Blake approached them. "Dylan has collected both laptops and is retrieving the mayor's office machine now."

"Good timing." Mina smiled. "We need to talk to the mayor's assistant again, and while we're there, we can make sure he has everything he needs."

"I'm sure he does, but it's always nice to have follow-up." Blake took the firm stance Nolan was beginning to associate with him when he wanted to make a point. "As long as it doesn't impede in our investigation."

"Don't worry," Nolan said. "We won't get in the way."

"Thanks again for everything." Mina spun and headed for the door.

Outside, she looked at her watch. "Almost five. We have to hurry if we want to catch Daisy and Dylan in the office before she locks up for the day."

She jogged to her car and clicked open the locks. Nolan got in with her, and she traversed the roads like someone with years of familiarity in navigating them. She made the drive through Lost Lake in what Nolan could only believe was record time, not speaking but keeping her eyes on the road.

He watched the clock on the dashboard tick down until it hit three minutes after five, and she screeched to a halt in front of the courthouse in a reserved law enforcement space.

She was out of the vehicle before it even stopped rocking, and he had to run to catch up with her and climb the steps to the main entrance. They jogged over marble tile floors to the last door on the right. He jerked on it, half expecting it not to open and Daisy to be gone, but there she was at her desk, typing away on her keyboard.

She looked up and shot to her feet. "Did you find Ernie's killer?"

"No. Sorry, Daisy." Mina crossed the room. "We have a few more questions for you."

She sighed. "Then I guess your guy in the other room will continue to do whatever he's doing with Ernie's work machine."

"Let me just check in with him, and I'll be right back."

Her phone dinged as she disappeared into the room, making Nolan curious. But if it was important she would tell him. Instead, he gestured for Daisy to have a seat. He sat across from her. "How are you holding up, Daisy?"

A soft smile spread across her thinning lips. "You're just the sweetest for asking. Mina's lucky to have you in her life."

"I don't know if being sweet is a positive trait for a deputy." He chuckled.

"Oh, that. No." She waved a hand with a sparkling amethyst ring. "I'm not talking about being a deputy. I'm talking about what's going on between the two of you."

His mouth started to fall open, and he clamped it closed until he recovered from the surprise of her comment. "There's nothing going on between us that isn't professional."

"You may not be acting on your feelings, but there's a definite chemistry between you two." She leaned forward. "I'm not one to gossip, but it always finds its way to my office. I heard that you had a summer romance a few years back."

Nolan shifted uncomfortably, considering his response. He liked Daisy. She wasn't a gossip but was well-meaning. "I figured when Mina deputized me that people would bring up our past again."

"Like I said, I don't pass information like this along, but word on the street is that you left her without saying goodbye."

"Not that I feel like I need to defend myself"—though he actually felt like he *did* need to with Daisy—"but I was suddenly called back to duty at the White House and was unable to say goodbye to her in person. I left a note with the hotel desk clerk to give to her. Problem is, he didn't pass it on."

She firmed her jaw. "I figured there was more to the story than what I was hearing. I pride myself in being able to judge someone's character. I might only have met you a few times, but I know you're a wonderful man."

A rush of blood heated his neck and face under her compliment. He said the first thing that came to mind that didn't have to do with his botched summer with Mina. "I didn't know if we would still catch you in the office."

"Normally I'm gone by now," she tipped her head toward the door to the mayor's office, "but I'm not going to leave that man alone in there with all of our confidential documents."

Nolan loved her fierce determination to protect the information even when it wasn't necessary. "I'm sure it's okay to leave him alone here. He wouldn't be here if he wasn't trustworthy. He works for a reputable agency and has likely undergone a variety of background checks and criminal searches."

"I don't know." Daisy sniffed. "He seems a little bit too laid-back to be trusted."

He almost laughed at her logic, but he controlled himself. "Since when is being laid-back something that means you aren't trustworthy?"

She let out a long sigh. "I guess I'm just being protective of the mayor's things since he's not here to protect them himself."

Nolan gave her an understanding nod. "I know you were a fine assistant to him, and he was lucky to have you."

Tears formed in her eyes. Nolan grabbed a tissue to hand to her, but he didn't know what to say to make things better for her. Thankfully, Mina returned.

She took a seat in the other chair facing Daisy's desk. "Did Mayor Sutton tell you that he had cancer?"

"Cancer? Ernie?" Daisy's eyelashes fluttered. "He didn't say anything about that." She lowered her arms to her chair as if it was too difficult to hold them up. "Was it bad?"

"Terminal, according to the medical examiner."

"Why wouldn't he have told me?" She closed her eyes and shook her head. "I could've helped him through any treatments he was having." She twisted the tissue in her fingers. "Seems like he wanted to handle it on his own."

"I think you're right," Nolan said, hoping to ease her

discomfort. "We don't know that he's told anyone, but then again, we still haven't located Becca to ask her."

"Well, hopefully he *did* tell her, and she was at his side." Daisy leaned back in her chair. "That could explain his weight loss. The secretive calls too. The cryptic calendar entries could've been doctor's appointments. He could've been talking to doctors when I stepped into his office. And even the hotel bill could be for a stay in Portland for medical tests or a procedure."

"You could be right on all of that." Mina gave an encouraging smile. "But also, if he was romantically involved with a woman, then he could've told her about the cancer, and she was at his side."

Daisy clutched the strand of pearls at her neck. "I'd hate to think he wouldn't trust me with such a big thing, but I know Ernie had his reasons for everything he did."

Mina got out her phone and held it out to Daisy. "This is a sketch of the woman who had lunch with Ernie."

Nolan sat forward to see it too. This must be the text she received when she'd gone to talk to Dylan.

"Do you recognize her?" she asked.

"Yes." Daisy's head flashed up. "That's Janice James. Ernie's personal attorney."

"Attorney?" Mina asked. "I thought everyone in town used Wally Carpenter for their legal needs."

"I think pretty much everybody does, but Ernie went to college with Janice, and she's always been his attorney, as far as I know."

Mina locked her phone, and the light died on the screen. "I've never seen her around."

"She practices in Medford, and he usually goes to see her there. I've only met her once, and that was several years ago." Daisy narrowed her eyes. "I wonder, since he had a terminal diagnosis, if he was updating his will. He might not have taken care of that since his wife died."

"I don't suppose you have a copy of his will," Nolan said.

Daisy shook her head. "Again, that was personal and not something I had any part of."

"Would that also be true of his insurance policy?" Mina asked.

"Yes."

Mina tapped her phone screen and held it out again. "Do you recognize this man, Daisy?"

She gave the phone a long look. "No. Should I?"

"He had lunch with the mayor yesterday. The waitress said they had a heated argument."

"I don't know him. I don't know any man who would argue with Ernie." She scrubbed her hands together, shredding the tissue she'd been holding. "I wish I could be of more help."

"You're doing the best you can, Daisy." Nolan smiled at her. "That's all you can do, and we appreciate your help."

"We do indeed." Mina shoved her phone into her pocket. "One final question, and we'll be out of your hair. You wouldn't happen to know his blood type would you?"

"Yes! Yes!" Daisy gave a vigorous nod. "Finally! Something I can help with. Remember when the Red Cross started doing regular blood drives here last year? We gave blood together every time they came. He's type O."

"What about Becca?" Nolan knew they were pushing their luck, but if she had the same type as the mayor, even knowing the mayor's blood type wouldn't rule out Becca having been shot at her house. "Did she give blood too? Do you know her type?"

A wide smile spread across her face. "In fact she did. She's A."

"You're sure of this?" Mina asked.

"Positive. One time, we joked about genetics and whether the A meant Ernie was her father. To kill time at the bloodmobile, Ernie looked it up online. He showed her that, though it didn't prove she *was* his child, it also didn't say she couldn't be. She must've gotten her blood type from her mother."

"Is there any question about Ernie being her father?" Mina asked. "I mean, I've never heard any talk about that around town."

"No!" Daisy slammed her chair forward and sat upright. "Absolutely no question. We were just joking around."

Or maybe there was some truth to it. What started out as a fun challenge might have raised Becca's suspicion, and she'd checked into it, then learned that Ernie really wasn't her father.

Nolan didn't think this was a solid lead, but it was surely something to look into. Especially with Becca's disappearance. Maybe they were looking at this all wrong. Maybe she really did have motive and took off after killing him.

18

Giving Daisy a smile, Mina rose from her seat. She was motivated more than ever to find Becca and the mayor's killer. Problem was, their conversation with Daisy now led her to believe they had to find out if Becca's blood type meant Ernie was her father. Or had she just found out she was adopted, been lied to all of her life, and in anger, killed her father?

Mina needed to speak with Dr. Osborne to see if he could answer that question, and if not, find someone who could. But first, she needed to give Dylan a list of items they could use his help with. He'd been involved in doing something he couldn't stop when she'd gone in earlier, and he asked her to come back later.

Hopefully, now was later enough. She entered Mayor Sutton's office, Nolan joining her this time. Dylan, focus fixed on his computer, didn't look up. She hoped he wouldn't get angry at being interrupted twice in such a short time.

"Are you in a spot now where I can give you a list of items we need your assistance on?"

He held up a finger, then went back to typing on his

laptop. A few minutes later, he looked up. "Had to finish that up so the final image would start." He leaned the chair back and clasped his hands behind his head. "So what do you need from me?"

"The first thing I'd like you to do," she said, "is to trace the IP address of the person who completed the online building lease for the escape room."

He gave an offhanded wave. "A cinch. I'll just need the web address for the form used to submit a reservation."

Mina took out her notebook and wrote down the request. "I'll text it to you."

"So what's next?"

"I don't know if you can do this, but Jude French, one of the Lost Lake Locators team members, doesn't have an alibi for the time of the mayor's death. Since the escape room was set up with memorabilia from all team members, that makes all of them suspects. But five of them have solid alibies. Not Jude. He was alone in his car on his way back from Portland, and no one can vouch for him."

"How can I help with that?" Dylan asked.

"He was on the phone for the entire trip," Nolan said before she could. "Can you determine which towers the call pinged from, so we can have proof he wasn't in town during the window when the mayor was killed?"

"Yeah, sure," Dylan answered. "Give me his phone number, and I'll give you a triangulation report. But..." He paused. "Here's the thing, and I gotta think you already know this, even if I trace the call, that only says where his phone was located. Not that he was with it."

"You're right, we do know that," Nolan said. "But it'll still help to have proof that he could've been in his car as he says."

Dylan picked up a pen and grabbed a notebook. "Okay, his phone number?"

Nolan shared the number from his phone's contact list.

Dylan looked up. "So far, this shouldn't take me long. What else do you need?"

Mina took a step closer. "We have an Instagram user who left negative comments on the mayor's posts. We'd like to locate him, but obviously his address and phone number aren't accessible on Instagram. He goes by Patriotic Puzzle." She jotted @patrioticpuzzle on a slip of paper and handed it to him. "Can you find out his real name and contact info?"

Dylan tucked the paper in a file. "I can, but I have to tell you, you're not going to like what I have to do to get it."

"I'm good with that, if you are," Mina said.

He chuckled. "I'm good with whatever I have to do to help locate a killer."

"Maybe keep your procedures to yourself." Nolan laughed.

Dylan joined in.

Mina didn't want to waste time joking around. "Can you also look into Becca's social media? We've done a review of her accounts to see if she mentioned a trip somewhere, but I wondered if you can write an algorithm, or whatever it is that you do, to see if anyone has posted negative comments. Or even if it seems like she might've had a stalker or someone who wanted to do her harm?"

"That's a little more complicated and will take a little longer, but yeah, I can do that as well." Dylan scribbled on his legal pad.

"We've also looked into both the mayor and Becca's finances," Nolan said. "We've learned that the mayor was selling off things through an auction house and on eBay. He's received several deposits from PayPal, and we're hoping to find out what he was selling. Is there a way for you to learn that?"

"Well, yeah, I can easily do it if I find his passwords and

logins on his computer." He tapped the large monitor on the desk. "I'll start on that after the image finishes processing. If no passwords are on here, you won't like how I have to do it."

"Same rules. Don't tell us what you're doing, and I'm good with getting the information from you."

"I have one more thing for you." Nolan explained about the personal items in the escape room. "Can you find out where the person who set up the room could've gotten our police academy graduation photos?"

Dylan frowned. "Not having any idea who the setup person was, I can't tell you exactly where they could've gotten the pictures, but I can scrape the internet and let you know if I can come up with them."

Nolan frowned. "I guess that'll have to do until we have a better suspect for you."

Mina wouldn't be disappointed. Not when this guy was going to find something in all of his work, she was sure of it. "Is it also possible for you to use a sketch we had made of our suspect to search the internet for him?"

"I could do it, but I'll only get sketches that resemble him in return, not real people." He intertwined his fingers and cracked his knuckles. "If that's all, take off. I'll get what you need as fast as I can."

Mina slipped her notebook back into her pocket. "Call me the minute you know anything."

"Don't worry," Dylan said. "I'm more than glad to brag about what I find when I find it." He laughed and waved his fingers at them, then turned his attention to his laptop.

Back in Daisy's office, they said goodbye to her and stepped out into the darkness of Main Street, where Founder's Day decorations had already been erected at the courthouse and were being strung up on storefronts and light posts. But it was the stars glistening overhead in the picturesque little seaside town that caught Mina's eye.

Nolan had once been very romantic under similar skies when she was involved with him. The more time she spent with him, the more she thought that could happen again. If she would only let it. But not knowing for sure that he'd followed up, she would keep him at arm's length. If tonight's meeting with the team didn't go past her parents' usual bedtime, she would stop by their house and ask if he'd visited and they'd sent him on his way without telling her.

"Before our dinner meeting, do you want to try to question Wade about what he'd argued with the mayor about?"

Right. He was thinking about business, as she should be doing. She nodded. "I doubt that he's still on his boat at this time of night, so let's go by his place."

In her car, she got them on the road heading toward the ocean.

"Where does he live?" Nolan asked.

"He has a small cottage that his parents bought when he was a kid. It's worth a considerable amount of money now due to its location near the beach. I know the mortgage is paid off, and he only has to pay taxes and utilities."

Nolan swiveled in his seat to face her. "If he needed money, he could've taken out a second or even third mortgage on the place."

"Can you ask Dylan or Hayden to look into that?" she asked. "All of Wade's finances, for that matter?"

"Hayden has his plate full helping with Becca, so I'll text Dylan."

She glanced at him. "Before you do, can you look up the registration page for the mansion and send that to him too?"

"Sure thing." Nolan got out his phone and tapped the screen. "Okay, here it is. Sending the link and request to Dylan now."

"Perfect." She thought ahead. "Maybe we should hold off on visiting Wade until we've had a look at his finances so we know if he's lying to us about them."

"Sounds like a plan." Nolan's phone dinged. "Dylan's on it."

She made a quick turn and pointed the car toward the inn. She still wasn't comfortable at the inn or with Nolan, but she was getting there. Or maybe her mind was too focused on the murder and missing woman to think about her discomfort all the time. It was only in down times, like right now, that she allowed her mind to wander.

She had to keep them talking, but about what? They passed her church, giving her a topic. "Since my church is the only one in the area with a contemporary worship service, I figured I would run into you there."

"I remembered you said you liked to go to the early service, so I go to the late one."

She shot him a questioning look. "You were avoiding me?"

He curled his fingers into fists on his knees. "That sounds harsh, but yeah, I guess I was. I know I shouldn't still be bothered by the fact that you didn't reply to my note, but I am."

Why had she brought this subject up? She could've talked about anything in town. Even the weather. But now she felt like she needed to defend herself. "I'll try to stop by my parents' house tonight after this meeting to ask them about your visit."

She pulled into the lot and shifted into park.

His gaze locked on hers. "You're going to see them because you don't trust me."

She killed the engine. "Yeah, that sounds harsh, too, but I guess you're right."

"I can see how that could be. You've spent five years thinking I'm the bad guy. It's hard to change."

"Are you speaking from experience?" Her voice was starting to give away her inner turmoil, so she took a breath. "Are you having a hard time accepting the fact that I never got the note?"

"Maybe," he said and fell silent for a moment. "But the more time I spend with you, the more I know you wouldn't lie to me."

"Ditto for me." She pulled the key from the ignition. "Maybe we can get through this together."

"I'd like that."

She considered squeezing his hand but pushed out of the vehicle instead. By the time they reached the conference room that smelled like tangy pepperoni, the rest of the team was seated, except El, who stood at the head of the table. A whiteboard behind her held the list of suspects in the murder investigation.

El turned to Mina and tapped the marker against the board. "Has this list changed since I spoke to you this afternoon?"

"It stands for now." Mina shared their conversation with Daisy and Dylan. "I'm hoping Dylan is as good as he claims, and by the time we end this meeting, he'll have given us something else to go on."

El nodded. "Help yourself to the pizza and salad while we run through the assignments from last night. Then we'll go through the list of suspects to see what connection, if any, they might have with Becca's disappearance."

Mina nodded and headed for the food laid out on a credenza. She grabbed a monster-sized slice of pepperoni pizza and a plastic container holding a ready-made salad and took her food to the table. She plopped down on the open seat next to Abby. If circumstances were different,

Mina thought she might be friends with the former sheriff due to their common experiences.

"Hayden," El said. "You're first on the list. What have you learned?"

"Before I start on the background checks, you should know that Becca hasn't used a credit or debit card since the mayor's death."

"That doesn't bode well for her going out of town," Abby said.

El gave a somber nod. "It does make me suspect foul play or that fear sent her into hiding."

"Her social media doesn't show her going away on a trip either," Hayden said. "Be it a day or a week or a month, she doesn't mention anything. So either she's wise on security measures—not posting when and where she's gone for would-be stalkers and burglars—or she really didn't go out of town."

"Hayden gave me a list of her social media friends," Jude said. "I was able to talk to the ones who replied to her posts most often. None of them knew about a trip. However, one of them said she wouldn't put it past Becca to make a quick decision to go somewhere for a long weekend and not tell anyone. She said Becca had a stressful job, and she often needed alone time to recover."

"I interviewed her supervisor and coworkers at the county," Reece said. "She didn't show up for work today or call in. The guy said it was unlike her to miss work. Her coworkers seconded that."

"Did they mention her need to recuperate from work?" Mina stabbed her salad with a plastic fork.

"Not in so many words, but her supervisor did say she's a hypersensitive individual, and she often took the plight of her clients to heart."

"So maybe she's holed up in a cabin or motel somewhere," Mina said.

Reece nodded. "I'm already checking with hotels, motels, and B&Bs in the area. I'll let you know if I find anyone matching her description."

Mina smiled at her. "Good work, Reece."

El dropped her pizza slice on her plate. "What about the list of people Daisy made of Becca's and the mayor's local friends?"

Jude held his pizza near his mouth. "That's me. I've interviewed all but two of them, and they don't know where she might be. One mentioned a spa she liked to go to, but she's not there. I'll keep after the friends I haven't been able to connect with yet."

"So we still don't know for sure that she's in danger." Mina looked around the table. "But since she never misses work without calling in, that's most suspicious."

The others nodded.

"I still have those friends to interview," Jude said. "But my gut says she isn't out of town. The mayor's a different story. Daisy couldn't come up with many friends. He only had acquaintances. His birdwatching club would be the closest, and they didn't have a clue who would want to hurt him."

El looked at Hayden. "What did you find out on Becca's and the mayor's background check?"

"Both are squeaky clean," he said. "Except the deposits and withdrawals I mentioned for the mayor. He's definitely been selling items in an auction house and on eBay."

Mina set down her fork. "I know he had some pricey sports memorabilia he collected over the years. He displayed it on shelves in his office, but I didn't notice if it was missing when we were there. I'll stop by his place on my way home tonight to see if the collection is missing."

"But it's odd, right?" Hayden said. "He has plenty of money. Why sell anything to get more? There has to be another reason. And why then take it out in cash?"

Jude shoved his empty plate away. "Maybe he was doing it for Becca. She told me she didn't understand his fascination with collecting and wasn't into it. If he took care of selling it, she wouldn't have to deal with it after the cancer took him."

Gabe scowled. "But she would've seen the items disappearing, which means the mayor would've had to tell her about his cancer."

"Or not," Nolan said. "He might've told her he was tired of it and wanted to get rid of it."

Jude shook his head. "I don't buy that and neither would she. Not based on how much of a fanatic he was about it. Or at least that's what Becca said."

"I can vouch for that." Mina stabbed a juicy tomato. "He *was* fanatical about it."

"Any thoughts on what this has to do with her disappearance?" El set down her water bottle.

Reece wiped her mouth with a paper napkin. "What if she was helping him sell the memorabilia, and she went to meet someone who took advantage of her?"

Mina swallowed a tomato dripping with ranch dressing. "I can't see the mayor letting her meet some stranger alone. He would take care of that himself."

"Not if his health got in the way." Abby looked around the room. "He might've had chemo or radiation that day and was too sick to deliver the sold item."

As if trying to recall something, Hayden cocked his head. "There's no indication that he was selling on any sites where he would deliver the items. But I guess eBay does allow local deliveries."

"In any event," Mina closed her salad container, "the

only thing that really makes sense is the mayor was being blackmailed. Otherwise, where would the cash be going?"

Nolan leaned back and grabbed another slice of pizza. "Maybe to Wade."

"I suppose he could be giving him money," Mina said. "At least both Daisy and Paisley said he gave him money, but why do it in cash? He could just write checks."

Reece held a bite of salad midair. "Could it be payments for his cancer treatments? Paying with cash not to leave a trail that Becca might somehow find?"

Mina doubted it. "The city has good health insurance policies for their workers, so I would think most of that would be covered by his insurance."

"Look into that further, Reece," Nolan said. "See if it leads anywhere."

"You got it, boss."

Nolan grimaced, but Mina had no idea the reason for his dislike of being called boss.

"Keep both teams updated on that," El said. "On another note, our alerts on Becca and her vehicle haven't turned anything up, so we're putting out an appeal to the public. Gabe and I didn't find anything when we canvassed the neighborhood, either."

"What she said." Gabe chuckled, but for some reason he looked uncomfortable. "We reviewed a few security footage videos from nearby neighbors. Unfortunately, their cameras didn't record any cars or people on foot in the timeframe of the mayor's death."

Nolan shot to his feet. "We have to be missing something. We've never had so few leads after someone's been missing for more than twenty-four hours. We need to check and recheck everything we've done. Keep after it, and don't let even the smallest detail escape you."

He was feeling the pressure of finding this missing

woman. No doubt about it. The same pressure that was eating away at Mina. Might he want to leave the mayor's investigation to head up his team's search for Becca?

It was becoming clear that Becca hadn't simply gone away for the weekend. Sure, they didn't have proof, but what they did have suggested foul play.

Should she release Nolan from the mayor's investigation and allow him to return to his team and the search for Becca? Something she couldn't decide right now. She would spend the evening pondering it and praying that she'd do the right thing to bring Becca home alive.

19

Promptly at eight a.m. the next day, Nolan held the door for Mina to gain access to the posh attorney's office located in an equally posh neighborhood. The five named partners' names—Janice James one of them—were engraved on the wall above the tall reception desk. The young receptionist, dressed in a formal suit of navy blue paired with a white collared blouse, looked up at them and smiled a smile she clearly didn't mean. Terse, if such a thing could be said of a smile.

He and Mina had agreed on the drive over that she would take lead, so he waited for her to approach the desk, then stopped behind her, ready to take any action needed.

She dug out her badge and displayed it for the receptionist, whose name tag read Angela. "I'm Sheriff Park here to see Janice James."

"Do you have an appointment?"

"No, but this is regarding one of her clients. If you give her a call, I'm sure she'll be glad to see me."

"I'm sorry, but she only sees people with appointments."

"I'm sure she'll make an exception in this case."

Angela crossed her arms. "I know she won't."

Nolan was surprised at how polite Mina had been, but it was getting her nowhere.

Still, with her taking charge like this, he got a chance to see her in action. Her easygoing approach was confusing him. Surprised him even. When he first met her, she was more aggressive, a take-charge woman. Something he found very appealing and something he had expected more of as she'd become sheriff.

"Look," she stated firmly, "I've asked you nicely. You haven't cooperated. I'm a law-enforcement officer, and I am here to see one of your attorneys. I know if you call her and tell her that I'm here to talk to her about her client, Mayor Ernest Sutton, she'll want to see me. Appointment or not."

Angela simply blinked up at her.

"Okay, other than me bringing you up on charges for obstructing a murder investigation, if you don't pick up the phone and call Ms. James, I'll be forced to create a scene in front of your clients." Mina was glaring at the young woman now. "I'm pretty sure if that happens, one of the partners will step out here, and I'll tell them how uncooperative you've been. If I have to do that, you might as well pack your things now as you surely won't be keeping your job."

Angela snarled at her. "Fine. But if I get in trouble, I'm holding you responsible for it."

Nolan wanted to laugh. There was no way this young receptionist was going to hold Mina responsible for anything.

She picked up the phone's handset and called Janice to explain the situation. She frowned as she hung up, then looked at Mina. "Have a seat. She'll be right out."

Mina crossed the room to a plush chair and sat, taking in several deep breaths and letting them out.

Nolan took the chair next to her and leaned close.

"What happened to the day when young people respected law enforcement officers?"

She shook her head. "When I was her age, I was terrified of being caught doing something wrong. Not only from cops, but from my parents. Principal. Teachers. That respect seems to have disappeared in a lot of places. More so in the big city, but we still have issues with it."

"I thought you were very diplomatic with her at first." He placed his hands on the arms of his chair and settled back. "In fact, I was kind of surprised. The younger Mina I knew would've come in here guns blazing."

"Yeah, you're right. I guess I've changed." She tilted her head. "Part of it came from having to supervise Abe. Since he ran for sheriff when I did and lost, he can be a challenge at times, so I've had to adjust my ways for him. I think it's made me a more patient person. Perhaps more understanding. In any event, a better supervisor and sheriff."

"That makes sense."

"Well, if you ignore how I blew up at him." She wrinkled her nose.

The side door opened, and a tall woman wearing a black suit and silky gray blouse stepped out. She wore impossibly high heels and looked at Mina with piercing blue eyes. "Sheriff? I'm Janice James. You wanted to see me. How can I help you?"

Mina crossed over to the woman, Nolan trailing her. Mina displayed her credentials and introduced both of them. "Can we step into your office?"

"I'm sorry, Sheriff." Janice raised her chin. "But I'm rather busy today."

"I think you'll want to hear about this in your office. It's regarding Mayor Sutton."

"Ernie?" Her perfectly plucked eyebrows drew together. "Did something happen to him?"

"Like I said," Mina didn't back down, "I think you'll want to hear this in your office."

Janice eyed her for a long moment, then pivoted on heels that Nolan couldn't imagine allowed her to remain standing much less perform such a quick maneuver.

Mina and Nolan trailed her down a wide hallway lined with closed doors to the last one. She slipped inside the room. They joined her and found her standing behind a glass desk with nothing but a small lamp and phone on it. The walls were lined with bookshelves holding official-looking law books, and the room smelled of her perfume.

She gestured at two black leather-and-chrome chairs by her desk. "Have a seat."

Mina sat first, and Nolan took a seat next to her, biting his tongue when he wanted to start asking questions. He couldn't. He'd promised to take a back seat. He might literally be sitting next to Mina, but he needed to keep his promise in mind.

Janice remained standing. "Now what's this about?"

Mina fixed her attention on the attorney. "I'm sorry to tell you, but Mayor Sutton has been murdered."

"Murdered?" Janice dropped into her chair and sat unmoving except for her eyelashes fluttering at the speed of hummingbird wings. "But how? Where?"

Mina explained, her tone sympathetic. "Do you know of anyone who would want to hurt him?"

"No." She frowned. "But then I wasn't involved in his day-to-day life, especially not his working life, so I wouldn't know." She took a long breath. "Poor Becca. I'm sure you told her first. How is she handling this?"

"Unfortunately, we haven't been able to locate her," Mina said. "Might you know where she could be?"

Janice gave a quick shake of her head. "I wasn't involved

in her daily life, either, so I don't have a clue. Perhaps she took a trip."

"Can you think of anyone who might want to hurt her?" Mina asked.

"Becca?" Janice's eyes widened. "No, she's the sweetest girl. Always thinking of others before herself. I can't imagine she would've made anyone mad enough to want to hurt her."

Mina shifted in her chair and leaned closer. "We've had reports that you've recently spent quite a bit of time with Mayor Sutton at the Rusty Hull restaurant. Can you tell me what you were doing together?"

"Updating his will."

Nolan couldn't believe she was being so forthcoming, but he was glad she was. Hopefully, she'd keep it up and provide the mayor's will.

"Isn't a busy restaurant an unusual place to discuss a will?" Mina asked.

She silently folded her hands on the desk. Her long nails were coated in a silvery-white color. "Probably, but he didn't want anyone to know he was making changes, and he hasn't been able to drive here to take care of it in my office."

"Is that due to the cancer?" Mina asked.

Janice gaped at her. "How could you possibly know that? He told no one except me."

"It was revealed at his autopsy."

"Autopsy." She clapped a hand over her mouth and took a long breath. "For some reason hearing that word makes his death seem more real."

"I know he was your friend as well as your client, and I'm sorry for your loss." Mina sat wordlessly for a moment. "I hate to have to ask you questions at a time like this, but I know you'll want us to find the person who killed him."

"Of course."

"Do you know why he hid his cancer from everyone?"

"To keep the time he had left as normal as possible. He especially needed that with Becca. He didn't want her to feel bad until it was clear that he wasn't going to beat the cancer."

Mina got out her notepad. "Why did he change his will?"

"I'm sorry." Janice stared at her hands. "I really am, but I can't help you. Attorney-client privilege continues even in death, and I'll need a warrant to ignore it."

Not a surprise, but Nolan had hoped for a different answer.

Mina didn't seem surprised either. "I can get a warrant, but all that will do is delay our investigation."

"Like I said, I'm sorry." Janice's eyes creased. "I simply can't share the details."

Mina crossed her legs and gripped the arms on the chair but didn't speak for a moment, and Nolan knew she was thinking. About what, he had no idea, but Janice didn't blink or move. A perfect lawyer pose, not stymied by anything happening around her. She probably was excellent in court.

Mina relaxed her hands on the chair. "About this latest will. Did Ernie have a copy of the document containing the final changes?"

Janice leaned forward. "I had no idea that he'd died, so I emailed it to him this morning right before you got here. I assume you'll be able to find it in his email."

Mina nodded. "He obviously wouldn't have signed it, and it won't be official."

"That's correct," Janice said. "He'd have a copy of the will we drew up after his wife passed away. Both electronic and paper. That's the document I'll present to the probate court."

"But you'll contact the beneficiaries about their inheritance, correct?" Nolan asked, not able to keep silent any longer.

"Yes, but not by gathering them all together as you see in TV and movies. Ernie has named me his executor. As such, I'll contact the beneficiaries after the will goes to probate."

Mina's phone chimed from her pocket, but she ignored it. "Can you think of any reason the killer might have associated the mayor's death with the Lost Lake Locators team?" She shared about the team and their purpose, the pride in her voice warming Nolan.

Janice looked him over as if seeing him for the first time. "Interesting, but no. Ernie never mentioned the team, and I know nothing about them."

"Might he have mentioned the refurbishment of the Portside Inn and Lighthouse?" Nolan asked, thinking Mina might not mind him asking such a question.

"Yes, I think he did mention that. But really just in passing as we drove by the location. He mentioned that he liked seeing younger people moving into town." She tapped a fingernail on the desk. "I know he didn't state who the occupants were, though. I would've remembered such an interesting team."

Nolan had hoped the mayor would've said something so they could figure out the connection, but he wasn't surprised the guy didn't discuss them with his out-of-town lawyer.

"Where were you Monday afternoon between three and five p.m.?" Mina asked.

Janice lifted her shoulders and angled her body like a viper about to strike. "Certainly you don't suspect me of killing him?"

Mina sat calmly, not at all bothered by Janice's antagonistic posture. "We just have to rule you out."

Janice sniffed as if it was too much for her to provide an

alibi. "I was in a deposition here in the conference room. I can get a written affidavit from all of the participants, if that will help."

"That would be a big help." Mina smiled. "Is there anything else you can think of that might help us find Mayor Sutton's killer or locate Becca?"

Janice relaxed her shoulders and narrowed her gaze. "Not at the moment, but then I never thought I would have to think about who killed Ernie. I only ever wondered how long I had left with my friend before the cancer took him."

Mina stood and laid a business card on the sparkling glass desk. "Please take some time to think about it. If you come up with anything you think might help us, I'd appreciate it if you'd contact me."

"I will." Janice slowly rose to her feet, acting like all of the fight had gone out of her and grief had settled in. "I'll show you out."

She strolled to the door at a slower pace than when she'd led them to her office and held it open. After saying their goodbyes in the waiting area, Mina and Nolan strode out to the hallway.

Mina turned to Nolan. "She may not have helped us in figuring out who *did* kill the mayor, but one thing is clear. She has a solid alibi, and we now have one less suspect."

"Good point." Nolan was glad she was optimistic. Too bad he couldn't find the same optimism. Not when they were no closer to figuring out how the mayor's death was related to him and his team and finding the real killer.

～

In the car, Mina got out her phone to check for a text she'd received while talking to Janice, but her phone rang in her hand, and she looked at the screen. "It's Dr. Osborne."

She answered. "Thanks for calling me back."

"You asked about blood types," he said in his usual straightforward tone.

"I've gotten the mayor's and Becca's types since I left the message with you, but I still need his deceased wife's type."

"Mary's? Why on earth would you want that?"

"Just to confirm that Becca is indeed the mayor's daughter."

He sputtered for a moment. "Don't tell me there's a question about that."

"Not really. Just a line of inquiry I need to close out."

"I have Mary's type on file from when she passed away, but I can't give that information to you without a warrant."

Of course not. Mina resisted slamming a fist into the steering wheel and searched for an easy solution to her problem. "What if I give you the mayor's and Becca's blood types. Can you look at Mary's and confirm that they are her biological parents?"

"I can give you the probability of it being true, but I can't state that it's so without a DNA test."

"That's good enough for me. The mayor had type O blood, and Becca's is type A."

"Hold on for a minute."

She heard fingers tapping on a keyboard in the background and wanted to urge Dr. Osborne to move faster. But she held her tongue so he could find the information they needed.

"I can tell you it's highly probable that Mary and Ernie are Becca's biological parents," he finally said. "Will that do?"

"Yes, thank you."

"Are you any closer to finding her or Ernie's killer?"

"Just like you can't tell me about Mary's blood type, I

can't tell you that. Sorry. I know you're friends of the family and would want to know."

"No worries. I understand. Let me know if you need anything else." He ended the call.

She shared the information with Nolan and then looked at her screen. "I missed a text from Dylan. Says to call him ASAP."

"Then call him," Nolan said, looking like he wanted to grab the phone from her hand and make the call himself. He was probably antsy after sitting nearly mute through that entire interview with Janice.

Mina appreciated his cooperation. She tapped Dylan's phone number and sat back to wait for his answer. "Dylan, it's Sheriff Park."

"I wondered if you were going to call." His frustration flowed through his tone. "I got a name and address for Patriotic Puzzle."

Mina's heart kicked hard. "Who is he?"

"Guy's name is Ty Rowe." Dylan rattled off a Lost Lake address.

"We're in Medford right now, but on our way back to Lost Lake, and I can head right over to his house."

"You should find him at home. He's in IT and works from home."

"If that's his line of work, I'm surprised you could trace his Instagram post and get his ID," Nolan said.

"He might be in the business, but he's obviously not very good at it." Dylan laughed. "Actually, if he's in IT it's surprising he's on social media at all. We know all the pitfalls and avoid it like the plague."

"True of most law enforcement officers too," Mina said.

"I'm sending you his picture right now," Dylan said. "Take a look and let me know what you think."

Mina waited for the photo to come through, then tapped

on it. She held it out to Nolan. "It's the guy Paisley saw with the mayor on Monday."

Nolan nodded, a blaze of excitement in his eyes. "Now that we know Ty Rowe and Patriotic Puzzle are one in the same, it cuts two of our many suspects down to one. Feels good to eliminate another one."

"Yeah," Dylan said. "Figured you'd like that. That's it for now, but I'll get back to you as soon as I have anything to report." He ended the call before Mina could thank him for his help.

She shoved the key in the ignition and gunned the engine a bit too forcefully. But, come on. It felt good. They had a solid lead to pursue for once.

"Hold on," she said to Nolan and whipped the vehicle out of the parking lot, the tires squealing as she rounded a corner.

"Don't sheriffs have to obey traffic laws too?" Nolan grinned at her.

She laughed but didn't slow down. She wasn't going to waste time. In the mountains between Medford and home, she had to be more careful, but not leaving the city. "By the way, I went by the mayor's house last night, and his office bookshelves were empty."

"So he's most likely selling the sports memorabilia. Maybe the auction house will know why he was selling it."

"If it was because of the cancer, I doubt he would've told them."

"Yeah." He gritted his teeth. "Doesn't seem likely."

"I also checked his files for a will and his insurance but didn't find anything. I would think he'd have kept the will at home, but maybe he has a safe deposit box. And he might have the insurance online only."

"I'll text Dylan to have him look for both things on the mayor's computers." Nolan got out his phone.

She pointed her vehicle into the Coastal Mountain Range and watched the wooded trees whizz by on the narrow country road heading toward the ocean. Normally she loved the peace of this drive. The time to reflect on God's beauty. To realize what a small cog she was in the wheel of life. All her problems would drift away. But not today. Today she had a larger-than -life purpose—a missing woman who might be alive, likely needing Mina to rescue her.

The pressure was immense. Greater than Mina had ever experienced. Nolan was sitting beside her, and she had three teams of professionals helping, and yet, she felt alone.

Oh, please let her be alive.

Nolan put away his phone and turned to look at her. "What about the other thing you were going to do last night?"

He would go there when she wasn't ready to discuss it with him, but she couldn't ignore his question. "You mean talk to my parents?"

"Yeah."

"By the time I finished searching the mayor's house, it was too late. I would've had to wake them up, so I didn't go."

"Honestly, I didn't think you would." He gave a bitter smile.

She stared at him when her focus should've been on the road. "Why would you say that?"

He didn't answer right away but took a few deep breaths. "I'm not sure you really want to let go of your anger with me."

Was he right? What if her parents had been duplicitous enough to have sent Nolan packing without ever telling her? Would it be even worse than Nolan having left her?

Oh, man. She just didn't know.

She faced the road again. On the surface, it made no

sense that she didn't want to know the truth about why he'd left the way he had. But she'd carried the anger for so many years, it was almost comfortable. Like a favorite pair of jeans she didn't want to get rid of even when they were worn out. It took more effort to let it go than to continue on the same path.

Nolan had bailed on her. He'd left her devastated, and she'd shut herself off. Closed down. Completely. Was that the effect of holding unforgiveness in her life? Did she need to forgive because she not only needed God to forgive her sins, but for her emotional well-being too? To be able to love and trust a man—anyone—again?

Oh, please, help me find it in my heart to forgive him. To move on. To trust.

Maybe he was right. Maybe she *did* need to make a point of seeing her parents. Not only for him, but for herself too.

"You could be right, I don't know. I'll go see them as soon as I can." She looked at him again. "But you know this investigation and finding Becca has to take priority over anything personal."

He sagged against the door. "I know."

She couldn't say anything else to change his disappointment. At least she couldn't think of anything else to say, so she clammed up and kept her attention on the drive. They remained unspeaking through the coastal range, down to the Oregon coast. Silence, save the tires running over wet pavement, filled the car. Not a comfortable silence. But one loaded with tension.

She approached an inexpensive apartment complex on the outskirts of town and breathed a sigh of relief. The complex was located far away from pricey, ocean-view housing. She wouldn't consider this a slum by any means, but it was definitely bargain accommodations. Two six-story blocks of apartments with outdoor concrete walkways and faded aqua doors greeted them, the blacktop lot crumbling.

Nothing about the sketchy location where her deputies often responded to callouts would deter Mina as she parked and raced for the third floor. She ignored the handrail and walkway railings with chipping paint. Nolan jogged up the steps behind her until they reached apartment 312.

She pounded on the door and stood back, her hand resting on her sidearm.

The door opened, and a tall, lanky man with thinning blond hair stared at her, a scowl on his face. "Yeah?"

"I'm Sheriff Park." Mina held out her credentials. "And this is my associate Nolan Orr. We're looking for Ty Rowe."

"That's me. What do you want?" He thrust out his chin in defiance. "I ain't done nothing wrong."

"I have some questions for you regarding your replies on Mayor Sutton's Instagram posts."

"That old geezer? Don't tell me he complained to you." Rowe frowned. "I didn't do anything illegal. Just speaking my mind, which the First Amendment allows."

"Do you mind if we come in and talk about this?" Mina asked, but she eased past him into an apartment that hadn't seen a vacuum cleaner, mop, or dusting cloth in quite some time.

She stopped near a black leather sofa holding a laptop and gaming controls. On the opposite wall, a large TV took up nearly the entire space. Below that, several different gaming systems filled rickety-looking black shelves.

She didn't sit, but he charged inside and plopped down next to the laptop. Nolan came to stand next to her, and they both looked down at him.

She cleared her throat. "You were seen on Monday having lunch with the mayor."

"So what?"

"You were having a very heated discussion with him," she said.

Rowe crossed his arms. "Far as I know, arguing isn't a criminal offense."

"What were you arguing about?" Nolan asked.

"What do you think?" Rowe rolled his eyes. "His stupid liberal politics. He'd give away the whole town's treasury on his do-gooder crusades if people like me didn't call him out."

"And your approach is more conservative?" Nolan asked.

"Well, yeah." He cocked his head. "Isn't that the only way to be?"

"Where were you on Monday between the hours of three and five p.m.?" Mina asked.

"In a stupid meeting." He shook his head. "We have a department meeting every Monday afternoon where they make us come into the office. It could easily be handled on a video call, but they just want to inconvenience us."

"Write down the company name and a list of the people who saw you there." Mina held out her notepad.

He grabbed it and started writing. "What's this all about anyway?"

"Just information we need for an investigation we're handling." Mina continued to watch him as he wrote. The moment he finished, she took back her pad and pen and pocketed them. "Thank you for your information."

Before he could question her about why she needed the information, she rushed to the door and down the walkway.

"Clearly he didn't know about the mayor's death," Nolan said, catching up to her. "But why didn't you tell him about it?"

She continued walking. "With his social media proclivity, he'd be all over the sites announcing it. I still rather it wouldn't get around until we have a good chance of finding the killer."

Which wasn't now, she didn't add and bring them both down. They didn't have a good chance of it at all. She had to look at that suspect list again and see how she should proceed from here.

In the car, Nolan strapped on his seatbelt and kept his gaze pinned ahead.

She got out her notepad to flip to her suspect list. "We're definitely narrowing down our list of legitimate suspects. Once we get the affidavits from Janice, she'll be ruled out. Same goes for Rowe and Harmony, once we verify their alibies. Jude and Becca really weren't true contenders in my book."

"But we shouldn't strike them off."

"No, but I'm not wanting to throw a lot of resources into looking into them at this point. That leaves the mayor of Seaside Harbor, Wade, and Smythe."

"The other mayor is a longshot at best, and I think Wade is kind of slimy, but I don't see him as a murderer. So it seems like we need to put more resources into finding Smythe, unless Dylan brings something to our attention or we run out of other leads."

"I agree with you," she said, looking at him. "In theory at least. But we have no way of finding Smythe unless someone recognizes his photograph or Dylan turns something up with the online registration for the mansion."

"We do still have the financial files for the county to review. That might reveal an additional suspect or point to the Seaside Harbor mayor."

"Abe might know something after his interview with the guy, and he has quite a few leads he hasn't reported on. We can get back to him on that."

"Why don't we stop by your office and talk to him,"

Nolan suggested. "Then if he doesn't have anything action-able, we'll head to the inn where we can spread out in the conference room and begin evaluating the town's records."

She nodded but wasn't any more eager to sit and review records than she figured he felt like doing. But investigations were often about doing the tedious work, and that's where solid leads could be generated.

Let that be the case today.

Oh, please.

Becca had been missing for over thirty-six hours, maybe more, and Mina was certain finding the killer was the key to finding her and bringing her home alive.

20

Mina stepped through the main door into her office vestibule, Nolan hot on her tail. A couple sat in the chairs, a redheaded woman with spiral curls falling softly to her shoulders, and a balding and fit man Mina put in his early sixties. Mina had never seen either of them before.

The woman jumped to her feet, her curls bouncing. "Sheriff Park?"

Mina glanced at Grace, the clerk manning the front desk.

Grace stood and cast an apologetic look her way, then mouthed, *Sorry*.

Mina took a breath, put on a practiced smile, then turned to the woman. "How can I help you?"

"I'm Cadence Vaughn, and I think my dad has information on Mayor Sutton's murder," she said.

"How so?" Mina asked, now honestly interested.

Cadence glanced at Grace and Nolan. "Is there somewhere we can talk in private?"

Mina hated to agree without knowing if this woman really did have legitimate information, but without any strong leads, she didn't want to turn it down.

"We can go to my office." Mina tipped her head at Nolan. "But Deputy Orr is very involved in this investigation, and he'll sit in."

Cadence gave a sharp nod. "I'd like to talk to you before my dad joins us. Mind if he waits here?"

Odd, but if that's what it took to get the information. "Fine with me."

Cadence stepped over to Grace, her high-heeled boots clicking on the ancient vinyl floor. "Would you mind keeping an eye on him? Make sure he doesn't leave?"

Grace frowned. "It's not really what I do."

"Please." Cadence's pleading tone would be hard to say no to. "It's important."

"Go ahead, Grace," Mina said. "We won't be long."

"If you insist." She plopped onto her chair and crossed her arms. "But please don't take too long."

"Follow me." Mina opened the secured door to the long hallway leading to her office.

The walls had recently been painted vivid white to brighten up the area, but it was still underlit and gloomy. The air smelled like burnt coffee and microwave popcorn, the two staples her team lived on. She entered her office door and came up short. Hayden sat behind her big wooden desk, his laptop in front of him.

"What are you doing here?" she asked as Nolan and Cadence stepped in behind her.

Hayden looked up and grimaced. "Sorry, I didn't know you were coming back. The internet's down at the inn, and El said I could work here."

He stood. "But now that you're back, looks like I'm sprung from solitary and put back in gen pop."

"General population," Cadence said.

Hayden's gaze flew to her, and he gave her an admiring once over, letting his gaze linger. "You know prison slang?"

"Cadence Vaughn." She returned his gaze with an equally interested one of her own. "Crime reporter for the Oregonian."

Mina spun on her. "Now wait a minute. You didn't say anything about being a reporter. If this is a ruse to get an interview, there's the door."

Cadence held up her hands. "This has nothing to do with my job. It's honestly about my father."

"She seems sincere to me." Hayden's focus remained locked on Cadence.

Mina knew a man's interest for a woman when she saw it, but she never expected it from Hayden. Under any other circumstances, he'd be the first person to call out a reporter and make her spill her guts.

"I guess I'll be going," he said, sounding like a little boy forced to leave a baseball game.

"Might as well stay." Mina motioned for him to sit, and he complied. She could use another set of eyes, even ones that were jaded by this woman's beauty. She turned to Cadence. "Have a seat and tell me what this is about."

Cadence took a seat and crossed her long legs incased in skinny jeans, and Nolan leaned against the bookshelf.

"So you're not local, Cadence." Mina pushed the in-basket on her desk out of the way and rested on the corner. "What's your connection to the mayor?"

"My father, Percy Vaughn, retired here about five years ago." Cadence peered at Mina, the intensity of a reporter on the hunt obvious. "He's an avid birdwatcher, and he met Ernie on one of his trips. They became good friends and often went birdwatching together."

Mina nodded. Mayor Sutton was as passionate about birds as he was about his sports memorabilia. "Go on."

"So when I heard that the mayor had been murdered," Cadence said.

"Exactly how did you hear when it's not common knowledge at this point?" Nolan hooked his thumbs in his pants pockets.

Cadence narrowed her big brown eyes and faced him. "I have my sources all across the state that I'm not at liberty to reveal."

"And you shouldn't have to." Hayden gave Mina a pointed look.

She wanted to argue with him, but this was the least of her worries right now. "So you heard about the murder. Then what?"

"Since I knew about Dad's friendship with Ernie, I knew he'd be distraught. So I got here as quick as I could to support him and ask if he knew anyone who might want to kill the mayor."

"For a story, you mean?" Nolan asked.

"I would—will—do a story, but not until I'm sure my dad's okay."

"He isn't now?" Mina asked.

Cadence shook her head, those curls shifting like a vortex of redness. "He's in the beginning stages of dementia, and he's often unclear as to what's actually happened. But when I questioned him about Ernie, he told me that the mayor asked him to keep a big secret."

Interest perked, Mina leaned closer. "And did he tell you what that secret was?"

"That's when things got vague. He said it has something to do with lots of cash Ernie was spending on something illegal." She splayed her hands over her legs. "No matter how many times I questioned him about the illegal thing, he couldn't remember what it was. Or he never knew. I thought maybe if he came here, and an authority figure gently questioned him, it might jog his memory."

"What if he implicates himself in something criminal?"

Hayden asked, sounding genuinely concerned for her father.

She gave him a quick smile of thanks. "If he does, then I hope you'll take into account that he's a man with dementia and may not have known what he was doing."

Tears glistened in her eyes, and Hayden grabbed a tissue box, then circled around the desk. He sat in the chair next to her and offered a tissue. "We'll make sure he's okay."

What in the world was going on with Hayden? This was so out of character for him. Mina was surprised he didn't actually reach up and dry her tears.

Mina got up. "Then let's go get him and let him tell his story."

Cadence joined her at the door, and together they went down the hall to the lobby. Percy wobbled to his feet and stared at Mina.

"I'm surprised I haven't met you before," Mina said to try to break the ice and comfort the older gentleman.

"Why would you?" His tone was sharp. "I'm not a lawbreaker. You don't need to arrest me. I want to go home."

"Now, Dad." Cadence twined her arm in his. "We're here to tell the sheriff about Ernie, remember?"

"Ernie?"

"You remember. He was murdered."

"Murdered?" Percy sagged as if he might collapse on the floor.

Cadence glanced at Mina. "Let's get him back to the office and maybe things will become clearer for him."

Mina unlocked the door again and held it open for Percy to go through first, then she held Cadence back a few steps. "Does he have someone to care for him?"

"He has a housekeeper who takes care of the basics, like cleaning and food. He's been lucid most of the time until recently, but we're getting to the point where he needs more than a housekeeper. I can't see putting him into a facility until absolutely necessary, so I'll likely be moving in with him for now or taking him home with me."

While she hurried to catch up with him, Mina offered a prayer for them. She couldn't imagine seeing her father lose his faculties this way. It had to be very difficult for Cadence.

Nolan remained leaning against the wall, and Hayden had taken a seat behind the desk. Cadence helped her father into a chair and sat next to him.

Mina resumed her spot on the corner of her desk and smiled at Percy. "Thank you for coming to see me, Percy. What can you tell me about Ernie's sudden death?"

"They killed him. Had to be them." His chin trembled. "He couldn't get the money fast enough. They wanted it now. All of it."

Mina clasped her hands together to keep her eagerness for answers in check. "Who are they?"

He shrugged. "Ernie didn't tell me. He didn't even mention the money. But I heard him on the phone."

Now they were getting somewhere. "Do you remember exactly what he said on the phone?"

"I...he..." Percy glanced around, a vacant look in his eyes. "I don't know."

"Think hard, Dad." Cadence squeezed his shoulder.

"I'm sorry. I'm sorry." His hands trembled, his gaze darting faster around the space, and he shifted in his seat. "I want to tell you, but I don't know."

Mina squatted next to him and pressed her hand over his. "It's okay, Percy. We all forget things."

Tears formed in his eyes. "Ernie didn't deserve to die."

"No he didn't." Mina paused for a moment. "Was someone blackmailing him?"

"Maybe." Percy tapped his foot. "I don't know. I just don't remember."

"That's okay." She smiled. "Do you know if Ernie was trying to keep a secret?"

Percy's eyes brightened. "He had one. He told me. About people."

"What about people?" Mina asked.

He shook his head. "I don't know. He wanted to help them though."

"Do you know how?" she asked.

He shook his head again and turned to his daughter. "I want to go home now, Cady. Please. Can we go home?"

Mina stood. "Of course you can. And if you think of the secret that Ernie kept or what he was doing with the money to help people, will you come back to see me?"

He nodded and swayed to his feet.

Cadence clutched her father's arm. "If he can't be on his own, I'll stay here or take him back to Portland with me."

"Don't wanna go. Live here." He fired an irritable look at his daughter.

Hayden jumped up and closed his computer. "We have internet at the inn again, and I know you want me to get out of your hair, Mina. I'll see them to the door on my way out."

"Thanks." Trying not to smile at his obvious desire to remain in Cadence's company, she handed her business card to Cadence. "My cell is on there in case you need to call me, but before you go, I'll need your contact information."

"I can give it to you, but your clerk insisted on taking it already."

Mina didn't want to keep Percy any longer. "I can get it from her then."

The trio exited, and Mina looked at Nolan. "This could be the lead we need regarding potential blackmail."

"Indeed," Nolan said. "But who are these people, and who did they need to be protected from?"

"I have the same questions." She slipped behind her

desk. "We also need to run a background check on both Cadence and Percy."

"Normally, I'd have Hayden do it, but clearly he's not the most objective person at this point." Nolan gave a wry smile.

"I'll get Dylan on it." She got out her phone. "If they check out, then maybe we'll know if this is a strong lead or if we're back to square one."

Nolan put the conversation with Percy behind him as he stood near Abe's cubicle in Mina's office. Abe crossed his arms in a defensive attitude. Whether his attitude was because he'd wanted to be Mina's sidekick instead of Nolan, or if he felt bad about not having additional information for them, Nolan didn't know. Because so far, all he'd mentioned was that he'd ruled out any law enforcement officers as potential suspects. The last thing the guy would want was for Nolan to question his work, but he'd been vague, and Nolan couldn't leave it at that.

"Is this for sworn staff only, or did you include the non-sworn staff?" Nolan asked.

Abe tightened his arms, the thick biceps straining his shirt sleeves. "I looked at everyone. It's not like we have people coming and going here very often." He glanced at Mina. "You're the only one on staff who's left town and come back."

"But I didn't leave the sheriff's department and come back," she clarified. "I hadn't started working here until I moved back to town."

Nolan didn't think her comment was important to the investigation, but it was clearly important to her to clarify what Abe was saying. Apparently, Abe still hadn't accepted the fact that she'd beaten him for the sheriff's seat and he remained a sergeant.

"What else do you have for us?" she asked.

He relaxed his arms. "Only two trophy companies in the county. I called them both and neither of them sold or engraved the trophies found at the escape room."

"It wouldn't be surprising if our suspect didn't purchase them locally," Nolan said.

"Yeah," Abe said. "I checked online too. Found a variety of companies that he could've gotten them from. Some have same-day delivery."

"Online is a good possibility since this is obviously a premeditated murder, and he had time to plan ahead," Mina said. "Go ahead and request credit card records for any of the suspects you can get a warrant for to see if we have any charges for trophies. In a store or online."

"You won't have to request Jude's records," Nolan said. "I'll ask him to provide them, and I'm sure he will."

"I had better luck with the caterer," Abe said. "Tide and Thyme handled the food."

"That new one in town," Mina said.

He smirked. "If you mean new in the last two years, then yeah."

"Has it been that long? Anyway, what did they tell you?"

"The order was placed online and paid via Zelle."

Nolan wasn't all that familiar with P2P, peer-to-peer, payments like Zelle, but he did know they consisted of automatic transfers from one bank account to another.

Mina gritted her teeth. "So it'll be harder to trace the payment than if done via credit card."

Abe nodded. "The order was picked up on Monday at four p.m. I showed our electronic sketch of Smythe to the owner. She said he was the one she dealt with. He was already dressed in his butler attire."

"Anything else the owner could share?" Nolan asked.

"He drove a plain white van that she thought might be a rental." Abe leaned back as if feeling more comfortable all of a sudden. "I'm calling all rental agencies in the county. Without a warrant, I'm hitting a wall. Still, I eliminated three companies who don't rent cargo vans. But then, they told me to check moving truck rental companies, too, so that's added just as many places back onto my list."

Mina gave a strong nod of approval. "Keep after it. What about the Seaside Harbor mayor?"

"It's a friendly competition."

"Says who?" Nolan asked.

Abe snapped his chair forward. "I didn't just take his word for it if that's what you're suggesting. I asked some of the city council members, and they agreed. Nothing there as far as having a real motive to kill Mayor Sutton."

"Sounds like you were thorough," Nolan said to put the sergeant at ease again.

Abe stretched his hands behind his head. "Daisy's alibis check out too. So that's at least two people off our list."

Mina shared their conversation with Cadence and Percy. "Hopefully, he'll remember something and get back to us. Until then, keep your eyes open for any groups of people that the mayor might have been involved with."

"You sure this dude knows what he's talking about?" Abe asked.

"No, but we have to treat this lead like any other." Mina gave the guy a tight smile. "Thank you for all of your work. Hopefully when the DNA and fingerprint information comes in from the Veritas team, it'll bring us some additional leads."

"Or somehow we figure out Smythe's real identity," Nolan added. "More than ever, he's got to be our prime suspect now."

"Still no luck on the burner phone he used to make arrangements with Harmony," Abe said. "Cell providers like to stonewall."

"Maybe Dylan will find something." Mina frowned. "Or we're barking up the wrong tree altogether, and there's someone we don't yet know about."

"It's time to look at the city records to see if someone might be embezzling money," Nolan said.

She nodded. "To that end, you can find me at the inn, where we'll work on reviewing the city's financial reports for the past six months. See if we can find any irregularities."

Abe nodded, but cast a suspicious look in Nolan's direction.

Nolan ignored him and left with Mina to go to her vehicle.

He wasn't eager to review boring financial records, but if they were successful, they might find another suspect, could track him down, and finally, finally locate the elusive killer before he harmed Becca.

21

Mina pointed her vehicle down Main Street, where business owners hustled around in the bright sunshine, decorating for the Founder's Day festival on Saturday. The first Founder's Day in a long time without Mayor Sutton. A wave of sadness hit Mina, her reaction stronger than she'd expected.

She shot a quick look at Nolan as he silently peered out the window. What was he so intently thinking about?

At a red light, she searched his face to see if something was troubling him, but he just seemed genuinely interested in the preparations and busy people around them.

"Looks like everyone is getting into a festive mood," he said.

"Founder's Day is a big deal here. People really come together to make it special."

"This will be my first year." A wistful tone crept into his voice. "Other than fireworks over the harbor on Saturday night, what can I expect?"

She gestured at Main Street. "This street will shut down to vehicle traffic. We have carnival rides, games, food, music, entertainment—you name it, we have it—for the whole weekend. I'm sure, as a local business owner, you've been asked to participate."

"Yeah. We're hosting kids arts and crafts at the inn."

She flashed a look his way. "No offense, but who on your staff has experience with children?"

"Does being a child at one point in life count?" He laughed.

She rolled her eyes as the light changed. She pulled into the intersection, careful of eager pedestrians ignoring the crossing signals. "I'm serious."

"Okay, in all seriousness," he said, "Reece has a younger sister—ten years younger—and has some experience, but mostly we looked things up on the internet. If we have any real issues, we'll be counting on parents to step in."

Made some sense. "At least she has more experience than I do. Or you, only having an older brother."

He swiveled to look at her. "You remembered."

"How could I forget?" She played it down, but she remembered every second they'd spent together. Especially their long talks at night, the moonlight showering them on the cliff as the ocean crashed on the rocks below. "It's because of him you're who you are. Or more like how your parents treated both of you, is how you've become who you are."

He sat silently for a moment. "It was really hard to live up to an older brother who achieved everything your father wanted him to achieve when you follow your own path—one your dad doesn't care anything about."

"I don't know how you lived under his thumb for as long as you did."

Nolan grimaced. "It's all in the past now. I haven't seen either of my parents in years. Not really since college. My team is my true family."

She'd witnessed that very thing back in the day. Each

team member had a reason for doing life on their own and had come together to form a kind of adoptive family. Not officially. But in all the ways that counted.

She'd even been a bit jealous until she thought about her almost idyllic upbringing here in Lost Lake. She glanced at him. "I've always been thankful to have what some people would say is a normal family and childhood. My parents always wanted me to do what I wanted to do. What fulfilled me. Even when I went into something as dangerous as law enforcement, they supported me."

But if Nolan was to be believed, they didn't support her in her relationship choice when they'd sent him on his way. She so didn't want to have that conversation with them. Not at all. She sighed.

"What is it?" he asked.

She felt his probing gaze on her. Should she tell him? Why not? "I don't want this thing from our past to ruin my relationship with my parents."

"Then maybe you shouldn't ask them," he said, but his tone held little or no conviction.

"Maybe." She left him with the vague answer as they reached the inn's parking lot. She parked near the main entrance and grabbed her metal water bottle and the stack of financial files from her backseat.

Nolan led the way to the conference room. At the long table, Hayden, Reece, and Jude sat behind computers, and Abby had a stack of papers in front of her that she appeared to be organizing. All of them looked up, their gazes expectant.

Nolan gestured for Mina to have a seat. She set the pile of reports on the table and took a chair near the end. He stopped at the head of the table.

"Long time no see." Hayden chuckled.

"Did you get Cadence and Percy off okay?" Nolan didn't comment on Hayden's obvious interest in Cadence.

Hayden nodded. "I got her phone number, too, just in case we needed to call her."

Mina smirked, but once again Nolan left it alone. "We're here to review city financial records, but let me give you a quick update first."

No one spoke, and they gave him their rapt attention as he recounted their morning.

Thank you for bringing this team here to help. I couldn't do this without them. Without Nolan.

"Anything to report on Becca?" Nolan dropped into a chair next to her and looked at the others.

Jude lowered the screen on his computer. "I'm about to take off and hunt down one of her friends who hasn't returned my calls. I'll let you know if I actually talk to her, and if she has anything to report."

Nolan scratched his neck. "Before you go, we need your credit card and bank statements for the past six months."

Jude arched a brow but didn't question the request. He obviously trusted Nolan not to ask for something that wasn't needed and would do as asked for the greater good, but she thought he deserved some reassurance. She explained their reasoning.

Jude lifted the computer screen. "I'll print them right now."

"You know this is just to rule you out, right?" Mina asked.

Jude kept his gaze pinned on his computer. "I do, but if my dad taught me anything that stuck—which isn't much— it was to never ever reveal your financial information to anyone else. To that end, I'll be redacting my account numbers before I turn over the statements. You need them, you'll have to get a warrant for them."

"Understood," Mina said, not questioning his reasonable response. He was estranged from his wealthy father, and money was a hot topic. She didn't want to bring all of that up when it wasn't necessary right now.

"I also need someone to look at our past cases," Nolan said. "See if we can spot a connection to the mayor."

"I can do it," Reece offered. "Anything in particular you think I should be looking for?"

Nolan slightly lifted his hands. "Could be a waste of time, but we have to look at every possibility."

"Waste of time or not, I'll do my best." Reece stood. "I'll get the files and get started right away."

"Anything else to report?" Nolan looked around the table. "If not, Mina and I are going to get started on the city financial records."

No one spoke. Not a word or even a movement, leaving the room as somber as when Jude's finances had been called into question. Maybe the others didn't think Nolan should've made the request when he knew his teammate—brother really—wasn't guilty. They might think he should've insisted on Mina getting a warrant. Maybe she should have, just to protect his relationship with his team.

Too late. She couldn't have a do-over.

He smiled at his team. "Feel free to offer to help with these records if you want."

The room was suddenly a beehive of conversation and activities, and Mina almost laughed at their willingness to avoid the mundane task.

She split the stack of reports in half, gave Nolan one half, and set to work on the other stack without a word.

Jude got up and went to the printer, then stopped in front of Mina and dropped his statements on the table. "I'm out of here to check in with that friend."

She looked up at him. "Thank you, and I'm sorry we needed to ask for these."

He didn't respond but spun and marched out.

"Guy's clearly not happy," Hayden said.

Hayden had been so quiet Mina had almost forgotten he was in the room.

"He's got thick skin," Nolan said. "He'll get over it."

"Either of you want lunch?" Hayden asked. "We could do delivery."

"I could eat." Nolan looked at Mina. "Anything you're interested in?"

"Fried clams, hush puppies, and fries from the Rusty Hull," she replied, wanting what she considered comfort foods.

"Sounds good to me too," Nolan said.

"I'm on board." Hayden looked down at his computer. "Anything to drink?"

"I'm good." She held up her water bottle.

He clicked away on his keys, and she started down the listings. She'd heard the budget reviewed at council meetings she'd attended, but these reports gave her a new appreciation for the seemingly unending line of items needed to run a city. Also gave her a frustration over how long it was going to take to get through this stack of papers.

The meal arrived, and Hayden distributed the containers, the contents filled the air with fried goodness. She'd planned to work through it, but Hayden closed his computer and Nolan slid his papers aside. So she moved her reports and lifted a crispy clam to her mouth. She didn't often allow herself to have fried foods, but was there any better food to eliminate stress? If so, she hadn't found it.

She bit into the crispy outside and tender inside of a hush puppy and groaned.

"My thoughts exactly." Hayden shoved the remainder of one into his mouth.

They ate, each obviously enjoying their food, but there was an underlying discomfort that remained in the room.

She searched for a safe topic to bring up to keep them occupied. "So, what've you been up to since I last saw you, Hayden?"

"Work. More work." He shoved several ketchup-tipped french fries into his mouth.

"No girlfriend?"

"Nope. Nothing serious anyway."

"You seemed pretty interested in Cadence." She held off biting her fry in wait for his reaction.

"That reporter?" Hayden tilted his head. "Why would you think that?"

"The pair of you were flirting like crazy." She shoved the crispy fry into her mouth.

"No way."

"Ah, man," Nolan said. "She's not wrong. Not at all."

Hayden fixed an imposing stare on them. Nolan had told her that the first day he'd met Hayden in the library, the guy had glared at him like this for no apparent reason. But as their study group gathered, he'd given everyone the same look, so Nolan hadn't taken it personally. She imagined it worked well when Hayden was an Oregon state trooper but otherwise, he could easily intimidate people.

Like right now.

She picked up a fry, swirled it in the ketchup, and changed the subject. "I thought one of the team would be married with kids by now."

Hayden shrugged. She'd caused him to shut down, and he wasn't likely to talk for the rest of the meal.

Of all the team members, he was the one who needed the most control over his life. Nolan might like to be in charge, but Hayden demanded control. Maybe that meant he couldn't let a woman into his world.

Maybe it stemmed from when he'd lost his parents as a teenager and had been put in foster care. Unlike a lot of the stories often told about foster care, he'd had a very positive experience, but he never fully connected with his foster family. Once he aged out of the program, he didn't stay in touch with them. He got through college on scholarships and hard work, and like the others on the team, replaced their nonexistent or dysfunctional family with each other.

Both men seemed kind of sullen, and she was likely to blame.

"Maybe you guys should consider arranged marriages," she joked to lighten things up.

"Oh, gross." Hayden rolled his eyes. "You're kidding, right?"

"Right."

He shuddered. "Trust me, I'm not that desperate for a woman in my life."

She looked at Nolan, wondering why he hadn't commented at all, and found him holding a fork of coleslaw at his mouth and watching her. Had her questions touched a nerve on his family or on the way he'd once thought she'd bailed on him?

She really wished they were alone and she could ask him, but Hayden was large and present in the room.

Nolan's phone rang. He looked at his screen and pushed his lunch plate away. "It's Dylan."

He tapped the phone. "Putting you on speaker, man, so Mina can hear you."

"Got something for you." Dylan's excited tone carried throughout the room.

"This about Wade?" Nolan asked.

"Better than that. I've identified your Smythe fella."

"You have?" Mina jumped to her feet. "Who?"

"He's one Zachary Tate. Lives in Seaside Harbor. Works in transport at the hospital. Professes to be a starving actor and has debt up to his eyeballs."

Adrenaline kicked Mina's heart rate up, and she planted her hands on the table to keep from pacing the room. "How did you find him?"

"I traced the login for the mansion reservation. He didn't bother to hide his IP address. Not a surprise. Most people don't do that."

Mina didn't care why he didn't hide the unique internet number assigned to his computer, she just wanted to know if it meant they could find him. "So do you have his physical address?"

"I do indeed. I'll text it to you." Dylan took a short breath. "And before you ask, I checked the hospital schedule to see if he's working today. He's off."

"Talk about first-rate service," Nolan said.

"Hey, you hired the A-Team of forensics." Dylan chuckled. "Still working on Wade, but I also have information on your graduation pictures. Located them online. I first found them at the academy. I had to hack their database to get the information. So either your suspect is a hacker, he hired a hacker, or he knows someone at the academy."

"If Tate didn't bother to hide his IP address, he's not likely a hacker," Mina said.

"Good point," Dylan said, "But he could've hired one."

"If he knows someone at the academy, it might mean he's in law enforcement," Nolan said.

Mina didn't like his implications. "Not at our office. My sergeant has investigated everyone who's worked there past and present and found nothing suspicious."

"He might've covered his tracks," Nolan said. "Or could be serving in another agency or even be private now."

Yeah, could be on the LLL team. She gave Nolan a pointed look. She hoped he didn't think she was beginning to suspect his team, but she wouldn't take time to clarify that. "And the other place you found pictures, Dylan?"

"The individual photos are used as rookie pictures at the agencies the team worked for on their first jobs," he answered. "Again it would've required hacking to access them, but all agencies? That's unlikely."

"So at this point, it's kind of a dead end." Nolan leaned back.

"Seems like it," Dylan said. "But you never know when the information could be helpful."

"We have another favor to ask." Mina told him about Percy and Cadence. "If I text you the information can you run a background check on them to see if they're legit?"

"Sure, but is this top priority?"

Mina glanced at Nolan to get his opinion.

"I wouldn't sit on it," he said. "Running the background on the dad could reveal who the mayor seemed to be helping."

"Okay, then I'll get someone else on our team to help out."

"Thanks, man," Nolan said. "Text me Tate's address."

"Will do." The call ended.

Expecting an instant text, Mina stared at Nolan's phone. She could sense Nolan staring at it too.

"Do you really have to check Cadence and Percy out?" Hayden asked.

Nolan peered at his teammate. "You don't need me to answer that question."

"Nah, I know you have to do it." Hayden rolled his shoulders. "They just seemed like they were telling the truth."

"As do many people who try to deceive law enforcement," Mina said.

"Yeah, you're right. Forget I even said anything." Hayden turned his attention back to his computer.

Silence consumed the room. Tension mounted. Mina wanted to do something to relieve it, but what? She couldn't prove Percy and Cadence were telling the truth, nor could she make the text appear. Still, she had to say something. "This is excruciating. Are you sure you still have a signal?"

Nolan glanced at his screen. "Full bars."

He'd no more than replied when it chimed.

"Hayden," he called out and rattled off the address. "Get the property up on the screen, and let's see if you can find a surveillance photo."

"On it." Hayden's fingers flew over the keyboard, clicking into the stillness of the room.

An electronic map appeared on the screen with the address highlighted by a red dot.

"Zoom in," Mina directed.

The screen whizzed closer in.

"I know that neighborhood." She shook her head. "And not because I have friends or family living there. It's a low-rent, high-crime area. Lots of drugs, petty crimes, and prostitution. Some assaults."

Nolan frowned. "Dylan said Tate had money issues, so maybe that's all he can afford."

"Whatever the reason, we're going to pay him a visit." Mina got up.

Nolan stood and planted his hands on his hips. "Not without looking at a surveillance photo, and not without backup."

She didn't like that he was suddenly demanding, but he was right. They should have backup, but... "As much as I'd like to have someone watching our backs, I can't afford to pull another deputy from patrol. The murder investigation already has us too extended as it is."

"I'll be glad to do it," Hayden offered.

"I don't know about that." She studied him, her mind racing over what to do.

"Think about his skills." Nolan apparently wasn't going to give up so easily. "He's former CBP and knows how to meld into the surroundings like he did down at the border. No one will even know he's there."

Nolan was right. A Customs and Border Protection agent would be highly skilled at surveillance and covert operations.

"What he said." Hayden grinned, a crooked boyish smile that belied the seriousness of their discussion.

His smile was infectious, but she wouldn't crack even a hint of one in return. "You're not an official deputy, and if something went south and you had to use force, my agency's reputation could be at stake."

"Simple," Nolan said as if deciding what to eat for dinner instead of a potentially life-altering decision like the one they had to make. "Deputize him too."

Mina frowned. "I don't—"

Nolan flashed up a hand. "Before you say no, he won't get involved unless you need him, but he'll be there if things get out of hand."

Unable to decide, she continued to stare at him.

Nolan met her gaze. "I haven't let you down or embarrassed your agency, have I? Hayden won't either."

She could hardly think straight when his puppy-dog eyes peered at her.

"Okay, fine," she said against her better judgment, then turned her focus to Hayden. "I'll sign you on, but you'll only act if and when I direct you to."

"Scout's honor." Hayden held up his hand as if swearing an oath.

"He really was a scout," Nolan said. "One of those over-achievers who stayed in all the way through high school."

"Good to know. If I need a fire started, I'll be sure to ask." She grinned, and they all laughed, but she didn't let it go on for long. "Get that satellite photo up so we can wrap this up before dark."

Hayden saluted and turned his attention to his computer.

Mina ran the op in her mind while she waited for the photo to appear. She had to wait for the final details to determine their actions, but she could at least get her mindset right for approaching a potential murder suspect.

Because one thing she'd learned on the job—she needed full focus whenever danger was present. Sure, she'd come under jeopardy as a deputy and sheriff, but today, making sure Nolan stayed safe and alive weighed even heavier on her than her usual goal to keep her deputies and county residents safe.

22

Nolan kept his gaze roving the area as he walked with Mina across the broken concrete toward Tate's apartment in the rundown complex. She kept her hand on her sidearm and her focus traveling around a litter-filled lot.

Tate lived in a worn and weathered three-story building with cedar-shake siding and lime-green doors. Nolan doubted the place had been updated since the sixties. It looked exactly like an apartment complex fitting the area surrounding them.

He didn't like leaving Hayden at the car, but they'd promised Mina that he wouldn't intervene unless things went south with Tate.

Mina stepped up to apartment 112 and planted her feet to look up at him. "Remember, I do the talking, and you keep your eyes open for any situation brewing."

He gave a sharp nod when his internal tension begged him to joke that she'd simply brought him along as eye candy, but this wasn't the time for any humor, and their stress would help keep them focused on situational awareness.

She pounded on the door and then stepped to the side,

moving him out of the way even more so Tate couldn't see them through the peephole and choose to ignore them or hit them if he started firing through the door.

The door opened the distance a chain lock allowed, and someone peered out. "Help you?"

Mina held out her credentials and identified herself. "Open the door, Tate. I'd like to have a word with you."

He closed the door and released the chain to open it a bit more. The guy wore sloppy jogging pants with a stained, gray T-shirt for University of Oregon. But most importantly, if he slicked back his black hair, Nolan could be looking at Smythe. Nolan resisted shooting up a hand in victory and waited for Mina to act.

Tate stared at her. "What could you want with me? I didn't break any laws."

He looked over her shoulder at Nolan, and his eyes widened. "It's you! You're one of the guys from the mansion. Don't tell me you reported me for locking the door and taking your phones? I didn't do anything wrong. It was just part of the script."

"Actually," Mina said. "Locking the door on guests is considered kidnapping, and I could bring you up on charges."

"Wait, what?" Tate shook his head. "It was just a job. I was following the rules. Following the script I was given. I was told everyone was in on it."

"How about we go inside and discuss this?" Mina asked.

"I don't know." He bit his lip. "It sounds maybe like I need a lawyer."

Nolan had had enough of this punk putting them off. He shoved the door fully open. "How about you let the sheriff in? If not, I'll be glad to press charges against you."

"Fine." Tate stood back.

Nolan waited for Mina to enter, then followed, eyeing

Tate all the way. "You answer every question we ask truthfully, or like I said, I can arrange for you to be put behind bars. And it won't be just one kidnapping charge, it'll be six. You'll never see the light of day again."

Tate swallowed, his Adam's apple bobbing in his scrawny neck. "What do you want from me?"

The small living room smelled like a combination of pizza and old socks. The space held only a cheap vinyl sofa, small television on a stand, and a table lamp sitting on the floor in the corner, casting deep shadows on the walls.

Mina turned to face Tate. "Who hired you to play the part of Smythe the butler?"

"I don't know. I never met him, and he never told me his name."

Nolan eyed him. "You expect us to believe you did this for someone you've never met?"

"Hey, when you don't know where your next meal is coming from, you take pretty much any job. This was a high-paying gig, and it didn't seem like there was anything illegal about it." Tate dropped onto the sofa, and the cushions squeaked. "Trust me, if I'd known locking you in the room was illegal, I wouldn't have done it."

"If you didn't meet the person who hired you, how did you arrange the gig?" Mina asked.

"It was all done on a site where local actors can be hired for various jobs. Things like birthday parties, singing telegrams. Stuff like that. We started out emailing through the site, and then I signed the agreement with him."

"How did he pay you?" Nolan asked.

"I got half up front and half after I finished the gig. Payment is arranged outside of the site, and you just notify the site that you received payment as promised or the person hiring you is blackballed to keep them from stiffing other actors."

"What form of payment did he use?" Mina asked.

"I asked for cash because then none of it would...you know...go to Uncle Sam."

"Something else we could report you for." Nolan stared at him.

"But what we're more interested in," Mina said, "is finding out how you received payment."

"We were scheduled to meet in person one day. Before we could, he dropped the money off in my mailbox with a note saying he had to go out of town at the last minute. He also emailed me the details of what I needed to do for a successful performance."

"Details like what?" Mina asked.

"He thought of everything and didn't cheap out on the things. I had to buy a custom tuxedo from a specific shop in Portland so he could be sure I looked like a professional butler. I got the feeling that the shop owner was going to report back to tell him I'd ordered it."

"Did the shop owner give you the name of the person who paid for it?" Mina asked.

"Nah, but I asked him a couple of times. He just clammed up, and I finally gave up."

"What's the name of that shop?" Nolan asked.

"Suited Elegance." Tate pinched his nose. "Kind of snooty sounding, am I right?"

Nolan ignored him. "What else did the man who hired you require of you?"

"He described how he wanted me to wear my hair slicked back and made a special point of saying that I had to wear white gloves all the stinking time, even before the performance began."

"He say why?" Mina asked.

"Yeah, get this. He wanted the night to be perfect and didn't want me to leave prints on anything, marring their pristine nature." Tate shook his head. "It made sense for the crystal and dishes, but not the food containers. Still, he was paying me a lot, so I did what he said."

Something about this didn't sit well with Nolan, but he would continue until he figured it out. "How did you get the food?"

"He had me rent a van to pick the meal up at the caterers. I had to do it on my credit card, but he gave me enough cash to reimburse me. Tide and Thyme is run out of some chick's house. At the mansion, I had to take the food trays and put them in the kitchen. Then I had to make sure the food was either kept cold or warm and would be ready to serve on time."

"And then, of course," Nolan said, "you had to greet us at the door and take our phones."

He nodded, but a sheepish look crossed his face.

"Didn't you find that odd about the cell phones?" Mina asked.

"No, the guy explained everything. He said all of you were in on the event and were going to be playing roles you'd agreed to play. He said that none of you wanted the performance to be interrupted by a phone call."

"And the fact that we all complained about giving you our phones didn't tell you otherwise?" Nolan asked.

Tate shook his head. "I figured that's what your role was so I improvised, as he instructed me to do."

"Did you clone or otherwise mess with our phones?"

"Nah, they just sat in the bag so you could find them when you were ready to leave."

"And when you gave in and told us the night was courtesy of one of our clients," Nolan said. "Was that part of the script?"

He laughed, then quickly hid his humor and nodded. "I

figured you would know that, since it was part of my script and all."

"Did you interact with Harmony Vance while you were there?" Mina asked.

"Yeah, she met me when I arrived, told me she would be upstairs watching television if I needed anything, and then she went upstairs. I felt bad for her being stuck there all night and went off script. Gave her a snack in the afternoon and took her a dinner meal, but then I never saw her again."

"So you locked us in the room after dinner, and then you cleaned up," Nolan said. "What did you do with the caterer's trays?"

"I loaded it all into the van and dropped things in a dumpster here at the complex before returning the van."

Nolan didn't much like this guy, but he didn't think he was lying. "And how did you get your final payment?"

"It was in my mailbox when I got home." He shook his head. "I sure wouldn't have left that much cash in this neighborhood. Not even in my locked mailbox, but that's the way this guy wanted to deal."

"How much did he pay you for the night?" Mina asked.

"Two grand." He clasped his hands together. "So you can see why I did it, even if some things were a bit sketchy."

"Did you help set up the escape room?" Nolan asked.

"Me? No. No way." He shook his head hard. "It was that way when I got there."

"We'll need you to send the emails that you shared with each other at the beginning," Mina said.

"Yeah, sure, I can do that." He bobbed his knee and let his gaze travel between them.

"Forward them to this email address." Mina handed him her business card and eyed him. "I'm not going to take you in tonight, but if I find out you lied about anything, I'll bring you up on charges. Don't leave the area."

"Hey, no way. I didn't lie. Besides, does it look like I can afford to go anywhere?" He stood and held out his hands. "No need to arrest me."

They left the apartment, and Mina turned to Nolan. "At least we got one thing out of that conversation we can follow up on."

Nolan nodded. "The minute we get back to the inn, we can look into that tailor shop. Maybe then, we can find a connection to the night and finally wrap up the murder investigation."

And hope that led to Becca's whereabouts, but he wouldn't say that aloud, in case he was wrong.

Frustrated, Mina didn't want to take time to eat, but Reece had arranged a dinner delivery from the local Italian restaurant. The food rested on a table near the wall. Most of the LLL team members were seated with plates in front of them. The smell of garlic and oregano wrapped around Mina, and her stomach rumbled.

"See," Nolan said. "I told you we needed to eat."

She might want to get straight to work, but they could kill two birds with one stone. "I guess we can eat and do an update at the same time."

"Indeed." He took the files and laptop from her hands. "Fix yourself a plate, and I'll put these down."

She really didn't need his help in putting files on the table, and she was just cranky enough that she almost snapped at him, but instead smiled up at him for his kindness. If they were to start dating after this was all over, she would have to get used to having someone in her life and not be so independent all the time. That would be a huge adjustment.

At the table, she picked up a large plate and scooped out ravioli, her mouth watering at the sight of the rich red sauce and thick noodle pillows.

Reece stepped in line behind her and retrieved a plate.

"Thanks for organizing the meal," Mina said. "We had a big lunch, and I didn't think I was hungry until I caught a whiff of the garlic."

"No thanks needed." Reece picked up a crusty slice of garlic bread. "It's kind of my thing on the team. We often get so involved in our investigations that we don't always remember to eat, and one thing I know for sure is, you have to maintain your own strength if you're going to be able to help someone else."

What she said made sense, and it helped Mina relax a bit and load her plate with spaghetti.

"It seems like you and Nolan have patched things up." Reece eased closer to reach the spoon in the ravioli.

Mina glanced back at Nolan who was heading to the table, and he gave her a sweet smile. "I guess so."

"Well, he seems far more relaxed and not tense with you, so it seems like from his point of view, things must be better." She looked over her shoulder. "Case in point, that smile meant just for you."

"Yeah, I guess you're right." There had been more of an easiness between them, but Mina had been too wrapped up in the investigation to give it much thought.

"You know it nearly killed him when you didn't respond to his note." Reece narrowed her eyes. "He basically lost interest in everything, including the job he loved, and was lucky he didn't get fired. He stopped eating and lost a lot of weight. When we all met in Portland for Christmas that year, we had to stage an intervention to get him to start eating properly. It's hard to imagine him that way now, but it happened."

She had no idea he'd reacted that badly or she'd had such an impact on him. She'd suffered too, but not to that extreme.

"If you're not serious, let him know now before he falls hard again," Reece warned. "Because I think this time it would kill him."

She walked away with her plate, and Mina watched her move to the table.

Nolan stepped into place next to Mina. "You two look like you were having a serious conversation."

"You know how it goes," she said and grabbed some bread, then spun for the table before he asked additional questions.

By the time he joined her, she'd gotten out her folder and was sharing with the team the conversation with Smythe. "Has anyone run across information on Suited Elegance?"

"Not me," Reece said.

The other team members murmured their nos.

"I'll dig into the shop to see what I can find," Hayden said. "Maybe even access their customer list."

"Sometimes the old-fashioned way of doing things is the easiest," Abby said. "We could interview the owner. If he's an upright guy, and he hears a woman is missing and someone's been murdered, he's more likely than not to cooperate."

Nolan reached for his water. "Are you volunteering to go?"

"Sure," she said. "I've got all the files in order until we get any evidence files from Veritas, and I *do* have the best interview skills of the team."

"Modest too." Jude laughed.

"I'm only speaking the truth."

"She's right," Gabe said. "You don't suffer as many years

as a sheriff as she did without learning how to ask the right questions and probe when you don't get the answers you want."

She shot Gabe a shocked look. "Suffer?"

"Admit it," he said. "If we polled everyone here but Mina, they would agree. Being a sheriff isn't the easiest job in the world and can be filled with more politics than policing."

"I wish I could say you're wrong, but you're not." Abby looked at Nolan. "I'll head out right after we finish this update. I can stay with a friend of mine in Portland tonight."

"Would that be Lauren?" Jude asked.

"It would." Abby grilled Jude with a gaze that Mina thought many a suspect had been treated to. "Why do you ask?"

"No reason."

"Hah!" Gabe said. "He's had a thing for her ever since he worked with her at the Bureau but was too chicken to ask her out. Why do you think it didn't work out with Becca?"

"Dude," Hayden said. "Lauren's way out of your league."

"I know." Jude honestly looked heartbroken.

Mina felt bad for the teasing, and she could help by redirecting them back to the investigation. "We do have other things outstanding."

"I ruled out the mayor having to pay for his medical treatments himself," Reece said, twirling her fork in her spaghetti.

"How did you manage that?" Gabe asked.

Reece put her fingers to her ear and mouth as if on the phone. "Hello, this is Betty Lou from plan services, and I surely hope you can help me today. We received a complaint about outstanding invoices and would like to confirm they've been paid."

Gabe rolled his eyes. "Good old Betty Lou rises to live another day."

The group laughed, and Mina assumed this was a character Reece used often.

She was all for lightening the tension, but maybe they needed tension to get them moving in the right direction. "We still don't know what the mayor's will contains. It's possible that it all goes to Becca, and his brother-in-law Wade, a sketchy guy, didn't think that was right. He was seen arguing with the mayor frequently. Could be about that."

"And could be motive for murder," Reece said.

"Would also explain abducting Becca," Nolan said. "If she was set to inherit everything, he couldn't let her live."

"I sure don't like that option," Reece said. "Because that means she's likely dead, and we have to keep hoping she's alive. If you need some help, I'd be happy to find the guy tonight and talk to him."

"Thanks," Nolan said. "Dylan's running background on Wade, so let me check in with him first to see if he located anything suspicious."

"Hold up," Hayden called out. "You might want to hang around here. I should be able to access the shop's financial records soon. We could get us a list of customers' names and narrow it down to who paid for the tuxedo."

"Good." Nolan smiled at his teammate. "In that case we'll wait here for Hayden's list, and Wade is all yours, Reece."

"I'm on it." She shoved her empty plate away.

Abby stacked her plate with Reece's. "You still want me to head to the tux shop?"

Nolan nodded. "It'll take several hours to get there, so it would be good if you were there first thing in the morning to question the owner in case we don't locate the information we need."

Abby stood and glanced at Jude. "Want to ride shotgun with me?"

Jude blushed. "If you seriously think you need someone with you, then yes. If you're just harassing me about coming to stay with Lauren, then no."

She ruffled his hair. "Sorry, I got this. Just making fun."

He stared up at her. "Do not mention anything about me to her when you get to Portland."

"Since you served together, she's bound to ask how you're doing."

"You can tell her I'm great, but keep it at that."

"Not a word about your crush." Abby mocked zipping her lips and turned toward the door. "Call me if anything comes up or if you need me to do anything else in Portland."

Nolan nodded. "Let's get this table cleared so we're ready to act on the list Hayden provides."

Mina grabbed her plate and Nolan's too, then took them to a bin Reece had set up for dirty dishes. She didn't stop to talk to anyone but did her job and returned to her seat to open her laptop.

Her phone rang. "It's Sierra."

She answered the video call and set the phone between her and Nolan. Sierra smiled. "Glad I caught you before we took off."

"Please tell us you have something for us," Mina said.

Sierra's smile evaporated. "Not any conclusions yet, but I wanted to let you know we're finished with the scenes and leaving town. Emory has already started DNA running from the samples that Grady took back last night, and she should have profiles in the morning."

Morning. That might be the time they finally had something concrete to act on. If, and it was a big if, they located DNA with a profile that returned a match from CODIS.

"I'll get started on fingerprints and other trace evidence in the morning," she said. "And Grady will finish his ballistics report then too."

"Did you locate anything at Mayor Sutton's place?" Mina asked.

She shook her head. "No. That is definitely not your crime scene. No blood evidence at all. Not even a trace left behind after any cleanup. Same goes for the escape room."

"You're sure?" Mina asked, and hoped she didn't take offense at it.

"Positive."

"Sorry to question you."

"No worries." Sierra gave a sweet smile. "I know the pressure you're under. It's stressful enough to have to locate a killer. Another to have to find a missing woman at the same time."

Mina was thankful this woman understood her plight. Sierra would do everything she could to provide a lead, but only God knew if the lead would come in time to save Becca's life.

23

Mina's phone rang, startling her awake. She glanced at the retro orange clock beside her bed. Four a.m. She grabbed her phone and sat up. She didn't recognize the number on the screen, but assumed it was related to either Becca's or the mayor's investigation.

She accepted the call. "Sheriff Park."

"Mina, it's Dylan."

Dylan? She blinked to clear her head from sleep fog. "I assume since you're calling at this time of night you have something for me."

"Man, do I ever. Becca's phone just pinged from a tower near Lost Lake."

The excitement in his tone raised Mina's excitement too. "Does that mean we can find her?"

"I can't guarantee that, but you should be able to find her phone. I have the exact coordinates of its location."

She stood and started to pace. "The phone company can be that precise?"

"No. But once it pinged on one of their towers, I opened the image I made of her computer. She had Find My iPhone turned on, and shazam! There it was. The address blinking up at me."

"Excellent," Mina said. "Any information on the property?"

"Google didn't map the location, but I found satellite images." His serious tone had returned. "They're grainy, but it looks like a small log cabin. Owner is a Knox Anderson."

Knox Anderson. Mina searched her sleepy brain to see if his name had appeared in their investigations. She especially thought through the names Hayden had provided tonight, those who turned out to be legit customers of the tuxedo shop. "Not a name I recognize."

"The mailing address on property records is for Portland. I did a quick search for him, and he's a big-time property developer. No connections to Becca or the mayor turned up, but that doesn't mean there aren't any."

"Property developer, huh? Not the kind of guy you'd expect to kill our mayor and abduct his daughter."

"No. But if this is a recreational or hunting cabin, the killer could be hiding out there."

"Do a deep dive on him just to be sure there's no link to the mayor or Becca."

"You got it."

Adrenaline raced through her body. "I need the coordinates. I don't want to get them wrong, so text them to me."

"I'll do it right now."

"Send me Anderson's address in Portland as well," she said. "Not like this isn't enough, but have you located any other information?"

"Why, yes. IT's golden boy comes through again." He laughed. "First is the mayor's will. He scanned the official one to his computer. Everything goes to Becca except for the boat called *Off the Hook*. That goes to a Wade Collins. But he also had a draft in his email of one he was working on with his attorney. In that one, everything including the boat goes to Becca."

"So he was cutting Wade out," she said. "If he knew about the changes, he'd have a solid motive for murder."

"Yeah, I mean if this boat is worth something."

"A couple hundred thousand."

Dylan let out a low whistle. "Losing that would be significant enough to end someone's life."

"And the second thing you found?"

"His insurance policy. He had a two hundred fifty thousand dollar policy. He's had it for years, but he changed it after his wife died to remove her as primary beneficiary. Becca receives everything."

"I guess this could be reason for murder, but nothing has changed recently, right? She doesn't appear to be in need of money, so why would she kill him now? I just don't see that happening."

"If she's with her phone, you can ask her that question."

"Send those coordinates. Keep me updated on anything else you locate. And, thanks." She ended the call and instead of waiting for his text, she phoned El.

Her detective answered on the fourth ring, her voice sleepy.

Mina explained the reason for her call. "Activate the SWAT team. We'll meet in the courthouse parking lot here in Lost Lake."

"Roger that," El said without question. "See you soon."

When Mina had assumed the sheriff's role, she'd organized a SWAT team, and they'd been training ever since. The team was comprised of five members including herself, El, and Abe, plus Deputies Banfield and Ewing. She hoped they would never need an emergency response team, but wanted to be prepared in the event of a school or mass shooting incident.

She tapped Nolan's icon on her phone. When he answered, she explained the situation. "We're meeting in the courthouse parking lot as soon as everyone can get here. You're welcome to come along, but you'll have to leave any breach to SWAT."

"Understood," he said without argument. "I'm on my way."

Mina had worked SWAT in Portland and knew what they might be up against when they arrived at the property. She would like to involve Nolan, but he hadn't trained with the team and could be a liability.

Dressed in a clean uniform, she brushed her teeth and washed her face, then raced toward the door. She lived only a short distance from the courthouse and was the first to arrive. She opened her trunk, put on her Kevlar vest from her go bag, and retrieved her rifle.

She sat behind the wheel and called dispatch as she waited for others to arrive. "Run warrants and record on Knox Anderson." She provided his Portland address.

"Roger that," the dispatcher said, and the radio fell silent.

Mina tapped her thumb against the wheel as she waited. Her adrenaline kept pumping, and she could hardly sit still, but it would be good to know if the property owner had any priors or warrants.

"Nothing outstanding or any priors," the dispatcher said. "Not even a traffic ticket."

"Ten-four," Mina said and stowed her radio.

A pair of headlights swung into the lot, and she got out of the car to wait. Nolan. Good. She was glad he arrived first so she could reemphasize his laid-back role on the op.

His vehicle lurched to a stop next to hers, and he was out of it in a flash. He wore his usual polo shirt and cargo pants, but had also added tactical boots and vest. He looked darkly dangerous as he hustled over to her, and their upcoming mission hit her full force.

A woman might be waiting and depending on Mina for the ultimate rescue. One mistake was all it would take to end her life.

Mina crouched in the woods and surveyed the log cabin with her binoculars. A faint light shone from the back of the house through a big picture window, but she spotted no movement inside. Still, she wouldn't move ahead. El was at her patrol vehicle, running the plates on a black Jeep Wrangler parked out front of the log structure. They'd had to leave their vehicles a good distance away so the engine noise wouldn't travel in these woods and alert their suspect.

Nolan, along with the rest of the SWAT team, were hunkered down with Mina waiting for El's return.

"I really don't see this Anderson guy being someone who would abduct Becca or kill the mayor," Nolan said. "Did Dylan find any connection between them?"

"Nothing yet," Mina said. "But he wasn't certain there weren't any."

"The guy would really have to go off the rails to do something like this," Abe said.

Mina lowered her binoculars. "Seems unlikely, but then, when I worked in Portland, I interviewed suspects you'd never expect to commit murder doing so."

A sound came from behind, and they all swiveled to see El slipping between trees. She dropped next to Mina. "Jeep is registered to Knox Anderson."

"Okay, so that says we have what appears to be an upstanding citizen at his cabin containing Becca's phone."

"It seems as if they're sleeping." El shifted in the long

grass. "I suggest if we can find an unlocked door, we enter silently rather than breaking down the door and forcing a hostage situation."

"I agree," Mina said. "One of us should go ahead and look for that open door."

"I'll go," Abe volunteered.

Abe would be Mina's last choice to send in as a scout. If any of them were trigger-happy, it would be Abe, and she could easily see him breaking protocol and causing the very situation they wanted to avoid.

"As lead on this investigation," El said. "I'd like to be the one to go."

"Then move," Mina said. "Check for the door. Do not enter. Return with a report."

El started to rise.

"Make sure your radio is off," Mina said.

"It's off, but I'll check it anyway." El fumbled with her radio and then scooted through the scrub to the clearing.

The detective stealthily advanced toward the cabin, darting behind tall evergreen trees, the pale moonlight highlighting her body just enough for Mina to see movement. She crept up the four steps to the front porch and rose to look into the big window. She edged to the door, checked the knob, then took the same path down to circle behind the building.

As Mina waited for El to reappear, she counted, forcing herself to remember to breathe. She'd reached fifty when El's body materialized on the side of the cabin.

She traced her steps back to them and settled next to Mina. "Front door is locked. Back door is unlocked. Front area is a kitchen-living room combo. Light is coming from the hallway that leads to the back entrance. Three doors in the hallway. One is closed. Likely bedrooms and bathroom. No sign of a security system or any kind of booby trap."

Mina quickly made a plan. "El and I'll go in. Clear the open areas and leave the closed door for last, at which time we'll announce ourselves and force our way inside it. Abe and Banfield, you have the front door. Ewing the back. Don't enter unless things go south."

"And me?" Nolan asked.

"Stay here until I call you."

His shoulders slumped, but he nodded. "I'll pray for a safe resolution."

"That's always appreciated." Mina stood, but left her rifle with Nolan. "Let's move."

She didn't bother taking El's circuitous route, but raised her sidearm and made a straight line toward the building. She paused at the front to let Banfield and Abe climb the steps to the porch. She checked the picture window to make sure there was still zero movement inside. Good. Nothing. She signaled for El and Ewing to follow her around back.

A gravel path led alongside the building that seemed to be in nearly new condition, but she chose the grass for silence. At the back, she climbed the three steps to a small porch to open the door. Thankfully, it didn't make a sound.

She glanced back at El and then stepped inside to flick on her flashlight and hold it out with her weapon. She tiptoed down the hallway, pausing to search a bedroom and bathroom.

Empty.

She passed the closed door and held her breath lest she make any noise.

In the family room, she swung her gun and light to the left, then the right, running it over the small kitchen and living area with a large stone fireplace, finding no one. She turned to El and shook her head.

"We go in," Mina whispered.

El spun and took long strides down the hallway. Mina followed and grabbed the doorknob.

"Police!" She pushed inside, and her light landed on a man asleep in the bed. He shot up.

"Police. Show me your hands."

"Hands!" El shouted. "Hands, now!"

He raised his hands and bent his head against their lights. "What's this about?"

"Becca," Mina said. "Where is she?"

"Becca who? I don't know any Becca."

"What's your name?" Mina asked.

"Knox Anderson."

Mina kept her gaze locked on him. "You own this place?"

"I do. Is that a problem?"

"Cuff him," Mina said to El.

She shoved her gun into the holster and went to the bed. "On your stomach. Hands behind your back."

"But I didn't do anything," he said.

"Now!" El snapped.

He complied, arguing all the way. Once securely cuffed, El helped the man sit on the edge of the bed.

Mina turned on the overhead light, and let her eyes adjust before checking the closet and under the bed. Nothing.

"Does this place have a basement or a root cellar?" she asked.

"Just a crawl space," he said.

Mina poked her head into the hallway. "Ewing, get in here."

He hurried down the hall.

"You and the others check the crawlspace for Becca."

"Roger that," Ewing said and strode away.

"I don't know why you think I have this Becca person," Anderson said. "But I don't have her, and I don't know her."

Mina locked her focus on him. "Then why do you have her phone?"

"Her phone? I don't—wait. Oh, man. That's it, right? I found a phone when I went hiking this afternoon. It was dead so I brought it home. When I went to bed, I plugged it in to charge. Figured if it didn't have a password, I could look at it in the morning. You know, to see who it belongs to and return it to the owner. Worst case, they would use their app Find My iPhone and come looking for it. I never expected the police to show up and cuff me like some common criminal."

His story sounded legit, but Mina couldn't take it at face value. "Please understand our point of view. We have a murdered citizen, his daughter is missing, likely abducted, and you're in possession of her phone. We have to be very cautious. I think you can understand that."

"I understand you needing to question me," he lifted his chin, "but I don't understand the need to cuff me."

He had a point, but... "I can see why you think it's a bit extreme, but I need to protect my deputies."

"Not hardly." He puffed out his chest. "If I *had* abducted this woman as you said, why would I plug her phone in here? Don't you think I'm smart enough to know it would then be traceable?"

Mina stared at him. "Just the fact that you know anything about a phone leading to your location raises suspicions for me."

He growled his frustration and glared at her.

Footsteps sounded in the hallway, and she poked her head outside the room.

"All clear in the crawlspace." Abe pressed his lips tight. He'd been looking for some action, and it hadn't materialized.

"The minute we get back to the office," she said. "I need

you to request a warrant to search his Portland home and any businesses he might own."

"Now wait a minute." Anderson started to rise.

El pushed him down. "You could be holding Becca or have held her in these locations. Or even left the gun that killed the mayor."

Anderson snarled. "I am seriously going to sue your joke of a small-town department when we get done here. You'll be sorry you treated me this way."

His offensive comment didn't bother Mina in the least. She knew she was doing the right thing. "We're not doing anything any other law enforcement agency wouldn't do in this situation. You can help yourself out if you remember where you found the phone and can show us."

He took several deep breaths. "I do and I can."

"Is it within walking distance?" she asked.

He nodded.

"Then take us there now." She eyed him. "Don't try anything or it won't go well for you."

He shook his head. "Why would I try anything? I'm not the criminal you seem to think I am."

"You can get some pants and shoes on before we go," Mina said.

"Thanks for the privacy." He glared at her, but grabbed his jeans from a nearby chair and slipped into them and a pair of athletic shoes.

Mina gestured at the doorway. "Detective Lyons, lead the way. Mr. Anderson, you'll follow her."

El stepped off, and Anderson fell into place. Mina trailed, her hand on her sidearm.

El opened the door and stepped out, then took Anderson by the arm. She strode down the steps and into the cool night at a solid pace. Thankfully, Anderson didn't drag his feet.

They moved down the gravel driveway and passed close to Nolan's position. Mina signaled for him to join them and told him what had transpired in the cabin.

"It'll be interesting to see where he found the phone," Nolan said.

"Indeed," was all Mina said as she wanted to concentrate on Anderson's behavior.

He walked with his shoulders back and didn't seem to hesitate. He didn't make any furtive moves or act as if he was going to try to take off. She really was believing his story, but there was no way she could let him go until they searched his properties or located Becca.

He took them to the road and turned right, traveling about a mile past their parked vehicles. He stopped near an odd-shaped tree.

"I found it here," he said.

"You're sure?" El asked.

He nodded. "The monkey puzzle tree is a dead giveaway. I hike a lot, and you don't see one of these often in the wilds of Oregon."

Mina had never seen a tree like it before. The branches were narrow, somewhat contorted, and covered with thick, dark-green triangular leaves.

Anderson jerked his head toward the side of the road. "The phone was in the ditch down there."

"Why were you in the ditch?" she asked.

"A car was coming down the road at a fast clip, so I was forced to step off for safety."

"Did you get a good look at the car?" Nolan asked.

"It was a newer model Ford Explorer. White."

"You didn't happen to catch the plates did you?" Mina asked.

He shook his head. "They were Oregon, but splattered with mud and not clear."

"So you picked up the phone and returned to your cabin?" El asked.

He shook his head. "I finished my walk. About two more miles down the road and back."

"Did you happen to see that vehicle again and where it went?" Mina asked.

"No. Was just me out here."

"Do you know if the houses around you are occupied, or are they recreational cabins like yours?" El asked.

He shrugged. "I've only owned this place for less than a year and stayed here maybe a half dozen times. I come here to unplug and get away from people, so I'm not about to go out looking for them."

Mina understood that. "So you didn't see anyone in the area? Like someone who might've been looking for this phone?"

"No one."

Mina turned to El. "When we get back to the cabin, we'll send Abe for the vehicle and you two can escort Mr. Anderson to lock up."

Anderson spun and fired an angry stare at her. "Wait a minute. You're saying you're going to arrest me? Lock me up?"

Mina kept her tone level to keep from making him madder. "We're going to detain you for now while we search your other properties."

"And then what?" His eyes narrowed even more.

"That will all depend on what we find in our search."

He growled at her again. This man could be bad news for her career. Seriously bad, like get-her-fired bad. But no matter the consequences to herself and the job she loved, she had to do what was right for Becca.

24

Nearing seven a.m. and a large cup of steaming coffee in hand, Nolan paced the inn's conference room behind Hayden. As the team's IT expert, he created a map of properties surrounding Anderson's cabin. Their theory? Whoever took Becca tossed the phone out the car window on the way to their property or on their way back.

Mina and El were sitting at the table, ready to access DMV records. The moment Hayden located the owner's name, they would search the database for anyone who might own a white Ford Explorer like the one Anderson claimed to have seen on the road. Not that this person was a suspect. Just driving on the road didn't mean they'd tossed the phone out earlier, but if not a suspect, they could've witnessed something important.

Meanwhile, Abe was booking Anderson in jail and getting the warrants for his Portland addresses. Reece had seen the light on in the conference room and had come by to bring coffee, muffins, and fruit. She'd always been the mother of the group, if anyone filled that role, and it wasn't unusual for her to do such a thing.

"Map's done," Hayden called out. "Putting it on the

screen now. Properties are labeled one to five. I'll start looking up property records."

"I'll take the first one." Mina sipped on her coffee, then poised her fingers over the keypad.

El sat forward. "I've got number two."

"Okay, good," Hayden said. "Just one listing for all of the houses on this road. It'll be quick to get to them."

"We should watch for Wade's name," El said. "With the will change, he's a good possibility for abducting Becca."

"He's so broke I don't see him as being one of our property owners," Mina said. "But he could be squatting with her in one of them."

"He's not the guy on top of the list." Hayden called out the first name.

Mina's fingers flew over the keyboard of her department-issued computer.

Hayden yelled out the second name.

El typed, her speed slower than Mina's, but her concentration was unwavering.

Nolan had suspected Mina would have a top-notch team working for her, and he'd seen evidence of it many times.

"Next up is Lawrence Osborne," Hayden said.

Mina's and El's hands stilled, and their heads popped up.

Nolan looked at his teammate. "Say that again."

"Lawrence Osborne." Hayden narrowed his gaze. "Isn't that the medical examiner's name?"

"It is." Mina sat back and stared at Nolan. "There could be other Lawrence Osbornes. Is there a different mailing address from the cabin for correspondence?"

"Let me see." Hayden checked his screen, then rattled off a Seaside Harbor address.

Nolan's gut cramped. "Is that the doc's address?"

Mina didn't answer right away, but rubbed a hand over

her face. "He lives in Seaside Harbor. I've been to his house, and that's his street, but I don't remember the exact number. Can you pull the address up on a map program?"

"On it," Hayden said, and the words had no more than left his mouth when the map appeared on the big screen.

Mina studied it far longer than Nolan thought was needed. This had to be a mistake. The good doctor couldn't be involved in the murder, could he?

"That's his place." Mina's tone had taken on an edge of resignation.

"This has got to be a coincidence, right?" El asked.

Nolan gave it some thought. "I don't know him like you all do, but he did mention in the autopsy about serving in the Army Medical Corps. So he's probably familiar with weapons."

Mina sat up straight. "But that doesn't mean he shot the mayor. What motive would he have? And why would he be out to get you and your team?"

Yeah, why? Nolan ran through everything he knew about Osborne. "He said he was glad we were restoring the building. What if he really resents us owning it after his parents lost it to the bank foreclosure?"

El rested her hands on the table. "That was years ago. Why wait to do something about it now? And why not target the bank? It's not like you're doing anything wrong by owning it."

She had good points. Ones Nolan might not be able to refute. "Maybe he had hopes of one day getting the property back, but now that I own it, he realizes that's not going to happen."

Mina let out a long breath. "Again, why target you? It's not your fault."

"What if that realization is what caused him to act now?" El looked between them. "Making you the scapegoat of killing the mayor, you'd go to prison and lose the property leaving it for him to buy again."

"Okay, say that's true," Nolan said. "Why kill the mayor? Why not just kill any old person and try to pin it on us?"

"I can't believe we're even having this discussion about Dr. Osborne." Mina got up to pace. "I honestly don't buy the suggestion that he killed the mayor and abducted Becca."

Nolan could understand her disbelief. He was nearly on the same page. Nearly. "I don't believe Anderson abducted her either, but you have him behind bars. The very least we can do is dig deeper into Dr. Osborne."

"He's right." El pinned her focus on Mina. "We need to forget that we know him, that we don't believe he's capable of this, and scrutinize him just as we will the other property owners in the area."

Nolan appreciated that El could put aside her trust in Dr. Osborne. "He's the only one with a connection to the case thus far. So I say we put him on the top of the list. If we discover the other property owners have a better connection, then we move them up the list."

"Agreed," Mina said, but her face had paled. "Which means we visit his property."

Nolan hated seeing her reaction. Hated causing her discomfort. Hated to put a man with a solid reputation on the suspect list, much less at the top of it.

Didn't matter what he liked or didn't like. He—they—had to do the right thing here.

Becca was counting on all of them to save her life and bring her home.

Mina sat back in her chair, the muffin and coffee roiling in her stomach. Even the smell of the nutty, fresh-brewed coffee filling the air made her want to hurl. A deeply intense desire to pick up the phone and call Dr. Osborne to resolve this issue had her reaching for her phone.

No. She couldn't and let her hand fall. She couldn't violate the oath she'd sworn to the people. She couldn't talk to him or give him a heads-up or even an inkling of the fact they were going to visit his property.

Not only did he own the home closest to the tree where the phone had been found, but he also drove a white Ford Explorer, and he could have been in the area yesterday. First, she would find out if he was in the office today. If so, they would be free to visit the cabin without raising any suspicions.

Preparing what she might say, she dialed his cell phone. It rang and the call went instantly to voicemail. A reprieve. For now. She didn't leave a message but tapped the number for his office instead.

Her call connected and his receptionist Nora's sweet voice came over the phone.

Nora was known for gossiping, a perfect person to answer as far as Mina was concerned. "This is Sheriff Park. I have some questions for Dr. Osborne. Is he available?"

"I'm sorry, Sheriff," Nora said. "He's taking a few days off this week."

Oh no. Did that mean he was occupied with Becca?

Mina relaxed tense neck muscles to keep her anxiety in check. "My mistake. I must've misunderstood him at the autopsy on Monday."

"Or not," Nora said. "This was an unexpected vacation." She took a long pause and came back with a lowered voice. "Between you and me, something had him so stressed he couldn't even think. Lots of appointments and angry patients left for me to deal with, I'll tell you."

"I'm sorry," Mina said sincerely. "He must've really needed the time. Did he say where he was going?"

"No, and that's odd. He usually tells me, but he must really not want to be disturbed. He made a point of saying not to call his cell phone. He also arranged for the doctor who handles calls for him when he's out of town to take over."

"Thanks for the information, Nora," Mina said, but wished she hadn't called.

"Of course, sweetheart." Nora's soft voice nearly had Mina in tears. "If he checks in, do you want me to tell him you called?"

"No, let's not stress him out more. I'll just check the autopsy report and maybe my answer is there."

"Sounds like a plan."

If Dr. Osborne turned out to be a killer and kidnapper, Mina could easily imagine Nora's resulting distress. The woman had worked for him for years and would be devastated. As would all of his patients. As would Mina.

Hah! What was she saying? She was already close to crying. Breaking down. Right here. On the job.

Unacceptable.

She took a moment. Flexed her fingers. Released. Flexed and released. Cleared her mind, then turned to the others. Focused on keeping a flat emotionless tone, she reported the information Nora shared.

"That makes Osborne sound even more suspicious," Nolan said.

Mina didn't want to admit it. To say the words aloud, but... "It doesn't sound good."

Nolan moved closer, almost forcing her to look at him. He'd been watching her, but she'd ignored him. If she looked at his face and found one of his compassionate gazes pinned on her, she would lose it.

"This might be a long shot," he said, "but our team shoots at Gunner's Haven to keep our firing skills up."

Where was he going with this? She looked up at him. "And?"

"Has Osborne ever mentioned going there? If so, we could get information about the type of gun he likes to shoot. Maybe it's chambered for the same caliber as the bullet that killed the mayor."

Mina thought back to her conversations with the doctor. "He's never mentioned shooting at all. In fact, he seems adverse to weapons of any kind. But I can call them."

"Got their phone number for you," Hayden said, working at lightning speed. He shared it.

Mina dialed and half hoped no one would answer.

No such luck.

"Gunner's Haven," the man said.

"This is Sheriff Park." She steeled her brain to think of this as a lead like any other lead in the investigation. "I'd like to speak to someone who knows about your membership list or regular customers."

"I'm the manager," the man said. "Roger Springer. I can help you."

She swallowed and forged ahead. "I'm hoping to learn whether Dr. Lawrence Osborne from Seaside Harbor is on your membership role or if he's a regular shooter."

"Oh, Larry, yeah," he said fondly. "He's a regular all right. Been a member here for years. I always found it interesting that a man who served as a medical examiner wouldn't be anti-gun. But he's a real enthusiast and comes in often."

Mina's heart sank. Could he really be their killer? It was seeming more and more like it. "Does he have a favorite weapon?"

"Say." His tone rose. "What's this about, anyway?"

"Just following up on a few outstanding items," she said,

trying hard to sound off-hand when her gut was as tight as a pair of handcuffs. "Do you think he has a favorite weapon?"

"Hmm." Silence followed. "I guess I'd have to say he fires his Glock 9mm more often than anything, but he really loves his HK MP5."

"So a submachine gun. And the ammo he uses for that? Anything special?" She held her breath and hoped he didn't mention copper-jacketed bullets like the one found at Becca's house.

"His go to is +P ammo, but it's a bit more expensive, and he doesn't waste his money on exclusively firing those here at the range."

"Doesn't the ammo change the way the weapon fires?" she asked.

"Yeah, but knowledgeable shooters like Larry will shoot primarily the less expensive ammo to familiarize themselves with their weapon. To get a track on where the firearm is shooting and its general 'feel'. In other words 'sight in'. Then they close their shooting session with several rounds of the higher pressure ammo to ensure they have the feel and sight of the better rounds."

"So in other words, he would do both." She thought for a moment. "Any way we can retrieve the bullets fired or casings ejected from his weapons?"

"There might be some in the trap from his last time here, but they'd be mixed in with others. No way I could tell you which ones came from his weapon."

She figured that was what he would say, but she still had to ask. "Do you know when he was there last? And did he bring his MP5?"

"Well, let's see. Yeah. Yeah. The last time he was here, he fired the MP5, but which day? I dunno. Last week though. I'm sure of that. If it's important, I can go back through the records and see when he signed in."

"I'll let you know if we need the information. Thank you for your help." Mina hung up and reluctantly shared the results of her call. "With that additional information, I have no choice but to consider Dr. Osborne a suspect in the murder of Mayor Sutton and the abduction of his daughter."

"I'm sorry, Mina," Nolan said. "I know you care for him and have worked with him for some time. It's got to be hard to think he could be behind any of this."

She lifted her shoulders, trying to make it seem like this wasn't a big deal to her, but it was. She never imagined someone she respected so highly could possibly do something like this.

She turned to El. "Call Abe. Share our details with him and have him get an emergency warrant to search Dr. Osborne's house and cabin. Until they come in, I want you and Ewing to watch his place. Nolan and I'll take the cabin. No one moves in until we have eyes on him."

"Do you honestly think he's our killer?" El asked. "I know several factors point to him as being our prime suspect, but still, he's a respected member of the community. A member of our crime-fighting team. So he could very well be innocent."

"As Nolan said, so could Knox Anderson, and he's behind bars." Mina rested her hands on her hips. "We can't treat Dr. Osborne any differently."

El gave a reluctant nod and pulled her phone from a cargo pocket. "I'll call Abe."

Nolan took Mina's arm and led her to the far side of the room. Not good. She expected his kindness as he tried to comfort her in this unusual discovery. He was very intuitive —especially for a guy—and willing to support her. He'd proven that when they were together before and now.

Could she ask for anything better in a man? She didn't

think so, and she really needed to resolve her issues with him as soon as possible.

He let go of her arm and made eye contact, that compassion in his expression where she expected to find it. "How are you feeling about this?"

She took a breath before speaking. "I can't pretend I like it, but part of me hopes that Dr. Osborne *is* our guy because we'll have solved the murder and perhaps found Becca too."

"You said you don't expect him to be holding her at his house, though."

"No, but I do think we could find something that might help tie him to the murder. Like the murder weapon and ammo. Maybe even bloody clothes or a rug."

Nolan continued to look at her. "Is there anything I can do to help until we depart?"

"Do?" She glanced around the room as she considered his question. "Just keep Hayden searching for information that might help either clear or convict Dr. Osborne."

"I can do that. But also know that I'm praying for a resolution and, for whatever we find, that you can accept it."

She clasped his hand and squeezed it, all the while looking into his eyes. "You really are as great of a guy as I remembered, aren't you?"

His eyes darkened, and he leaned closer. "And if you'll let me, I'd like to show you how great we could be together again."

She'd opened her mouth to reply when El called her name. Mina released his hand. "To be continued."

"Promise?" he asked.

"Promise," she said and hoped she wasn't letting the day's emotions get to her and wasn't leading him on.

25

Before departing to surveil Osborne's cabin, Nolan escorted Mina to the team's equipment room. She carried the tension of the day on her shoulders like a heavy weight pushing them down. He wanted to help alleviate it, but he didn't know how or if he could.

Her jaw dropped when she walked into the room and turned full circle. "Man, oh man, this is something. You must have a ton of money tied up in the inventory."

More than she realized. "You can't put a price on rescuing someone. We don't want to be caught without the right equipment when someone is missing and needs our help."

She waved her hand toward the floor-to-ceiling shelf holding their camera gear. "Seven different gadget bags?"

"One for each person and a spare in case one is malfunctioning." He tried to keep any pride of ownership from his voice as this wasn't about the items they'd accumulated. It was about how they used them. "We each chose a camera and various lenses. Some are interchangeable with different bodies, but for the most part we stick with our own gadgets."

She tilted her head. "Why different cameras?"

"It was just preference starting out, but then we discovered along the way which brands were the best." He blew on his fingernails and polished them on his chest. "Mine seems to produce the best quality photos and has the least amount of mechanical issues."

"I would expect you to choose the best one. You said you were a photo buff. You took so many pictures when we were together." She narrowed her eyes. "I don't suppose you kept any of them."

He had. All of them, every picture, but didn't want to answer and seem like a fool for hanging on to them when he'd thought she'd dumped him. But he wouldn't lie. "I don't know why, but I have them all. In a box in storage."

"Would you show them to me sometime?" She smiled softly up at him.

His heart somersaulted in his chest. "I'd be glad to get the box for you, if you want."

She broke eye contact. "Maybe we can look at them together."

"Maybe," he said, but was he ready for that? Not if she hadn't learned to trust him again. Better to move on now and do their job.

He grabbed his gadget bag. "I can handle taking any photos we need. Help yourself to whichever binoculars you'd like to use."

She moved to their shelves of binoculars, both regular and night vision. She tapped the NVGs on a lower shelf. "I'll grab a pair of goggles for both of us. They won't be of use in daylight, but who knows how long we'll be watching the place."

"Sounds like a plan." He reviewed the contents of his bag, making sure to have both a wide-angle and a selection of telephoto lenses. Satisfied, he closed the bag and reached for an empty tote to stow the binoculars and NVGs.

"I'll take a signal jammer too. Wouldn't want the doctor to use his cell phone." He picked up a device they used to block electronic signals. "What about a drone?"

"We can't legally fly one over his property without permission," she said. "And if he's guilty, I don't want anything to prevent us from successfully prosecuting him."

"Let's bring one along, just in case. It's better to have it and not need it, than to need it and not have it."

She looked up at him. "You really do have a first-rate surveillance business here."

"Like I said." He zipped up the tote. "We're dealing with people's lives, so we need to have the best tools available to increase the odds of bringing them safely home."

She cocked a hip. "And I suppose you have an assortment of weapons as well."

"Follow me." He shouldered the bags, grabbed a drone, and left their equipment room. He set down the items to unlock a nearby door. "Our armory, as small as it might be, used to be a single guest room. We've reinforced the walls, door, and locks to keep everything secure. As you can see, we removed the window."

She let out a low whistle, and he took the time to admire their weapon collection featuring various handguns, rifles, and even semi-automatics mounted on the upper walls. A store of ammo was neatly arranged and labeled on shelves below. And one wall held a hanging rack and dryer for Kevlar vests.

Her gaze flashed up to his. "Don't tell me you need all of this?"

"Need? Nah." He grinned. "A lot of the weapons we only use at the firing range, but like I said, we never know what we're up against. If someone has abducted another person, they're already walking on the edge, and it's best to be prepared in case we push them over."

She smiled back at him, reminding him how wonderful it would be to have a relationship with a woman who understood what his job required and his need for gadgets and weapons.

"I have my rifle and handgun," she said. "Bring what you want to take along."

He took a submachine gun and ammo, though he doubted they would need it. Still, he preferred it to a rifle.

"I figured you'd take that." She laughed and stepped into the hallway. She hung one of the gadget bags over her shoulder.

He made sure the door locked and was secured, then grabbed the other bag, and they took off for her patrol vehicle. They didn't speak as she maneuvered out of the inn's parking lot and onto the road that led to Dr. Osborne's cabin.

The miles clipped by, and Nolan really didn't know what to say. Was it appropriate to have a personal discussion when they were on the way to try to rescue an abducted woman? Their issues seemed trivial compared to the life and death situation Becca faced if they didn't get to her on time. That was, if she was still alive.

He just couldn't do anything but ponder helping her, so he sat back and watched the rural scenery pass by. God's handiwork on display. Majestic trees. Soaring hawks. Babbling brooks. Mountains. All right in front of him and a reminder that if God could make and oversee all of this, He could help Mina and Nolan work out their issues.

Mina slowed and clicked on her blinker.

It was go time, and he sat up straighter to take in the surroundings.

She pulled onto a small dirt road that the map told them would overlook Dr. Osborne's cabin. She killed the engine. "Perfect lookout, and we can't be seen from below."

"I'll grab the camera and binoculars." He opened the door as silently as possible and went to the rear hatch to retrieve the equipment. Back in the passenger seat, he handed the binoculars to her and opened his gadget bag to select a lens and screw it into the mount.

She lifted the binoculars over the steering wheel and leaned forward. "Wow, these have really good clarity."

"I told you. Nothing but the best for us." He chuckled, but it was forced.

"No movement at the cabin," she said. "Dr. Osborne's vehicle is parked in the clearing."

Nolan lifted his camera with a telephoto lens, and snapped a succession of photos taking in the entire area. He confirmed a small cabin in the large clearing as they had seen on the satellite images Hayden had retrieved and the white SUV parked near the door. Shades were drawn on all the windows, and lights were on in two of the front rooms.

"This clarity is so good, I should be able to see movements behind the blinds," she said keeping her eyes on the binoculars. "Your aunt must've left you a lot of money to afford all this top-of-the-line stuff."

"She did. A good chunk of change. But also, the team members bought into the business so they would each have a stake. We used that money for the equipment."

"From what I've heard around town, you've been very successful in finding people."

"We have," he said, careful not to sound prideful. "By God's grace. So far everyone we've found was alive, but I know the odds are against us for that continuing."

"You've got to expect that in your business, though, right?" She turned to look at him. "I mean, we all know the longer a person is missing, the more likely they're no longer alive."

He nodded, but kept his eyes on the viewfinder. If he

looked at her, he knew he would see her concern for Becca there, and he couldn't let any emotions get to him. He had to stay levelheaded. "By the time families come to us for help, the police have investigated for some time. It's only when they come up empty-handed that the families hire us as a last resort."

"That's got to be hard." She turned back to the cabin. "What made you decide to get into such difficult work?"

"Goes back to my earlier days before the Secret Service. When I was a deputy in Portland. I was first on scene for a missing girl. Four years old. Taken from her bed. No suspects. No one ever found. Not even the little girl." The full force of that past experience coupled with the present tension hit him, and he had to stop talking or he might lose it.

"And that stuck with you," she said. "I can see that. I have a homicide investigation from Portland that I'll never forget. Not because it was unsolved, but because it was a husband killing his wife, and the brutality he used is beyond comprehension."

She shuddered, but lowered her binoculars to look at him. "It's nice to be able to talk to someone who under-stands what this job does to people."

"I agree." He shifted to face her. "But honestly, I just like talking to you about anything."

"I feel the same way."

Music to his ears. "Do you think you can talk to your parents? To find out once and for all that I'm not lying to you?"

"I can, and I plan to." She fell silent. "But you know if they admit to warning you off and then not telling me about it, I'm not sure I'll be able to forgive them."

"What if they lie and say I never came there?" he asked. "How will you feel about me then?"

"I don't know. I just don't know." She looked away. "I'm having a hard time forgiving you. Not that you even need forgiveness if you did indeed leave me the note. Every time I think about how badly it hurt to have been left like that, I let the pain take over my common sense. My faith. The knowledge that I need to let it all go no matter what happened." Her fingers tightened on the binoculars as if she were squeezing them to death. "Add my family into this, and I don't know what I'll do."

She shuddered, then lifted the binoculars and pointed them at the house.

Okay, then. The end of their discussion. But it wasn't the end as far as he was concerned.

Please let her parents tell her the truth but not at the expense of their relationship. I can't be responsible for coming between them.

Mina's phone vibrated from the holder on the dash. He'd never been more thankful for an interruption in his life. He spotted Sierra's name on a video call.

"Answer," he said. "She could have evidence."

Mina tapped the button. "Sierra."

Sierra smiled broadly. "I have DNA from Becca's house."

"And?" Mina and Nolan asked at the same time.

"And we have three viable profiles from the portable AC filter." She took a breath, and Nolan wanted to push her along. "Mayor Sutton's as expected, as well as Becca's."

"And the third person?" Mina asked.

Sierra frowned. "It belongs to your medical examiner. The AC unit likely picked it up while he was on scene. It was on the bullet casing too, which I found odd, but he must've accidently contaminated the scene."

Mina shared a quick look with Nolan. They both knew he'd never gone to that scene.

"Looks like you both find that odd," Sierra said. "But

maybe this will help you figure out what's going on. Did he also touch the invitation envelope for any reason? Because he left his DNA on there too."

What? The invitation too? Nolan shouldn't be surprised. If Osborne killed the mayor, he also arranged the night at the mansion and would've sent the invite. But he'd been so careful thus far, so why would he have touched or even licked the envelope? The only reason that made sense was that he didn't think they had his DNA on file. So where did Sierra get it?

"He's not law enforcement," Nolan said. "And his DNA wouldn't be in CODIS, so how do you know it's a match to him?"

"We have his profile on file here for elimination purposes for an investigation we did years ago." Sierra fell silent for a moment. "I'm sorry, I can tell this bothers you. You never like to hear that one of your professionals might've slipped up."

"He didn't slip up on the job," Mina said, her tone low. "He was never at the scene in a professional capacity nor did he handle the envelope after we took it into evidence."

"Oh. Oh-h-h!" Sierra's expression held the same measure of surprise as her tone. "That's a different story then. Do you have reason to suspect him of the mayor's murder?"

"We do," Mina said. "We're actually watching his cabin right now as we think he has Becca inside."

"Oh, wow." Sierra shook her head. "I'm sorry to hear it could be him, but at least you know it, and now you have forensic evidence to help you prove it."

"Thanks to you and your team," Nolan said.

"I appreciate the thanks, but none is needed." She smiled. "One last thing before I go. If you remember, we cast the shoe print outside Becca's window. I was able to identify it from the shoeprint database as a size eleven men's Brooks Adrenaline. So if you locate this brand and size in Osborne's possessions, we can match it to the print."

"We'll let you know. Thanks again." Mina ended the call and raised her binoculars.

"It's Osborne, then," Nolan said. "No question."

"I'm not sure if I should be glad because we're outside his cabin and will soon be able to arrest him or be disappointed and disgusted because he's the medical examiner."

"Yeah, being right for once is painful."

"We have movement behind one of the windows," she said, her tone lifting.

Nolan raised his camera again and began clicking. The door soon opened, and a woman was shoved out onto the porch, a gun to her back—Osborne, the man holding it.

"It's Becca," he said, though Mina would've come to the conclusion already. "Dr. Osborne is our guy. He really abducted Becca."

"Yeah," she said, her tone now low and melancholy. "I'd like to say it's not what it looks like, but the gun tells us it is."

She bent down to her radio and called for backup, requesting them to arrive silently so they didn't spook Osborne.

"At least Becca is alive." He watched Osborne march her down the steps toward the woods, the gun firmly in the middle of her back, then lowered the camera to look at Mina. "Looks like he might be planning to kill her now."

"Yeah," was her only response.

"Backup won't likely arrive on time."

"Yeah," she said again, but lowered her binoculars to meet his gaze.

"Then it's up to us," Nolan said. "It's our job to find a way to apprehend Osborne and bring Becca home alive."

Mina would rather be anywhere, doing anything else, other than creeping up on Dr. Osborne, where he held Becca at gunpoint. Dr. Osborne, for goodness' sake! The man she respected and looked up to. She really didn't want to arrest him, but it didn't matter what she felt. She had to do her job.

Handcuffed, Becca trembled in the harsh wind. "You don't have to do this. You don't have to kill me."

"But I do, don't you see?" Dr. Osborne asked. "I can't let you live, or you'll tell everyone I killed your father."

She lifted her shoulders and eyed the doctor. "Then you should be a man and take responsibility for killing a defenseless person."

Dr. Osborne growled. "Maybe he was defenseless, but he wasn't innocent. He deserved to die."

She shook her head. "But why? If you're going to kill me, isn't it time you finally tell me what this is all about? I know you've been worried I would escape and tell others, but it's the end now. If I'm dead I can't tell anyone."

Mina didn't know how Becca kept her composure and was able to speak of such things without falling apart.

Dr. Osborne planted his feet as if he'd reached a decision. "Taxes. It's all about taxes. My parents were struggling for years to keep their business afloat. They went to your father for help. Asked him to lobby on their behalf to reduce the taxes on the inn so they could afford to stay in business. But would he do it? No, absolutely not."

"So that's it?" Becca's eyes narrowed. "You blame him for your parents losing the inn and that's why he had to die? Seems lame to me."

Mina had to agree. This was one of the weakest excuses for murder she'd ever heard.

"It's not lame." Dr. Osborne waved his gun. "I didn't

really think anything of it until Nolan Orr and his team showed up in town. Then your dad arranged for tax breaks for his business so he could afford to operate the inn." Dr. Osborne glared at her. "A newbie! Your father takes the side of a newbie over a couple who'd been in business their entire lives. People he knew. I went to school with your dad, and he didn't care one bit for my parents."

"I'm sure he had a reason." She lifted her shoulders again. "Did you ever ask him?"

"Sure," Dr. Osborne said. "But he gave me the stupid line about if he gave the inn a tax break, he would have to give a break to all of the resort-type businesses in town, and the tax revenue would fall too dramatically. Then the county wouldn't be able to operate. But Orr's business wasn't at all related to the resorts so they could have a break and not set a precedent."

"That makes sense to me," Becca said.

"Of course it does." He waved his gun wildly. "Your father is the one who made the horrible decision. My father is the one who lost his business."

"Did you ever try to lobby for him before he lost his business?"

Osborne let out a long sigh. "Dad was really old-school and wouldn't accept any help from me. He said if he couldn't manage to get a tax break on his own, he didn't deserve to run the business."

"And now? How are your parents doing?"

Tilting his head, he didn't answer right away. Perhaps he didn't expect her to inquire about their well-being when he had her at gunpoint.

"Okay, I guess," he said. "But just okay. I moved them to Florida so they didn't have to get up every day and see the inn sitting empty and decaying as was happening before Orr bought it. I made sure they were comfortable, but every time

I visit, my dad talks about how he'd rather be running the inn than anything else."

"So when Nolan and his team took over the inn, you decided to get revenge."

"Oh, I decided to get revenge a long time before that, but I had to find the perfect way to kill him and not take the fall for it." Dr. Osborne smiled in a disturbing way Mina had never seen from him before. "When Orr took over the inn, I knew I could set it up to point in their direction."

Becca shook her head. "But surely the sheriff will figure out they're not guilty."

"Could be. She's pretty sharp, but she'll still have to investigate all the members of the Lost Lake Locators team. Word will get around. No one will trust them again, and they'll be forced out of business. The inn will be offered at a reduced price that I can afford to pay, and I can bring my parents back."

Remaining calm, Becca arched an eyebrow. "What if she suspects you?"

"Hah! No way." He snickered. "I played my part perfectly. No one suspects me, and that's why you have to die. I can't go to prison. My parents need me to buy the inn back."

Becca started shaking. "I could just go away. Live somewhere else."

"Like I can trust you not to want me to pay for your father." He waved the gun toward the tree. "Over there. Move slowly and don't try anything."

Becca didn't move. "If you shoot me, there'll be blood everywhere, and the police will find it."

"Like I said, they don't suspect me so why come out here? Secondly, if you dig in the pile of leaves you'll see I came prepared. Go ahead. Start scattering the leaves."

She brushed the leaves away with her feet and looked up. "A tarp."

He'd really planned ahead. Mina didn't want to be impressed, but she was. He'd seen enough murders in his day or heard enough details to plan what he thought would be the perfect murder.

"We have to intervene," Nolan whispered.

"Agreed," she said without hesitation. "I'll go in. You cover me."

She took a step, but he squeezed her arm. "Be careful. I can't lose you again."

His voice choked off. Her heart clutched. The feelings swimming inside her caught her by surprise. But she wouldn't admit them, or he might try to stop her.

She gave him a tight smile before stepping through rotting leaves and vegetation. Her footfalls were silent. Neither Dr. Osborne or Becca showed any indication of hearing her. She stopped fifty feet from the doctor to keep from scaring him.

"Dr. Osborne," she called out, her hand on her sidearm at the ready.

He spun, his gun waving. He locked gazes on her, then turned to the side and waved his gun at Becca. "Don't move. Either of you."

Mina held up her hands. "There's no need for the gun, Dr. Osborne. I'm not here to hurt you. I heard everything you told Becca, and I'm here to help you."

"No, you're not. You're here to arrest me." He glanced at Becca, then back at Mina. "Now you put me in a real predicament." His gaze traveled over the area, his eyes unfocused and wild. "I'm not going to prison, and I don't want to kill you, but I will if I have to."

"No, you won't." She took a few steps closer. "You really aren't a killer. You took an oath to save lives, not take them."

"Some people just deserve to die. My cases as a medical examiner show me that."

"Say that's true," she said to keep him focused on her. "Who gets to decide who should die? Should you? Should I? Should Becca over there?"

"Stop talking," Dr. Osborne said. "You're just trying to confuse me. I'm not a criminal, and I'm not going to prison."

"But you *are* a criminal." Mina firmed her stance. "You committed murder. Kidnapping. You need to pay for your crimes."

"I've always respected you, Sheriff, and enjoyed working with you, but you've stuck your nose in where it doesn't belong." He shook his gun. "Get over there with Becca."

She slowly moved forward, hoping when she reached him that she could disarm him, but as she approached, he backed away. She couldn't reach him without taking a bullet. Her only hope at this point was to talk him down. If she couldn't, then there was only one option. She would put herself between him and Becca.

Mina would likely take a bullet, but then Nolan would take Dr. Osborne out before he could kill Becca too.

26

Nolan didn't like what was happening in front of him. Didn't like it one bit and his gut tightened. Osborne had moved out of his comfort zone for a sure shot with his handgun, and he had to get closer. He dashed from tree to tree until he was as close as he could get without alerting Osborne to his location. Mina had moved next to Becca and was whispering something to her.

"Stop that." Osborne waved his gun again, this time wildly. He was skilled with a weapon and shouldn't misfire, but it didn't matter what his skill was right now. He was losing his grip on reality. "Since there are two of you, you can quickly get that tarp laid out."

Nolan couldn't wait until the tarp was down. That would be too late. He had to try a surprise attack now. He inched closer. Silently. Carefully placing his feet.

Mina caught sight of him and gave a slight shake of her head. Nearly imperceptible, Osborne didn't pick up on it.

Nolan returned her shake with a stubborn one of his own. He wouldn't stop and risk her life. He'd give his life first, if that was what it took to save her. Becca too.

Please don't let Becca see me and react.

The women spread out the tarp, the sound and action serving as a distraction while he closed the final twenty feet to his target. He took a silent breath and let it out.

Mina held one corner of the tarp and Becca the other. They backed away from each other. The camouflage vinyl fluttered in the breeze.

Now! Go!

He took off, not caring about the sound his feet were making as he all but flew over the ground.

Five feet away, Dr. Osborne turned, his gun outstretched. His eyes flashed open. He fired.

Pain razored into Nolan's upper arm, and he hit the ground.

The doctor advanced on him, gun pointed at him, and an angry glare in his eyes.

"Run," he yelled at Mina and Becca.

Osborne raised his gun and spun.

He was going to shoot them.

"No!" Nolan wrapped his good arm around Osborne's legs, taking him down. His gun fired, the report sounding like a cannon in Nolan's ears.

He scrambled on top of the doctor and tried to wrestle the gun free. One hand alone didn't work. He clawed at the man's gun hand.

Osborne ripped it free and started to crawl away. Turned onto his back and lifted the gun, aiming the barrel at him.

Nolan had failed. Big time. He prepared himself for a fatal bullet.

Please keep Mina and Becca safe.

Mina appeared above them. "It's over, Dr. Osborne. Drop your gun. My weapon is trained on you, and I'll use it if I have to."

Osborne struggled for a moment longer, but then let out

a sigh and dropped the gun. Nolan lunged at him, secured the gun, and held him in check.

Mina stowed her sidearm and cuffed the doctor, leaving him lying on the ground. She went to Nolan and gently touched his shoulder. "Look at your arm."

He didn't want her to make a fuss over such a minor injury. "It's fine."

"It's not fine. It's bleeding. We have to stop it." She pulled a large white handkerchief from her pocket and tied it around his arm.

"A handkerchief?" He grinned at her, but kept his weapon fixed on Osborne. "I didn't know anyone still carried them."

She blushed bright red. "Something I learned from my LT in Portland. You never know when you'll have to deliver bad news to someone, and it's always convenient to have one in your pocket to hand over to them."

"Or in my case," he smiled at her, "use it to stop bleeding."

"I found many uses for it over the years. One of these days I'll share them with you." She gave him a playful smile.

"I'll hold you to that." He almost whooped for joy at this investigation being over and finding Becca alive, but opted for professionalism and held his emotions in check. After all, Becca had lost her father and was grieving. Maybe just starting to grieve now that she was free and didn't have to worry about her own life.

Mina leaned down to her radio. "Come in, El."

"Go ahead." El's voice came over the radio.

"Suspect in custody about a mile east of the cabin. Becca is alive and well. Require medical assistance."

El released a long breath over the radio. "I'm three minutes out. Will get the ambulance dispatched."

"Roger that." The radio squawked and went silent.

Nolan's arm throbbed, but he didn't want Mina to see that it bothered him. He tried to move like normal as he helped Osborne into a sitting position. Becca remained seated behind the tree.

"Let me check on Becca." Mina went to her and unlocked her cuffs. They talked for only a few moments when Becca got up and firmed her shoulders.

Mina gave the young woman a side hug, and they stepped through leaves to join Nolan again.

Mina continued to stare at Osborne as if she couldn't believe he really was their killer. Nolan didn't have the same problem she did, but then he hadn't worked with this man for years.

"I'm sorry, Mina." Osborne cast her a pleading look as he began sobbing. "I'm really sorry. I didn't mean for any of this to happen. I didn't want to kill Ernie, but my father wouldn't avenge himself, so I had to do it. I couldn't stand by and let someone take advantage of him like that and get away with it."

"And what do you think he's going to say about all of this?" Nolan asked.

Osborne's sobbing ramped up. "I'm going to be an embarrassment to him. His only child, I was his pride and joy. The doctor son he'd groomed me to be since I was a little boy. Important in the community and certainly too good to run an inn. Too good to help him out too."

He let out a shuddering breath. "And now, I'll be his convicted son. The rest of my life thrown away. He'll die while I'm in prison. My mother too. Both of them alone, without me."

Mina actually gave him a compassionate look that Nolan couldn't possibly muster. "And now that you've avenged him, do you feel any better?"

He looked up at her, his expression despondent. "No.

Not at all. I feel worse. Terrible. And I'm embarrassed for having done such a thing."

"Hah!" Becca shouted. "Embarrassed? Embarrassed? You kill my father, and your main feeling is embarrassment? How about remorse? How about guilt? How about the same things for abducting me? You might've been kind and treated me okay these past few days, but I feared for my life each and every hour of each and every one of them. I will never get those days back and never feel safe again."

Osborne shifted his focus to her. "I'm sorry. I am. I do feel guilt. And remorse. For your father and you, and especially now for trying to kill you too. It was one thing to let my rage take over, another to do this."

"I don't buy the rage thing, either." Becca fisted her hands on her hips and glared at him. "Rage makes you act in the spur of the moment. You planned this. Every bit of it. That's cold-blooded murder."

"No. No." Osborne shook his head. "It's not like that. Try to understand. I was so angry I could hardly see straight. Wasn't in my right mind, even as I planned it. But now, I can see how very wrong it all was."

"You'll have plenty of years to think about that in prison," Nolan said, not buying this *I'm sorry for myself* routine either. More likely he was sorry for having been caught. "I'm equally angry over you setting my team up to take the fall."

"You bought the inn. It could be no one else." He shook his head. "And then to discover the cancer in the autopsy, and it was all for nothing."

"Cancer?" Becca's eyes flashed open. "What about cancer?"

"I'm sorry, Becca," Mina said. "I didn't want you to find out like this, but your father had terminal cancer and didn't have long to live."

She blinked. Closed her eyes and blinked again, tears now starting to flow. "He didn't tell me."

"He didn't tell anyone," Mina said, "except the attorney who was revising his will."

"But why? Why keep it a secret?" She swiped a hand over her eyes. "I could've—would've—been there for him. Made it easier."

"He wanted his last days to be as normal as possible," Nolan said, as if that could make things better for her.

She shook her head. "It still stings, but at least I know I would've lost him no matter what this creep chose to do."

"That's a good way of looking at it," Nolan said.

"How did you catch on to me anyway?" Osborne asked.

Mina shared all of the details. "One thing we haven't figured out, though. How did you get the police academy graduation photos for the escape room?"

"Oh those." A prideful look crossed Osborne's face. "That was a nice touch wasn't it? I have a friend who runs the academy, and he gave them to me."

Mina glared at him. "When we take your formal statement, we'll be wanting his name."

"No, no." He swung his head side to side. "I don't want to get him in trouble."

"Just like you had a choice in doing this," Nolan said. "He had a choice in helping you, and he made the wrong decision. He needs to pay for it."

Nolan heard footfalls and swiveled to see El, along with Deputy Ewing, charging toward them. His adrenaline had subsided, and his arm started throbbing more. He felt a bit lightheaded, but swallowed to fight it off. He couldn't let Mina see that he was suffering. She'd been casting him worried looks, so he had to keep it together for her as she still had a lot on her plate to deal with here.

"El, good," Mina said. "Take Osborne into custody, and make sure Becca is seen by a medic."

She nodded and glanced at Ewing. "Get him in the back of the patrol car."

Ewing advanced on Osborne, and Nolan stood. He had a rush of lightheadedness and closed his eyes for a moment while he breathed deeply. When he opened his eyes, Mina was watching him. He smiled at her to tell her he was okay, and she turned her attention back to Becca.

The young woman's face had paled, and she was shivering. Shock. She was likely in shock. That wasn't a surprise in the least.

Mina squeezed Becca's shoulder. "Go with Detective Lyons. I'll check in with you later to get your statement while it's fresh in your mind. I don't want to bother you now, but we want to be sure Osborne goes away for as long as possible."

Becca gave a firm nod, but didn't speak.

El clasped Becca's elbow. "Come with me, and I'll make sure you're taken care of."

Tears formed in her eyes. "You might be able to help with my physical issues, but there's nothing you can do to make up for the horror of watching my father be murdered."

Tears flowed in earnest, and she stumbled like she might collapse. El put her arm around her and supported her as they walked toward the cabin.

Nolan gritted his teeth and watched El lead Becca away.

Mina joined him.

"Becca's right," Nolan said. "Only a trained professional will be able to help her move on after seeing him murdered and then being kidnapped too."

Mina grimaced. "I'll make sure she has someone."

"I can't imagine the trauma she experienced standing next to her father as he was gunned down. That's bad enough, but then becoming Osborne's prisoner for days." Nolan shook his head. "I wish we could've found her sooner."

"Me too, but we located her in time, and that's all that matters." Mina studied his face. "Tell me about your arm. Do you need to see a medic or should we go straight to the ER?"

"Let the medics treat Becca."

Mina shoved her hands in her pockets, but immediately removed them and plunged them into her hair. "You shouldn't have done that. He could've killed you."

"Better he kill me than you."

"Says you." She stared into his eyes. "My heart nearly stopped when Osborne shot you. I don't know what I'd do if anything ever happened to you."

He liked hearing her declaration, but she still hadn't fully committed to a future with him. "I don't think I could live without you again either."

She stilled. "So what are we going to do about it?"

He took her hands in his. "That's up to you, honey. I'm fully invested in this thing between us, but you have to decide if you can trust me—trust us going forward in a new relationship."

27

Nolan stood with his teammates on the inn's veranda, overlooking Founder's Day in full swing on Main Street below. In a few hours they would be responsible for hosting the kid's art project, but for now they were free to enjoy the day.

If they could, after Mayor Sutton's death. They'd been so focused on finding Becca and bringing Dr. Osborne to justice, that they hadn't properly dealt with things, and there was an uneasy undercurrent in the team.

Jude slid onto the railing. "It's so crazy, man. I still can't believe the ME was responsible for killing the mayor."

Reece dropped into the wide porch swing next to Abby. A shaft of sunlight crossed her face, and she lifted her hand over her eyes. "It might blow us away, but we didn't know him very well. Can you imagine what the locals must think?"

Nolan had spoken to several people, and he'd also talked to Mina, who relayed the town's shock and dismay. "It's a surprise. A big one. A shock, really. I've heard there was no inkling that he wasn't the kind doctor he portrayed himself to be."

Gabe narrowed his eyes. "Just goes to show you don't know people like you think you do."

The zeal in his tone said he could only be thinking of one thing. His family—a bunch of criminal slackers who he'd left behind when he graduated from high school. He hadn't known their proclivity for crime until he reached his freshman year, and his father was arrested and convicted of armed robbery. He'd survived four years of being razzed about that in his small town.

Hayden perched next to Jude. "Too bad Percy Vaughn hasn't remembered whatever secret he claims the mayor told him. I'd like to put that to rest too. And find out where that money was going."

"Dude." Jude grinned. "You're only interested in finding out if Cadence has moved here."

Hayden socked his teammate in the arm. "You're wrong. I honestly want to know if Percy remembered anything."

"I believe you." Jude's grin widened. "Not."

Nolan stepped between his teammates before they really started duking it out. "Has anyone heard from Percy or Cadence?"

"Actually, I have." Hayden shifted on the railing. "I've gone by a few times to check on him."

"Ri-i-ght. To check on Percy." Jude chuckled.

"Hey, I liked the old guy," Hayden said. "He still doesn't seem to remember who the people were that he thought the mayor was helping with his money. We may never find out."

"Dementia is a bear," Abby said. "Remember to keep praying for Percy *and* Cadence because it doesn't only affect the one with the disease."

"In case anyone is interested"—Hayden glanced around the group—"Cadence is going to take her dad back to Portland after Founder's Day. He wanted to stay for the mayor's memorial presentation tonight."

He swiveled to look over the town, and Nolan couldn't get a take on how his teammate felt about her not moving here to take care of her dad, as she'd once mentioned.

"Hey man," Hayden said. "Isn't that Mina coming up the hill?"

Eager to lay eyes on her, Nolan pinned his focus on the road.

"Come on, guys." Abby got up and stretched. "Let's get ready for the art project and let these two have some time alone."

Reece stood. "Tell Mina we said hi."

Hayden got up and rested his hand on Nolan's uninjured shoulder. "Good luck, man. We're all pulling for you two."

"What he said," Jude said as he passed by.

"You got this, man," Gabe said. "If only I could be as confident in that art project. Maybe if we fail, I can offer rides on my motorcycle."

Nolan laughed, which he knew was Gabe's intent, but still, his palms started sweating. He hadn't seen Mina since the night in the ER, when the doctor cleaned and bandaged up his arm and pronounced him good to go. They'd spoken on the phone, and she'd been vague about talking to her family. If she'd done so or was even going to, he had no idea.

And then what? Would she be able to forgive him if she thought he was guilty of abandoning her? Had she talked to her family and was on the outs with them, blaming Nolan for that?

His gut clenched. He wanted to see her, but he didn't at the same time. Didn't matter what he wanted. There she was, walking up the hill toward the inn, and he hoped all would be revealed.

She was dressed in uniform, the khaki pants and shirt emphasizing her curves. The blond waves in her hair were tucked up behind but still shone in the sunlight. The uniform wasn't a surprise. She would be on duty for Founder's Day, like most of her deputies, to make sure no one got out of control during the celebration.

They'd been blessed with a warm, sunshiny day for this time in March when it typically rained and the skies were cloudy and gloomy. The sun glistened off the waves gently rolling in from the ocean behind him and lit up the landscape that had turned a lush green from all the rain.

Maybe the calm waves were a sign to Nolan that all was calm with Mina. He didn't usually believe in signs, but he was grasping for anything today. He'd had time to replay every minute he'd spent with her, to rehash the recent phone calls, and knew that just like back in the day, he still loved her. Loved her completely and forever. The marrying kind of love.

He was prepared to ask her to marry him, but he hadn't bought a ring. Wouldn't buy a ring until he knew their past had been resolved.

He couldn't wait at the entrance any longer and jogged down to meet her at the edge of the parking lot. She looked up at him and smiled. That dazzling smile that sent his heart racing.

Was she telegraphing something good was about to happen?

"Mind if we go to the lookout?" she asked, her smile wavering.

"Of course." He turned to let her go first.

"If I have to take my phone out, I'll be sure to keep a better hold on it." She laughed, but it was a nervous laugh.

Was it because she was bringing up the last time they saw each other before he'd left? Or was it just because she was remembering their time together in the past, and she was going to hold that against him and refuse to see him in the future?

They strolled side-by-side toward the lighthouse the team had decorated in old-fashioned red, white, and blue bunting, matching the other businesses in town to celebrate the day Lost Lake had been officially founded.

Locals milled around the place, most of them calling out a hello to Mina, and giving him a sharp nod of acknowledgment. The positive greeting from them was all he could expect at this point. He was still too much of a newcomer to receive the same warm welcome their elected sheriff was getting.

They reached the railing on the cliff's edge, the ocean spreading wide before them. The sun continued to glisten all the way to the horizon, and magnificent blue waves undulated toward them, crashing on the rocks with a frothy white intensity before receding.

She planted her hands on the metal rail and shivered.

"If you're cold I can give you my jacket," he said.

She shook her head. "Not cold. I'd just forgotten how brutal the waves were against the rocks."

"I've heard stories about people losing their lives down there."

"Nothing recently, but I remember several boating accidents when I was a kid. And there was also a suicide."

His turn to shiver. "I can't imagine being desperate enough to jump into that churning water."

She turned to look up at him. "I can't either. But I do remember feeling very desperate when you left."

He couldn't wait any longer to ask about her decisions. "Did your parents confirm I'd stopped by to talk to them, and they sent me on my way?"

"No."

That one word felt like he'd taken another bullet. "Oh."

"Because I didn't ask them." She peered into his eyes. "I didn't want to hear them admit it aloud and put a rift between us. Besides, I didn't need them to confirm your story. I believe you. Completely."

His heart soared. "So you're okay with our past, and we can move forward?"

"I'm not only okay with it, I can't wait to start dating."

This was too good to be true, and he had to know why in order to believe it. "What changed?"

She chewed on her lower lip. "I spent the last few days in prayer, which I have to admit I didn't do back when you left. I was very much like Dr. Osborne. I let my anger get to me. But I finally asked God to help me release my anger and trust you."

"What will happen once your family knows we're dating again?" He locked gazes with her. "They'll ask about me. Ask if it's a good idea to date a man who 'abandoned' you. You'll have to confront them then."

"Maybe so."

No. More than maybe. "I can't help but believe they'll think I told you what happened, and they'll feel the need to defend themselves."

She stepped closer to him. "Maybe it'll all come out in the open. I don't know. But I'm of the mindset that it will be what it will be. I have to live my life as I see fit, and I don't need to stir a hornet's nest. I just need to let things lie. If they want to bring up the past, then we'll discuss what actually happened."

He looked around. "I wish there wasn't a crowd here and you weren't in uniform so we could seal our new relationship with a kiss."

"You'll have to be patient." She smiled up at him. "I'm on duty until six, but then if you're agreeable, I'd like to have dinner, take a turn around the fairgrounds, and go to the fireworks with you."

Of course he would say yes. They'd lost so much time

when they could've been together, and he would never get it back, but they could begin fresh tonight.

"*If* I'll have dinner with you?" he asked so loudly the people nearby turned to look at them. He lowered his voice. "You know I will. Our past is all behind us, and we can move forward."

"Yes," she said. "I like the sound of that. Our past is behind us, and we have a promising future together."

He could barely keep his hands to himself, so he shoved them into his pockets. "Should I pick you up at six or do you want to meet me somewhere?"

"I like the thought of you picking me up for our first real date." She fixed a flirtatious smile on him. "Do you know where I live?"

"Um, yeah, maybe I figured that out." He chuckled.

"Then see you at six." Her laughter trailed behind her as she walked through the crowd, greeting people as she disappeared from view.

A moment of anxiety hit him. No, she was just disappearing from his view, not from his life. Never that again.

Mina peered at her reflection in the full-length mirror in her bedroom while Abby and Reece looked on. She rarely dressed up. Any formal affairs she had to attend lately were due to her job, and she just made sure she wore a fresh uniform.

She especially didn't often wear dresses, but Reece found out about the date and dragged Mina aside to ask if she had anything special to wear. Mina confessed she didn't, and Reece insisted on providing a feminine dress with a top that showed off curves she rarely displayed, tight at the waist, and then yards of fabric in a flowy skirt.

Reece clapped her hands. "Perfect. Nolan won't know what hit him."

Abby raised an eyebrow. "More likely he won't recognize you at all."

Reece swatted her hand at Abby. "Don't be such a goof. Of course he'll recognize her. He's in love with her. How can he not know who she is? Especially when she smiles at him, which we both know she'll do once she sees him all dressed up too."

Mina hadn't known they were working with him too. Or maybe they weren't. He knew how to dress up from his work. After all, she first saw him in a tux this week. How much dressier could he get than that?

Oh, man. She was totally out of her comfort zone. She turned to look at Reece. "Are you sure this is a good idea? He's never seen me looking like this. If he wanted a blingy girl, then he would've fallen for one instead of a maverick like me."

"We can be both," Reece said. "Or at least I like to think I've managed to do both."

Mina stared at the slender woman who had always looked like a model to her. "Um, Reece, I think you fall more on the feminine side of the spectrum."

She smoothed her hands down her sleek navy dress. "You could be right. It's all those years of modeling in college. It's hard to unlearn some of the things I was taught twenty-four/seven."

"Honey," Abby said. "It's not just that, it's in your DNA."

"Okay, fine. I'm a girly girl in law enforcement. Maybe not law enforcement anymore, but you get the point."

They laughed together for a while, and then satisfied with their work, Reece and Abby departed. Mina wasn't so confident and kept studying herself in the mirror. She glanced at the clock on her bedside table. Five minutes until six. Nolan would be arriving anytime. She couldn't dress like this. She just couldn't. It wasn't her. She had to change.

She went to her closet. The doorbell rang, and she stopped in place as if her parents caught her doing something wrong. She didn't have time to change, and she would have to open the door dressed this way. Whether she remained in this silly dress depended upon his response.

Thankful her mother at least made sure she knew how to walk in high heels, she started down the hall, each step raising her level of panic. She hadn't felt this nervous since high school prom, when she dated the boy her parents wanted her to go with but she didn't have a relationship with. The night was disastrous, and she sure didn't want tonight to be that way.

At the door she wiped her hands on her frilly skirt and pulled the door open.

Nolan stood there, dressed in black slacks and a white long sleeve shirt with the collar open. He looked devastatingly handsome, and her heart fluttered, but gone were her nerves. She didn't care what she was wearing, she was going on a proper date with the man she loved.

"You look fabulous." He took her hands and twirled her around. "I don't remember ever seeing you in a dress."

"Reece's idea."

"Reece, huh? Did she have to talk you into it?"

"Yeah. I don't mind wearing it, but I feel uncomfortable and very self-conscious." She freed her hands and smoothed the skirt again.

"Do you want to change?"

How did she answer that? "Do you want me to change?"

"I want you to be as comfortable as you can be tonight so we have a great first date," he said with certainty. "Not the kind of date that Reece would like us to have, but what we'd like."

"Then come in and have a seat while I put something else on." She laughed as she headed to her bedroom, and called over her shoulder, "But promise me when Reece is disappointed, you'll help me talk her down."

She discarded the dress and took the time to hang it up so Reece could have it back as neat as when she brought it. She put on a pair of khaki slacks that were her idea of dressing up and paired it with a frilly blouse her mom had gotten her. Satisfied this was a good compromise, she left the room.

Nolan came to his feet and ran an appreciative look over her from head to toe. "Now that's the Mina I know. Not that I didn't love the dress, because I did. You looked beautiful. But you're more beautiful when you're you than when you're what someone else wants you to be."

Oh, man. Could he have said anything better? "I'm really glad to hear you say that. After Reece left, I was going to change but ran out of time."

"Then let's go and have fun." He held out his arm.

She snuggled hers into the crook, and they started off for the night she'd only ever imagined in her dreams.

Her home was within walking distance of closed-off Main Street. The loud sounds and garish lights of carnival rides and concession games greeted them. A food stand run by her church's youth group filled the air with the savory scent of frying onions and hamburgers and the sweet scent of cotton candy and funnel cakes at nearby food carts fought for dominance.

Her stomach growled.

"I guess that's my cue to say let's eat." Nolan laughed. "Where do you want to get dinner?"

"I know this is kind of lame for a first date, but the church's youth group makes the best burgers and onion rings ever. The business association at the end of the midway does seafood, but we eat that all year long, and I don't have burgers often."

"You never have to twist my arm to have a burger." He grinned, a boyish smile that was lopsided and adorable.

She scooted closer to him, and he wrapped his arm around her waist. She liked that. Liked that they were announcing to everyone they were a couple. After their breakup had gone around town many years ago, people would be speculating. So what? She and Nolan would show them it had just been a misunderstanding, and they were back together for good. She was probably jumping ahead, but at least she hoped it was for good.

They perched on stools at the burger stand, and as much as it was great to be together, the burgers and onion rings were so good they inhaled them. The rest of the night was a dream as they got on rides, and he won her a pink teddy bear at the ball pitch. But all too soon it was time for the fireworks, and they climbed through the cool night to the inn.

"The team reserved a blanket for us," he said, "But we don't have to sit with them."

She looked up at him. "I mean, I like them, but five extra people on our first date isn't what I had in mind."

"Me neither." He took her hand and led her toward the lookout.

The sky over the ocean sparkled with more stars than she could count, and the moon glistened off rolling waves. A magical night.

The team had roped off a section on the inn's property to save the space for their night. After all, there had to be some perks of owning the place during such an event. Everyone was present, sitting on blankets. When they approached, the others looked up at them.

"You *did not* change." Reece pouted.

"Don't make a big deal about it," Nolan said. "Not everyone is as comfortable dressed like that as you are."

Reece frowned. "At least tell me you got to see her in the dress."

"I did, and she looked beautiful in it, but she's just as beautiful now."

Gabe groaned. "If I'd known this sappy talk was the price of admission to the fireworks, I would've skipped the night."

Abby socked him in the arm. "You're just jealous that you don't have someone special."

"Trust me," Gabe said. "When or if there's someone special in my life, I won't be laying it all bare like this."

"We'll see." Abby smirked.

Nolan picked up a wicker basket and no one tried to stop him. "We're going to head down the cliff a little bit to watch the fireworks. See you later."

Nolan took her hand, and they started away from the group. As they walked, memories of their kisses long ago came back, and her heart skipped a beat in anticipation.

He continued down the cliff, passing locals and sending their tongues wagging. She could hear some of the comments. They weren't mean, but she and Nolan had obviously surprised people.

He directed her through long grass and past a large boulder to a private space. Setting down the basket, he dug out a blanket and unfurled it. The soft breeze caught hold, fluttering it in the air before the fabric landed on the tall grass. "I should've thought to mow over here today, but then I guess if the grass was short other people would've come over here too."

"It's perfect." She sat on the blanket and was thankful she wasn't trying to maneuver around with a frilly dress.

He dropped down next to her and reached into the

basket to pull out a bottle of sparkling cider and two glasses. "I thought we might want to toast the beginning of our relationship."

"That's so sweet of you to think of that." She slid closer to him. "We can do that. We should do that. We will do that. But first this."

She reached up and cupped his face, feeling his strong jawline beneath her fingers. It'd been so long since she'd touched him, and she thought she'd never do it again. Yet she'd dreamed of him, of touching him, kissing him more times than she'd like to admit.

He gently ran a finger over her cheekbone, then slid his hand into her hair to release the soft waves from the clip Reece had put in and let them fall over her shoulders.

"So many memories are hitting me right now." He clasped the back of her head and pulled her closer. "But we have to forget those and start over. Start again. This time it won't end."

His head came down, his lips pressing against hers, demanding, urgent. She hadn't expected a soft kiss. Not after all they'd lost. The time they'd lost. And she didn't want one. She wanted this. Exactly this.

She slipped her arms around his neck, and he pressed a muscular arm around her lower back and drew her close. She felt safe. Like she didn't feel any other time in her life. Difficult law enforcement experiences that always troubled her vanished, which rarely happened, and she had no fear. Was at peace.

He deepened the kiss. His lips were soft but urgent. She matched him with the same urgency. He'd always known what she liked. What she expected. What she wanted.

He knew her in a way no one else had ever known.

An explosion sounded in the sky and lights flashed above the ocean.

With a groan, he pulled away and looked at her. "So when we're old and our kids ask us what it was like to be together when we were young, can I tell them when I first kissed you, I saw fireworks?"

She laughed, her heart happy and filled with unrestrained love. "I mean, you can tell them that, but it's not true. This certainly wasn't the first time you kissed me."

"And it wasn't the first time I saw fireworks when I kissed you either."

She swatted a hand at him, and he grabbed it to press his lips on the back side. "Okay, fine, I didn't see actual fireworks, but I might have with the way I felt. With the way I feel now. I loved you then, and I love you now."

"I love you too." She ran a finger over his lower lip. "So where do we go from here?"

"The shortest dating relationship and engagement ever recorded?" He slid an arm around her back and turned them both to watch the colorful explosions in the sky.

She settled her head on his shoulder and the night sky lit up while a soft breeze blew over her. "I'll have to revoke your deputy status now."

"I expected nothing less, but tell me there are rights that come with being the sheriff's first man."

"Ah, Nolan." She giggled. "I don't think there are first ladies or first men that go with this elected position."

"And here I was looking forward to putting on my tux over and over throughout the year and going to special events with you."

"You couldn't have been more sarcastic."

"Oh, I could've been, but I wasn't." He laughed but then it stilled. "In all seriousness, I *am* going to ask you to marry me. But not tonight. Not while we're still fresh in the emotion of the shooting and all of that. But once that settles down, we'll make things official." He tipped her face up by the chin to look at him.

She swiveled and put her arms around his neck. "There's nothing more that I want in this world, Nolan Orr, than to marry you and make up for all of those lost hours."

Thank you so much for reading *Lost Hours*. If you've enjoyed the book, I would be grateful if you would post a review on the bookseller's site. Just a few words is all it takes or simply leave a rating.

You'll be happy to hear that there will be more books in this series. Read on for details.

I'd also like to invite you to learn more about these books as they release and about my other books by signing up for my **NEWSLETTER** at https://www.susansleeman.com/sign-up-2. You'll also receive a FREE e-book copy of *Cold Silence*, the prequel to my Cold Harbor Series, when you do. If you're already a subscriber, you can sign up again and get the free book and it won't put your name on the list twice, but you will receive welcome to my list messages.

LOST LAKE LOCATORS SERIES
When people vanish without a trace and those who go looking for them must put their lives on the line to bring them home alive.

Book 1 – Lost Hours - March 3, 2025
Book 2 – Lost Truth - July 7, 2025
Book 3 – Lost Cause – November 3, 2025
Book 4 – Lost Lake - March 2, 2026
Book 5 – Lost Girls - July 6, 2026
Book 6 – Lost Light – November 2, 2026

For More Details Visit -
https://www.susansleeman.com/lost-lake-locators/

LOST TRUTH - BOOK 2

A vulnerable reporter. A hidden truth.
Lost Lake Locator Hayden Kraus is thrust into a high-stakes investigation as he investigates the disappearance of a beloved local resident. He delves deeper and crosses paths with Cadence Vaughn, a fearless and resourceful investigative journalist determined to uncover the truth behind her father's mysterious murder—a case she believes is connected to the investigation. The case quickly becomes a complex web of deception, corruption, and danger.

And an investigator pushed to extremes.
Despite initial friction, Hayden and Cadence realize they need each other to expose the powerful forces at play. As they piece together clues, they uncover evidence pointing to a sinister cover-up. The threats escalate, and they face increasing danger, but the bond between them strengthens. When they have to risk everything to bring the truth to light will that include risking a future together too?
Preorder Lost Truth Now!

SHADOW LAKE SURVIVAL SERIES

When survival takes a dangerous turn and lives are on the line.

The men of Shadow Lake Survival impart survival skills and keep those in danger safe from harm. Even if it means risking their lives.

Book 1 – Shadow of Deceit
Book 2 – Shadow of Night
Book 3 – Shadow of Truth
Book 4 – Shadow of Hope – April 8, 2024
Book 5 – Shadow of Doubt – July 8, 2024
Book 6 – Shadow of Fear – November 4, 2024

For More Details Visit -
www.susansleeman.com/books/shadow-lake-survival

NIGHTHAWK SECURITY SERIES
Protecting others when unspeakable danger lurks.

A woman being stalked. A mother and child being hunted. And more. All in danger. Needing protection from the men of Nighthawk Security.

Book 1 – Night Fall
Book 2 – Night Vision
Book 3 – Night Hawk
Book 4 – Night Moves
Book 5 – Night Watch
Book 6 – Night Prey

For More Details Visit -
www.susansleeman.com/books/nighthawk-security/

THE TRUTH SEEKERS
People are rarely who they seem

A twin who didn't know she had a sister. A mother whose child isn't her own. A woman whose parents lied to her. All needing help from The Truth Seekers forensic team.

Book 1 - Dead Ringer
Book 2 - Dead Silence
Book 3 - Dead End
Book 4 - Dead Heat
Book 5 - Dead Center
Book 6 - Dead Even

For More Details Visit -
www.susansleeman.com/books/truth-seekers/

The COLD HARBOR SERIES

Meet Blackwell Tactical- former military and law enforcement heroes who will give everything to protect innocents... even their own lives.

Prequel - Cold Silence
Book 1 - Cold Terror
Book 2 - Cold Truth
Book 3 - Cold Fury
Book 4 - Cold Case
Book 5 - Cold Fear
Book 6 - Cold Pursuit
Book 7 - Cold Dawn

For More Details Visit -
www.susansleeman.com/books/cold-harbor/

ABOUT SUSAN

SUSAN SLEEMAN is a bestselling and award-winning author of more than 60 inspirational/Christian and clean read romantic suspense and mystery books. In addition to writing, Susan also hosts the website, TheSuspense-Zone.com.

Susan currently lives in Oregon, but has had the pleasure of living in nine states. Her husband is a retired church music director and they have two beautiful daughters, two very special sons-in-law, and four amazing grandsons.

For more information visit: www.susansleeman.com

Made in the USA
Columbia, SC
02 May 2025

57444847R00178